The Ruse

Ivy Ford

Published by Ivy Ford, 2024.

This is a work of fiction. Similarities to real people, places, or events are entirely coincidental.

THE RUSE

First edition. November 15, 2024.

Copyright © 2024 Ivy Ford.

ISBN: 979-8230333050

Written by Ivy Ford.

Chapter 1: In the Crosshairs

The alley is a grimy ribbon of concrete and shattered dreams, the kind of place where even the rats have given up on escape. Neon signs flicker overhead, casting sickly green and yellow light on the puddles below, mixing with the stench of sweat, grease, and decay. My feet slap against the wet ground in frantic rhythm, the sharp click of my heels a constant reminder that every step is one closer to something worse than the last. Behind me, the sound of boots pounding the pavement grows louder, chasing me through the veins of this godforsaken city.

I don't have time to think, don't have the luxury of a plan. My heart is hammering against my chest, a steady thrum of panic. My breaths are shallow, coming in bursts, as if the very air of New Chicago is trying to choke me. The lights above flicker, casting erratic shadows along the alley, but they can't drown out the feeling that I'm being hunted. They know me. They always know me. And there's nowhere left to hide.

I round the corner sharply, my shoulder slamming into the brick wall, sending a jolt of pain through my arm. My hand reaches out instinctively to steady myself, but I don't stop—I can't stop. The alley twists ahead, narrow and suffocating, but it's my only option.

Then, in a blur, I collide with something solid. A wall of muscle, a weight like nothing I've ever felt before. It's so sudden, so violent, I stumble backward, heart skipping a beat, but the arms that catch me are unyielding. The man—him—holds me fast, his grip firm, unwavering.

I blink up, disoriented, but even as the world sways around me, I know him. I've seen that face in the underworld's whispers. Jaxon Pierce.

A bounty hunter. A shadow that hunts in the corners of the city, an elusive, cold-hearted figure whose name strikes fear into the hearts of even the toughest criminals. The stories—they don't do him justice. He's colder, sharper, more ruthless than anyone dares to say aloud. And now, in this moment, he's holding me, his fingers digging into my arms as though he's trying to squeeze the answers from my skin.

His eyes are icy blue, sharp as shards of glass, cutting through the chaos like a predator zeroing in on its prey. The dim light reflects off the hard angles of his face, making him look even more dangerous. His jaw is set, lips tight in an expression that speaks of a man who's seen everything the world has to offer—and didn't care for much of it.

"Didn't think you'd be this much of a mess," he murmurs, voice low, like gravel dragged across steel.

I swallow, mouth dry, my heart still racing. His presence overwhelms me, the scent of leather and something faintly metallic hanging around him, like the air after a storm. My mind scrambles for words, but none come. I know better than to try and talk my way out of this. I'm caught—there's no getting out of this.

"What do you want?" I force the words out, even though my voice shakes more than I'd like to admit.

Jaxon's grip tightens for a second, like he's contemplating something, before he lets me go, pushing me away with a single, deliberate motion. He takes a step back, eyeing me like I'm a puzzle he hasn't quite figured out.

"You're not exactly the type to run from a bunch of street thugs," he says, his voice dripping with suspicion. "What are you mixed up in, sweetheart?"

I almost laugh, but it comes out as a broken cough. "You think I'm the one mixed up in something? I'm running for my life here. They'll kill me if they catch me. They don't care about anything but their agenda." My words tumble out in a rush, each one an attempt

THE RUSE 3

to throw him off the scent, to keep him from asking questions I'm not ready to answer.

Jaxon stares at me, his eyes calculating, like he can read everything I'm trying so hard to hide. He tilts his head slightly, just enough to let me know that the thought of helping me is something he's weighing, not for kindness—but for something else.

"You always run this fast, or are you just saving your best moves for the big players?" His lips curl into a slight, mocking smile, but it's colder than any insult I've ever received.

There's no warmth in him. None at all. His presence is like the wind before a storm—tense, unrelenting. I've dealt with dangerous men before, but there's something different about him. Something unsettling.

I try to steady my breathing, the panic bubbling beneath my ribs, and fight the urge to bolt. "I don't have time for your games," I snap, my voice a little sharper than I intend. "I've got bigger problems than a bounty hunter looking for a paycheck."

Jaxon looks at me for a long moment, his gaze unreadable, but I can feel the tension radiating off him. He's weighing me, and whatever conclusions he's drawing, they don't sit right with me.

"Guess we're both running from something, then," he says after a pause, his tone hardening. "But I'm not here to save you."

The sound of footsteps echoes from the far end of the alley, growing louder. I can't waste any more time. I glance past Jaxon, eyes scanning the shadows, but I know the odds are against me. The thugs are closing in.

"I didn't ask you to," I mutter, spinning on my heel and darting forward, pushing past him.

But Jaxon's hand is suddenly on my arm, gripping tight enough to stop me dead in my tracks.

"Guess you're going to need some help," he says, voice rough, a hint of something almost like amusement in it.

I stare at him, frustration bubbling up in my chest.

"Why?"

He shrugs, not offering any explanation, and for a second, I hate him for it. But the sound of shouting behind me—louder now—forces me to swallow the fury.

"You're either with me or you're not," I say, voice low, tight.

He doesn't answer right away, but when he does, it's with a decision that feels too final, too dangerous.

"Let's get out of here first," he mutters. "Then we'll talk."

I can feel his fingers still wrapped around my arm, his grip just firm enough to remind me that he's not letting go. The heat of his palm sears through the thin fabric of my jacket, but it's the tension in his body—muscles taut, ready to spring—that's really got me on edge. If I had any sense, I'd pull away, keep running, but the alley behind us is closing in. I don't know if it's the adrenaline, the exhaustion, or the fact that there's no one else left to trust, but for some godforsaken reason, I don't fight him.

"How do you want to do this?" His voice is low, rough, as if the words have been dragged out from the depths of a much darker place.

I glance over my shoulder, hearing the gang closing in, their voices now cutting through the night air—loud, angry, and full of promises I don't plan on keeping.

I swallow, turning back to Jaxon. "You're not planning to drag me off to some cage, are you?"

He raises an eyebrow, his expression unreadable. "Not unless you give me a reason to."

I force a shaky breath, trying to quell the nerves that are knotting themselves in my stomach. It feels almost absurd, standing here with a man who's made a career of chasing people like me, and yet, there's a strange safety in his presence. Something about the way he stands—so sure of himself, even in the face of danger—reminds me of someone who's survived more than his fair share of close calls.

"Well," I say, shaking my head in disbelief, "I'd rather not find out if you've got a cage handy."

I turn my back to him, eyes darting up and down the alley. The footsteps are louder now, their owners getting closer, and there's nowhere to go but deeper into the maze of city streets. My mind is working overtime, trying to form some plan, some escape route, but nothing comes to mind.

"I'm not asking for charity, but I'll take it if you're offering," I add, more out of desperation than hope. "Can you help or not?"

Jaxon doesn't answer right away. He seems to be weighing the question, his gaze flicking briefly to the shadows where the thugs are lurking. I can see his mind turning, running through scenarios.

"I don't do charity," he finally says, his lips curling in that half-smile I've come to recognize as his default. "But I can get you out of here. For a price."

I clench my jaw. Of course. He's a bounty hunter. He'd never do anything for free. But right now, I don't have much of a choice.

"What's the price?" I ask, trying to sound less desperate than I feel.

He considers this for a beat, eyes flicking toward me, and for a moment, I wonder if he's going to ask for something ridiculous—some kind of trade I can't possibly offer. But then, as if the answer is as simple as breathing, he tilts his head, his gaze hard.

"Don't get in my way," he says.

I stare at him, confused. "What does that even mean?"

"I'm not here to babysit," Jaxon clarifies, voice gruff. "You make a move, you get caught, you're on your own. You stay out of my way, and I'll make sure we both get out of here in one piece."

I nod, though my stomach churns at the thought. "Deal." I don't have time to think about it. The gang is closer now. Their laughter echoes off the walls of the alley, mocking and relentless. The sound grates on my nerves, pulling me into full-on survival mode.

Jaxon steps forward, his hand brushing against my back as he takes the lead. The contact is brief but unmistakable, his body warm and solid in contrast to the cold night around us.

We move fast, not speaking as we weave through the maze of alleys. Jaxon doesn't look back. He knows I'm there, but he doesn't need to check on me. He's already made the decision. It's either I keep up, or I don't. I think about bolting a few times—about cutting and running when he's not looking—but something stops me every time. Maybe it's the fact that the gang would catch me before I made it a block, or maybe, just maybe, I'm starting to believe that Jaxon might get me out of this mess alive.

We take a sharp right, the narrow alley leading into a dimly lit street. I'm already sweating, my heart pounding with the effort to keep up, but Jaxon doesn't slow down. His long strides eat up the distance between us and the thugs that are still hot on our trail.

I hear their shouts now—faint, but close.

"You're not going to outrun them," I say, panting.

Jaxon doesn't answer, but his pace doesn't falter. He keeps pushing forward, faster now, as if he can sense the exact moment when the thugs will turn the corner. He's a man who knows how to move in a city like this, how to stay one step ahead of the predators that lurk in every shadow.

Then, without warning, he ducks into a doorway to our right, motioning for me to follow. The door is barely open—just enough to slip inside. We're in, just as the first of the gang members rounds the corner.

I press my back against the cool stone of the building, holding my breath. The thugs don't see us. They're too focused on the alley we just left behind, too caught up in the hunt.

Jaxon's chest rises and falls with each breath, his face inches from mine as he peers through the crack in the door. His presence fills the narrow space between us, suffocating and magnetic. His eyes meet mine for a moment, and I feel a flicker of something—an unspoken understanding, a fragile alliance forged in the fires of necessity.

"Keep your head down," he whispers, voice a sharp command.

I nod, and we wait.

The minutes stretch, a slow agony, as the thugs mill about just outside, unsure of where we've gone. I can feel the weight of Jaxon's presence next to me, his body a constant reminder that in this city, survival isn't about bravery. It's about knowing when to run and when to hide. And right now, hiding feels like the smarter move.

The sound of the thugs shouting outside fades into a muffled hum, the heavy beats of their boots retreating as they begin to give up their search. My pulse still races in my ears, my skin flushed with the rapid, desperate rhythm of survival. I stay pressed against the cold stone of the doorway, my body taut with the anticipation that the moment we move, we'll either slip out unnoticed or get caught in the middle of the next catastrophe.

Jaxon doesn't flinch. He's steady, the stillness of him as unnerving as his silence. I can feel the heat radiating off him, but he's not even breathing hard, the way someone accustomed to danger does. I wonder how many times he's been in this exact position—the calm before the storm. For him, it must be second nature.

"I thought you said you didn't babysit," I whisper, unable to keep the edge of sarcasm out of my voice.

His lips twitch in what I think is the closest thing to a smile he's capable of. "I'm not babysitting. Just trying to make sure you don't get us both killed." His tone is low, clipped, but there's a thread of something darker buried underneath it. I can't quite place it, but it's there.

I try not to react, but there's a part of me that wants to scream that I'm the one trying to survive here. I'm the one who's running, not him. But I bite my tongue. Arguing with a man who has the entire city's bounty hunter network in his back pocket seems about as productive as arguing with a brick wall.

Minutes stretch into eternity as we remain still, waiting, the sound of the thugs' retreating footsteps slowly fading. The cool air feels like it's pressing in on us from all sides, the darkness thick with tension. I should feel safer, but there's something about the way Jaxon's body is so close, about how his presence seems to swallow up the space, that makes me feel both grounded and trapped at once.

"Think they're gone?" I finally ask, my voice low, unsure whether the question is aimed at him or more at myself.

Jaxon's eyes flick toward the crack in the door, the only hint of movement in the otherwise still night. His gaze sharpens, his posture shifting just slightly, a subtle signal that he's assessing the risk. "Not yet," he murmurs, the words laced with a warning.

I glance back at him, confusion flitting through me. "Then why are we still standing here?"

"Because they're not gone," he says simply, as if it's the most obvious thing in the world. "They'll circle back. I know these streets. And I know their type."

"Right," I mutter. I don't like the thought of being bait. Being stuck, waiting for the inevitable, feels like surrender. "So what's the plan?"

Jaxon takes a moment, the faintest flicker of something in his eyes. It's the same look I saw in his face when we first collided in that alley—something like recognition, but with a touch of disdain. As if he's already decided I'm trouble, but trouble can be useful, sometimes.

"We get to the rooftops. From there, we move fast," he says, his voice a clipped command that brooks no argument.

THE RUSE   9

"Rooftops?" I repeat, almost incredulously. "Are you trying to get us both killed?"

Jaxon doesn't answer, his focus returning to the crack in the door. The tension between us is palpable, thickening with every passing second. I can feel the weight of the decision hanging in the air—whether I follow this man or risk whatever's waiting for me out there on the streets below. He's not exactly reassuring, and I'd be lying if I said I didn't want to scream at him to just let me go. But every part of me knows that's not an option.

So I nod, but only just. "Lead the way."

Without another word, he slips through the door, his movements fluid and precise. I follow, my heart in my throat as I try to keep my breathing steady. The narrow hallway is dimly lit, dust particles floating in the shafts of light that spill in through the windows. Every creak of the old building underfoot sounds like a warning, but Jaxon doesn't hesitate. He moves with purpose, his footsteps quiet but sure.

We ascend the narrow stairwell, the air growing colder with each step. I'm hyperaware of every creak and groan of the building, the distant shouts of the gang still echoing down below. I feel the weight of every minute passing, the risk inching higher with each move.

At the top of the stairs, Jaxon gestures to the window. "We climb out here."

I eye the gap, unsure how exactly it's going to work. There's nothing but air between us and the next rooftop. "You're kidding, right?" I say, my voice coming out sharper than I intended.

"Nope," he says, his voice deadpan. "The ledge is wide enough. You'll make it."

I glance over at him, my heart pounding as I take a step back. He's calm, his focus trained ahead, but there's a flicker of something behind his eyes—something too calculating, too cold.

"You've done this before, haven't you?" I ask, voice laced with disbelief.

"I don't do anything I haven't done before," he responds easily, and with a single motion, he's out the window, vanishing into the night like he's done it a thousand times.

I stand frozen for a beat, my mind racing. Then, the footsteps—heavy, determined—are closer than I thought. The gang's not far behind. There's no time to hesitate. My pulse racing, I grab hold of the window ledge and pull myself outside. The cold air hits me like a slap, and I feel the immediate pull of gravity, my stomach lurching as I make my way onto the narrow ledge.

The city sprawls below, a sea of lights that seems so far away. I glance back at Jaxon, but he's already ahead, a dark silhouette against the backdrop of the night sky.

"You coming, or are you just going to stand there?" His voice is distant, but the challenge is clear.

I take a deep breath and follow.

As I step carefully along the ledge, trying to ignore the dizzying drop below, something shifts in the air—an unmistakable crackle of tension. Then, a shout from behind me. The gang's found us.

Chapter 2: Unlikely Allies

I never should have agreed to this.

But here we were, trudging through the damp alleys of New Chicago's underbelly, a tangle of shadows and filth where even the rats knew better than to stick around. The air felt thick, like the city itself was holding its breath, waiting for something to break. My boots slapped against the wet pavement, every echo a reminder that I had no business being here, no reason to trust the man at my side, yet somehow, there I was, tethered to him like some fool caught in a slow-moving disaster.

Jaxon. Even his name made me itch with irritation, and yet... I couldn't stop looking at him. He wasn't a man you could ignore, even if you tried. He was tall, broad-shouldered in the way of someone who spent too much time in places where muscles and fists solved problems. His dark hair was perpetually in that just-messy-enough-to-be-cool state, and there was this... this magnetism about him that made me want to punch him and kiss him all in one breath. A walking contradiction, as infuriating as he was impossible to resist.

"You know, you're really something else," I muttered, wiping my hand across my brow to keep the sweat from getting into my eyes. It wasn't the humidity that made me sweat—no, it was the way he made every part of me feel like I was one bad decision away from losing control.

Jaxon glanced over, a crooked grin tugging at the corner of his mouth. "I've been told," he replied, voice low and gravelly, like it had been worn down by years of bad decisions.

I wanted to respond, but the words stuck in my throat. Damn him for being so damn charming.

We passed a neon-lit strip club on the corner, its buzzing sign flickering like it was about to give up on life entirely. The smell of stale cigarettes and cheap perfume clung to the air, and I wrinkled my nose, stepping around a puddle that looked suspiciously like it might be more than just rainwater. The city had a way of making even the most familiar places feel unfamiliar, unsafe.

"We're close," Jaxon said, his voice snapping me out of my thoughts.

I glanced at him, his dark eyes scanning the alleyways with an intensity that made my skin prickle. "Close to what?"

He didn't answer right away, instead leading me into a narrow passageway between two crumbling buildings, the walls adorned with graffiti that seemed to pulse with the rhythm of the city's heartbeat. I followed, unsure if this was where I wanted to go, but knowing that the longer I hesitated, the more likely I'd end up regretting it.

Jaxon stopped at a rusted fire escape and turned to face me. His eyes were hard, calculating, like he was making some kind of decision. "You sure you're ready for this?" he asked.

I raised an eyebrow. "Do I look like someone who's not ready?"

He shrugged, and for a moment, his gaze softened, just a flicker of something human behind the mask of menace he wore so easily. "I've seen a lot of people get swallowed up by this city," he said quietly. "The kind who think they can walk through it without paying the price."

I snorted. "You think I'm scared of a little danger?"

A smirk tugged at his lips. "I think you're a lot more cautious than you let on."

I bristled. "You don't know me."

"Yeah," he said, taking a step closer, lowering his voice until it was barely a whisper. "But I will."

I fought the urge to step back, my heart doing that strange, unpredictable dance in my chest. "So what's the plan, genius?"

Jaxon's eyes flashed with something dark, something I didn't want to name, and for the first time since we'd started this ridiculous partnership, I wondered if I'd made a mistake. But it was too late to turn back now. He was already moving, climbing the fire escape with the kind of ease that made it clear he was no stranger to the rooftops of this crumbling city.

I followed reluctantly, keeping a good distance between us. It wasn't the climb that bothered me—it was the fact that, in moments like this, I couldn't help but wonder whether Jaxon's plan was the one that would end up getting me killed.

When we reached the top, the city spread out before us, a canvas of neon lights and darkened streets. Somewhere down there, a crime lord pulled the strings, and somehow, we were both tangled in the web.

"We find him tonight," Jaxon said, his voice grim as he surveyed the city below.

"How?" I asked, crossing my arms.

He hesitated, as though weighing his words carefully. "We follow the money. And the people. Everyone's got a price, even the ones who think they're untouchable."

"Is that why you're doing this?" I asked, more to myself than him. "For the money?"

Jaxon shot me a look that could've cut glass. "I'm not here for the money. I'm here to end it. To burn it all down."

The weight of his words hung between us, heavy and suffocating.

I swallowed hard. "And I'm here because I've got a score to settle."

For a long moment, we just stood there, looking at each other across the space that separated us. Something crackled in the air, an unspoken understanding that neither of us could ignore. He wasn't my ally. He wasn't even a friend. But for tonight, we were in this together, two halves of something neither of us fully understood.

"We go in quiet," Jaxon said, his voice now a soft command. "Get close. And we make sure no one walks out alive except for us."

I nodded, the finality of his words sinking in. This wasn't just about money. Or revenge. This was about something far darker, something that would change us both before it was over.

And somewhere deep inside, I knew that whatever happened next, I'd never be the same.

The night had taken on a new weight, as though the entire city knew something was about to shift. I could feel it in my bones, an unsettling hum that didn't quite reach my ears, but pressed against my skin like an electric charge. The buildings loomed over us, dark sentinels, their cracked windows staring blankly as we passed. I walked a little faster, the silence between Jaxon and me stretching, thick and tight.

Jaxon's every step was measured, calculated. He moved like someone who had spent too many nights in places where being loud or careless meant someone didn't make it out. I envied him, just a little, for the way he made danger look effortless, like it was an old friend he could trust without thinking twice. I, on the other hand, had spent most of my life avoiding it—getting by with my quick wit and faster feet, rather than relying on fists or guns. But the world had a way of twisting things, didn't it?

"Don't fall behind," Jaxon muttered without looking at me.

I shot him a glare. "You act like I'm the one lagging behind here. You're the one with a death wish."

He grinned, the faintest flash of amusement in his eyes. "You'll catch up."

"Ha. You think so?" I couldn't help the biting edge to my voice. "Because last time I checked, I didn't need a lesson in how to stay alive from you."

For a second, he didn't respond. Then, in that same low tone that always seemed to hold a hundred unspoken words, he said, "Maybe not. But it's always better to have someone watch your back."

I would've responded, but something about the way he said it made my throat tighten, and for the first time in hours, I realized that, just maybe, I wasn't the only one who didn't want to die tonight.

We slipped deeper into the labyrinth of alleyways, moving past flickering streetlights that barely made a dent in the overwhelming darkness. Somewhere ahead, I knew, was the heart of the city's rot—the crime lord we'd both come to destroy. But that didn't make it any less dangerous. If anything, it made it more so. The deeper we went, the more the city seemed to close in on itself. Every corner felt like it was waiting to swallow us whole.

"How much further?" I asked, my voice almost lost in the space between us.

"Not much." Jaxon's voice was sharp now, all business, and I couldn't decide whether that was comforting or disconcerting.

"Great," I muttered. "I love it when you say that. It's like a promise, but with no actual details."

He shot me a sideways glance. "You've got a smart mouth for someone who's about to get killed."

"Well, at least I'll die with some style," I quipped, even though I wasn't sure how much longer I could keep up the act. There was something about this place, the way it gnawed at you, that made every second feel like a countdown.

We rounded a corner, and I froze. I hadn't seen anything. No flashy signs or neon lights. No hint of the glitzy, dangerous underworld I was used to. But I could feel it now, creeping up on me, the weight of the place pressing down like a threat you couldn't ignore.

"This is it," Jaxon said, voice barely above a whisper.

I followed his gaze to a nondescript door nestled between two crumbling walls. The kind of door no one would look at twice unless they knew what it meant. The door wasn't even marked, but the feeling in my gut told me all I needed to know. This wasn't a place for amateurs. This was where the real work got done.

I took a step forward, then stopped. "How do you know?"

Jaxon didn't answer right away. Instead, he pulled something from his jacket—a small, almost delicate-looking device that flickered to life as he tapped a few buttons.

"What the hell is that?" I asked, raising an eyebrow.

"A key," he said, still focused on the device. "It'll get us in."

A key. To a place like this? I wasn't sure if that made me more nervous or less.

"Seriously, Jaxon," I pressed. "You just—"

He held up a hand. "This isn't a game, okay? If we get caught here, we're done. You need to stay sharp."

He didn't say anything else, just stepped forward and pressed the device against the door. The faintest hum echoed, and the door clicked open. It felt wrong, like we were stepping into a trap, and I should've backed out while I still could. But my feet wouldn't move.

"After you," Jaxon said, his eyes gleaming in the half-light.

I stepped through, not bothering to look back, knowing that if I hesitated now, I wouldn't go through at all. Inside was worse than I imagined. The room stretched long and narrow, lit only by the harsh glare of overhead fluorescent lights. The air smelled like chemicals and blood, and my stomach turned.

I didn't need to ask what we were here for. Every inch of this place reeked of desperation and danger. But as I glanced around, something flickered in the corner of my eye—a movement that didn't quite belong. I tensed, my hand already reaching for the knife at my side.

Jaxon wasn't looking at me anymore. His eyes were locked on something further ahead, where the shadows seemed to thicken in a way that didn't make sense. He took a single step forward, his movements so precise that I felt a chill.

THE RUSE

"Don't look at it too closely," he said quietly, his voice barely audible over the beating of my own heart.

I followed his gaze, squinting into the shadows. And that's when I saw it—the figure watching us from the far end of the room. The kind of figure that made everything else fade into the background. They weren't alone. And neither were we.

"Looks like we've got company," I muttered.

Jaxon's lips curled into that familiar, dangerous smirk. "Let's say we keep them from noticing us for a little longer, yeah?"

I had no idea how long that would last.

The silence stretched thin, the kind that feels like the whole world is holding its breath. There was no sound but the faint buzzing of the overhead lights, each flicker adding to the tense rhythm of the room. I stood frozen, my eyes fixed on the shadowed figure at the far end of the room, the figure that shouldn't have been there. They were still—too still—but the air around them crackled with danger. Whoever they were, they weren't just a bystander. They were waiting. And I was about to find out what for.

I glanced at Jaxon, his body rigid as he stood just slightly in front of me, as if instinctively blocking me from whatever was coming. He didn't need to say anything; his posture was enough. He was ready for this—whatever this was. I, on the other hand, felt the familiar surge of panic creeping up my spine. This wasn't part of the plan. We hadn't come here to deal with... whatever this was.

"Stay close," he murmured, his voice low, controlled. I nodded, though my heart hammered in my chest, a wild rhythm that betrayed my outward calm.

The figure stepped forward, just enough to break the shadows around them, revealing a face that made my blood run cold. The man was tall, with sharp features and eyes that gleamed with a knowing sort of malice. His lips curved upward into a smile that made it clear he had been waiting for us. Waiting for me, specifically.

I tensed. "You don't look like the welcoming committee," I muttered, my fingers brushing the handle of my blade.

Jaxon's eyes darted over to me for a split second, a warning—stay calm, stay smart. But there was a slight twitch at the corner of his mouth, the kind that told me he was itching for this. He was used to this—he thrived on this kind of tension. Me? Not so much.

"Didn't take you for the type to sneak around, Jaxon," the man's voice was smooth, almost lazy. It dripped with something foul—condescension, maybe, or amusement. "You've been busy."

"I could say the same to you," Jaxon shot back, his tone cool, the rhythm of the exchange familiar. "You're not here to make a deal. So, what's your angle?"

The man's smile didn't falter, but his eyes flicked to me briefly, taking me in with an unsettling level of interest. "You've got an interesting companion, Jaxon," he said, his voice almost playful. "Not quite what I was expecting. But then again, you always did like to mix things up."

I shifted uncomfortably under his gaze, suddenly feeling very exposed in this dimly lit room. I had no idea who this man was or how he knew Jaxon, but I could tell he was more than just an obstacle. He was part of the machinery that turned this city's darkest corners. Part of the reason we were here in the first place.

I looked at Jaxon, trying to read him, but his expression was unreadable. He was always so damn good at that, keeping everything locked behind that steel-cold mask of his. Whatever history he shared with this guy, it was more than just business.

"Not interested in a chat, pal," I said, my voice steady despite the sudden surge of adrenaline. "Get to the point."

The man chuckled, a low, mirthless sound that bounced off the walls. "A little impatient, aren't we?" He stepped closer, his boots echoing with each step. "But then, I suppose that's the thing about people like you—always looking for the quick way out."

Jaxon's hand subtly moved toward his side, and I knew that in an instant, he'd have a weapon in hand. But there was something about this guy that didn't sit right. He wasn't just some lackey or hired muscle. He was... familiar with the game. Too familiar.

"I'm not here to make deals," the man continued, his eyes flicking back to Jaxon. "I'm here to deliver a message." He paused, letting the words hang in the air like a weight. "Your time's up, Jaxon. The game's over."

I didn't even have time to react before the man lunged. It was fast, too fast. A blur of motion, and before I knew what was happening, Jaxon had already shifted, blocking the attack with a speed that made me dizzy. The sound of a metal blade scraping against bone filled the room, and the man staggered back, a surprised look on his face. But the expression that replaced it was something darker, something colder.

"You're still trying to play this game," Jaxon said, his voice a calm, dangerous whisper. "I thought we were past this."

The man wiped the blood from his mouth with the back of his hand, his smile widening. "Maybe you should've stayed out of it, Jaxon. But now that you've made it personal..." He shrugged. "Guess there's no going back."

I didn't know what kind of history they shared, but I could tell that Jaxon wasn't going to walk away from this unscathed. His jaw was set, his eyes hard. But there was something behind them that made my stomach turn, a flicker of doubt, maybe. Or was it regret?

"Get ready," Jaxon said suddenly, his voice sharp. "He's not alone."

I barely had time to react before more figures emerged from the shadows—silent, like phantoms. A part of me wanted to scream, to run. But I wasn't about to leave Jaxon hanging, no matter how much I wanted to walk away from this madness.

The man who'd spoken before raised his hands, almost mockingly, and the others spread out, surrounding us.

"Guess it's time to finish what you started," he said, his grin returning in full force.

The room was closing in. The tension was suffocating. We were trapped, and as I met Jaxon's eyes—finally seeing the flicker of something other than cold calculation—I knew that whatever happened next, nothing would ever be the same.

And then the lights went out.

Chapter 3: Secrets and Shadows

The safe house was a wreck. Not that I was expecting luxury, but there's a certain standard to desperation. The flickering light overhead cast an eerie glow on the cracked walls, which trembled with every gust of wind that rattled the thin, broken windows. The floor creaked in protest as I shifted my weight, standing just a few feet away from him, watching. I wasn't sure what to make of the man hunched over the map in front of him. He was absorbed in it, every line and marker etched deeply in his mind, as though his survival depended on understanding every curve of that city better than his own skin. I watched him, silently, my gaze tracing the sharp angle of his jaw, the way his fingers pressed against the paper as if it were the only thing in the world he could trust.

His eyes flickered up, sharp and unsettling, catching me in the act of studying him. He didn't even need to ask what I was thinking. There was no point in pretending we were anything but what we were—two survivors thrown together by fate and circumstance, bound by nothing but mutual distrust.

"You think you've figured me out, don't you?" His voice was low, barely above a murmur, but it still felt like an accusation.

I leaned against the crumbling wall, my arms crossed, resisting the urge to shiver in the cold that crept in from the cracked windows. "I haven't figured you out. I'm just trying to figure out what the hell you're planning."

His laugh, short and bitter, sent a chill down my spine. He stood up abruptly, sweeping the map off the table as if it were a useless thing, a distraction. The way he moved—quick, almost predatory—was enough to make me flinch, but I didn't. It wasn't fear I felt, but something else. Something raw and stirring that I couldn't name.

"You think I'm planning something?" His eyes flashed in the dim light. "You think I'm some villain in a story that's supposed to make sense?"

I opened my mouth to respond, but the words caught in my throat. His question wasn't just a challenge; it was a crack in the armor of his cold detachment. A question to himself, maybe. The vulnerability it hinted at made me pause, just long enough for him to notice.

"You're not making this easy," I said finally, the words blunt, though a part of me wondered why I cared.

His lips pressed into a thin line, and for a long moment, the only sound was the low hum of the flickering light above us. He seemed to weigh my words carefully, measuring their meaning in the silence. When he spoke again, his tone was far more controlled, as though the mask was back in place. "I never meant to make it easy. But you, you're not like the others. You're different. And I don't know if that makes you a liability or... something more."

There it was again, that crack, barely noticeable unless you were paying attention. And I was paying attention. The way he glanced at me, almost as if expecting me to lash out, to call him out on his cryptic nonsense. But I didn't. Maybe because I understood more than I cared to admit.

The truth was, I didn't know what to make of him. Every instinct screamed at me to keep my distance, to walk away from this mess before I became entangled in whatever shadows he was chasing. But there was something about him that refused to be ignored. Something that pulled at me, an invisible thread tying my fate to his. Whether I liked it or not.

I took a step closer, the sound of my boots echoing in the quiet room, my voice quiet but firm. "You think I'm a liability? You're wrong."

THE RUSE   23

He didn't move, just looked at me, his gaze hard and calculating. "I'm not wrong. People like you—people who ask too many questions, poke around where they shouldn't—they don't last long in this line of work. You can't keep acting like you're still in control."

"Maybe I don't want to be in control," I shot back, the words coming out sharper than I intended. "Maybe I'm just trying to survive like everyone else."

His eyes narrowed, and for a second, I thought he might lash out, but he didn't. Instead, he turned away, raking his hand through his hair, as if my words had caught him off guard. "Survive? You think that's what this is about? Surviving?" His voice grew quieter, more contemplative, though there was still a bite to it. "You think I'm here because I want to survive?"

I didn't answer right away. What was I supposed to say? That he was here because of something more, something far darker than survival? That there was something beneath the surface of his cold exterior—something he was afraid to confront, let alone admit?

The silence stretched between us, thick and charged, before I finally spoke. "Why are you here, then? What is it you're running from?"

He froze, his back to me now. The tension in the room thickened, the air suddenly charged with something neither of us were willing to name. It was as though my words had opened something—something fragile and dangerous. He didn't turn around, but his shoulders tensed, his breath coming in shallow, controlled bursts.

"You wouldn't understand," he muttered, his voice low, almost to himself. But I heard it. The flicker of something deeper—something darker—just beneath the surface. And for the first time, I wondered if he even understood it himself.

He didn't move after that, the stillness in the room almost unbearable. I could feel the weight of the words I'd thrown at him, hanging between us like a storm cloud waiting to burst. Every instinct in me screamed to say something else, to fill the silence with something less loaded, but I couldn't. I wasn't the type to back down from a fight, and something about the way he stood there, tense and unnerving, made me want to push until he cracked.

But then, without a word, he turned around. Slowly. Deliberately. His eyes met mine, not with the sharpness I expected, but with something else—something darker. I couldn't quite place it, but the air in the room seemed to shift. "You don't get it," he said, his voice barely a whisper. But I heard it, clear as day.

"What is it I'm missing?" I asked, unable to keep the sarcasm out of my tone. It wasn't that I wanted to be hostile; it was more like a reflex, a way to keep the distance from the suffocating closeness that had started to creep up between us.

He didn't answer immediately, and for a moment, it was like we were locked in a quiet standoff, each of us waiting for the other to make the next move. His gaze flickered to the floor before rising back to meet mine, the same guarded expression covering his face, but now there was something else there too. A flicker of regret? Or maybe fear. I wasn't sure.

"You think I'm some kind of... monster, don't you?" The question was low, bitter, as if he was already bracing for the answer.

I didn't want to say yes. Not exactly. But how could I not? Everything about him screamed danger, screamed secrecy. And yet... and yet there was that flicker again, something underneath the surface, something I couldn't ignore.

"You're not a monster," I said carefully, testing the waters. "You're just... complicated. In the worst possible way."

He huffed out a bitter laugh, stepping away from the table where the map still lay, forgotten. "Complicated? Is that what you call it? Maybe that's the problem. You don't see the whole picture." He moved closer, his presence so overwhelming it felt like the walls were closing in on me.

I swallowed hard. "I'm not sure I want to see the whole picture."

A shadow crossed his face, and for a brief second, I could almost swear I saw something akin to regret. Or maybe it was just my mind trying to make sense of everything that didn't quite add up. But before I could hold onto the thought, he spoke again, his voice low, like a confession he didn't want to make.

"You think I'm just some guy with a past I can't escape," he said, his eyes fixed on the floor. "And you're right. I can't. But it's more than that. It's..." He stopped, rubbing a hand over his face as if the words were stuck in his throat.

"Then spit it out," I said, the impatience in my voice cutting through the tension. I didn't care about his past. Not really. I just wanted to understand him, even if I hated what I'd find out.

"I'm not running from my past," he said suddenly, his voice sharp as a knife. "I'm running from what I'm going to become if I stay in this game much longer."

The words hung in the air, unspoken, as if they had the weight of years behind them. I felt the cold chill of the room creep further under my skin, and I took a step back, my hands instinctively reaching out to steady myself against the crumbling wall. I wasn't sure what he meant, but I wasn't about to ask. I had the feeling that knowing more about him was a dangerous thing, something that would take me further down a path I wasn't ready to walk.

"Then stop," I said quietly, almost to myself. "Stop running."

He looked up sharply, his eyes hardening with something close to anger. "You think it's that easy?" His voice was tight, every word carrying the weight of something old, something that had broken him. "I can't just walk away. You don't get to choose your path when you've already crossed a line that can't be uncrossed."

The words hit me harder than I expected. I felt a pang of something deep, something that made me wonder what he had done, what he had seen, to make him so sure that the past had him locked in its grip. It was clear that whatever he'd been through, he didn't believe there was any way out.

I couldn't imagine what it must feel like, to be so trapped in your own life, to be so certain that there was no redemption. I wanted to reach out to him, tell him there was another way. But something stopped me. Maybe it was the way he looked at me, like he knew exactly what I was thinking.

"You don't get to tell me what to do," he said, his voice cold now, almost detached.

"I'm not telling you what to do," I shot back, frustration building in me. "But you need to stop acting like you're some martyr. The only one holding you back is you."

He took a step toward me, and for a brief moment, the distance between us felt smaller than ever. His breath was warm against my face, and I could smell the faint hint of smoke on his clothes, the sharp tang of alcohol still lingering on his skin. I didn't move, didn't even flinch. Something in his eyes made me want to stand my ground, to prove that I wasn't afraid of whatever he was trying to throw at me.

"I didn't ask for your help," he muttered, barely above a whisper, his lips just inches from mine. "And I sure as hell don't need it."

The words stung, but I didn't back down. I couldn't. Not now. Not when everything between us felt like it was teetering on the edge of something—something raw, something dangerous.

"You'll need it eventually," I said, my voice steady, though my heart was pounding in my chest. "And when that time comes, don't expect me to be the one to save you."

He stepped back, his jaw clenching, as if the words I'd spoken had physically struck him. I felt an odd rush of satisfaction at the way

THE RUSE

his composure faltered, but it was quickly replaced by an unsettling emptiness that crept over me. I could hear my pulse in my ears, the thudding like a drum, and I couldn't quite shake the feeling that we were spiraling into something neither of us could control.

For a moment, neither of us spoke. I watched him, standing there in the dim light, his posture stiff, like a man bracing for a blow. The silence between us felt thick, as though we were both too afraid to move. It was a tension I could almost taste in the stale air—heavy, suffocating. And yet, I couldn't look away. I couldn't tear my eyes from him.

His voice broke the silence, and it was quieter this time, more measured. "You think you can walk away from me when it all goes south? You think you'll be able to just... let it go?"

His words cut through the air like a sharp blade. I froze, every nerve in my body going rigid. He was right. I had no idea what I would do when things fell apart, when the lies unraveled, when the secrets buried beneath the surface rose to the top. It was so easy to say that I wouldn't get involved, that I wouldn't let him drag me deeper into his world of shadows, but somewhere inside, I knew that wasn't true.

I crossed the room, deliberately slow, each step making the floorboards creak under my boots, the sound breaking the quiet like a gunshot. "Don't assume you know me," I said, my voice low, controlled. "I'm not some naive fool who thinks she can change you. I'm not some damsel in distress waiting to be rescued."

His eyes flickered, a flash of something—amusement, disbelief—before the mask slipped back into place. "I didn't think you were." He leaned back against the table, the sharp edge of the map digging into his side. "But I still think you're in way over your head."

"I'll be fine," I shot back, the words too quick, too certain. But I wasn't fine. I wasn't fine at all. It was easier to say it than to believe it. Easier to stand there and pretend that I wasn't already unraveling, piece by piece, in this crumbling room with him.

The silence lingered again, thick and heavy, until finally, I couldn't take it anymore. I had to know. I had to understand. "Why don't you just tell me what the hell you're running from?" The question came out sharper than I intended, but it felt like the only thing that mattered. If he was going to be this insufferable, this impossible, then at least I needed something real to hold onto, something solid amidst the chaos.

He sighed, a long, almost pained sound, before pushing himself off the table with a sharp motion, pacing in front of me like a caged animal. I stood still, watching him with equal parts curiosity and wariness. The space between us had become something more now—something electric.

"I don't have to explain myself to you," he muttered, his voice tight.

I tilted my head slightly. "But you want to, don't you? You want someone to understand. Even if you hate the idea of it."

He stopped in front of me, close enough that I could feel the heat of his body. It was all too much—his proximity, the tension, the rawness of the moment. "You think understanding me is going to make this easier for you?" he asked, his voice now a low rasp, each word coated with bitterness. "You think you're going to find some kind of peace with me after everything I've done? After the things I've seen?"

I didn't answer right away. Because I didn't know. I didn't know what I thought anymore. Part of me wanted to walk away, to turn my back and leave him to whatever dark corner of the world he'd crawled out from. But there was another part of me, a part I wasn't willing to acknowledge, that wanted to stay. To keep pushing. To get answers from him, even if those answers could destroy everything.

"Tell me, then," I said quietly, "why do you think I'm still here? After everything?"

He looked at me, his expression unreadable. The seconds stretched on, and for a moment, I thought he might turn away. But then he spoke, his voice barely above a whisper, full of something I couldn't place.

"Because you don't know how to walk away. Not from me. Not from this."

I swallowed, the words hitting me harder than I'd expected. He was right. I didn't know how to walk away. The truth was, I was in this too deep now. And I didn't want to admit it, but I had come to rely on him—on his presence, on the weird, maddening pull between us. As much as I wanted to hate him, as much as I wanted to run, there was something else there, something raw and dangerous. Something that couldn't be ignored.

I took a deep breath, stepping back slightly. "Maybe you're right. Maybe I don't know how to walk away. But that doesn't mean I'm going to follow you blindly into whatever mess you've made for yourself."

For a split second, I thought I saw something in his eyes—some glimmer of relief, of release—but it vanished as quickly as it appeared, hidden behind the mask once more.

"I don't need you to follow me," he said, his tone clipped. "I need you to stay out of my way."

The words felt like a slap. But I held my ground, meeting his gaze. "I won't," I said simply. "I'm not going anywhere."

The silence that followed felt heavy, suffocating. And then, just as I thought we might be on the edge of some kind of breakthrough, the door behind us creaked open.

We froze.

I barely had time to react before the figure in the doorway stepped forward. Someone I didn't recognize. Someone who shouldn't have been there. And the last thing I saw before the world around us went black was the glint of a blade in the stranger's hand.

Chapter 4: The Enemy of My Enemy

The night air was thick with the promise of trouble, a humid veil that clung to the skin, slick and suffocating. I hated it. I hated how it made my shirt stick to my back and how every breath felt like it was laced with danger. But I didn't have the luxury of being uncomfortable—not tonight.

Jaxon's silhouette cut through the darkness in front of me, his movements effortless, like a predator on the hunt. He was always calm, always composed, and always several steps ahead of me. It was a skill I'd come to begrudgingly admire. And tonight, as we crept towards the dilapidated warehouse that was the center of the gang's operations, that calmness was starting to rub off on me. Or maybe it was just the fact that we both knew what was at stake—more than just another criminal operation. This was bigger. Much bigger.

He paused at the edge of the building, one hand resting on the rough brick wall, the other lifting a small device to his ear. His jaw was tense, lips thin, as if he could hear something beyond the hum of the city. He didn't speak—just nodded once, then turned his gaze towards me. His eyes, always calculating, flicked over my figure with that familiar intensity, and for a moment, I could have sworn there was something else in them. Something deeper.

"You ready?" he asked, his voice low and controlled, like he was already on the edge of some decision I couldn't quite fathom.

I wanted to say no. Wanted to pull back, to step away from the danger, but the truth was, I'd already crossed that line the moment I walked into this mess. "Let's go," I replied instead, pushing all the hesitation to the back of my mind. There was no turning back.

Jaxon led the way again, his body an extension of the shadows, moving through the darkness like it was his natural habitat. The warehouse loomed ahead, a hulk of steel and stone that looked as if it had been abandoned decades ago—fitting for a crime syndicate that hid in plain sight. We circled the building until we found the back entrance, an old metal door that was barely hanging on its hinges. Jaxon pulled out a small tool and in a matter of seconds, the lock clicked open.

Inside, the warehouse smelled of rust, stale beer, and something more metallic. The walls were lined with shelves filled with crates, but I knew it wasn't just contraband stacked high. This was bigger. I could feel it in my bones, the same way you can sense the storm before the first raindrop hits your skin.

We moved silently, Jaxon's footsteps so light they barely made a sound. Me? I was all clumsy and self-conscious, but somehow, I kept up. We reached a set of narrow stairs leading to the second floor, and that's when the first sign of something truly wrong hit me—voices. Low murmurs, but unmistakable in their urgency.

Jaxon motioned for me to stay low. I didn't argue. We crept up the stairs, the old wood groaning beneath our weight, the faint echo of footsteps above telling me we weren't alone. The top of the stairs opened into a large room—dimly lit, with men milling about, a few hunched over tables, others arguing in hushed tones. And there, at the far end of the room, was a figure I recognized immediately.

Marek. The crime lord. His reputation had spread far enough that even I knew his name. But tonight, he wasn't the monster I had expected. No, tonight, he looked like a man on the edge of losing everything. His shirt was wrinkled, his tie crooked, and there was a nervous twitch to his fingers as he ran them through his graying hair. The man had been the puppet master behind the scenes for far too long, but whatever deal he'd struck had apparently gone sideways.

"What is this?" one of the men demanded, his voice rising. "You said we'd be safe! Now they're everywhere—"

"Shut up!" Marek barked, his voice sharp with panic. "We've got bigger problems than your little turf war! Do you think The Wraith is going to give a damn about your petty squabbles? He wants it all. And he's coming for us."

The mention of The Wraith made my skin prickle. I'd heard whispers about him—no one knew who he was, or where he came from. But everyone knew he had a way of making people disappear, leaving behind nothing but a whisper of smoke and blood. He was a shadow in every sense of the word, and tonight, I could feel him looming over everything, just out of sight.

Jaxon's grip tightened around my arm, his eyes never leaving the scene unfolding in front of us. "He's not just a ghost," he muttered, more to himself than to me. "The Wraith is someone with eyes everywhere."

I nodded, my throat dry. I had the sinking feeling that whatever this meeting was about, it wasn't just some power play. Marek wasn't scared of losing his position in the gang—he was terrified of The Wraith's reach.

But then, as I looked closer, I noticed something that made my stomach twist. There was something off about Marek's demeanor, something... forced. He wasn't the only one afraid of The Wraith. He was also in over his head, tangled in a conspiracy that had already swallowed him whole.

I glanced at Jaxon, but his expression was unreadable. His face was a mask, but I could see the slight tension in his shoulders, the way his fingers twitched at his side. He was thinking, processing. I knew this was more than just a routine job for him—it was personal.

"Let's move," he said suddenly, pulling me out of my thoughts. There was no time to waste.

I followed, my heart pounding in my chest, as we made our way deeper into the shadows. The enemy of my enemy wasn't just some faceless criminal. This was a war that would change everything, and if I wasn't careful, it would swallow us both whole.

The hum of the fluorescent lights overhead made my skin prickle, each buzz like a warning bell that we were being watched. I'd expected some form of confrontation, but nothing prepared me for the icy knot of tension that lodged itself in my stomach as we slipped deeper into the warehouse. The layout was simple—high ceilings, expansive space—but every corner, every crevice felt like it was holding its breath, waiting for something bad to happen. My steps were light but shaky, betraying the calm I tried so desperately to project.

Jaxon's presence beside me was a strange comfort. He moved with the quiet grace of someone who had spent a lifetime sneaking around corners, hiding in the shadows, always a step ahead of whatever was lurking. But tonight, I could feel something else—a certain awareness between us that hadn't been there before.

We reached the far end of the building, where the walls narrowed into a makeshift office area. The door was cracked open, the faint glow of a desk lamp spilling into the dark hall. We exchanged a glance, one that could have said a million things, but neither of us spoke. The air around us was taut with expectation.

"What's the plan?" I whispered, though I already knew his answer.

Jaxon's eyes flicked to the door. "We go in fast. No room for mistakes."

I nodded, feeling the pulse of adrenaline rush through me, making my fingers twitch at my sides. Fast. There was a sharp edge to his voice that hinted at urgency. The kind that usually meant something was off, that we were walking into something much bigger than just another drug deal or arms stash.

Without another word, Jaxon pushed the door open, his body shifting seamlessly from shadow to light, his gun raised in one fluid motion. I was right behind him, my own weapon drawn, but my heart was in my throat.

Inside, Marek stood with his back to us, talking to a man I didn't recognize—tall, wiry, his face obscured by a hood. It was the kind of face you'd forget the moment you turned away from it. The kind of man who didn't need a name to be dangerous.

"Everything's set?" Marek's voice cracked, desperation lacing his tone.

I didn't need to hear more. We were too late. This wasn't just about control over the city's criminal underground. This was about something far darker, something that made my skin crawl and my heart skip a beat. My instincts told me that Marek was trying to cut a deal, to save whatever part of himself he still could. But the cold reality was that he had no leverage. The Wraith wasn't someone you could bribe or negotiate with.

"Who's your friend?" Jaxon's voice sliced through the tension, calm and direct, like a blade finding its mark.

The man in the hood didn't flinch, but Marek's eyes went wide. He didn't even turn around at first, but his hand trembled as he reached for the desk, knocking over a glass of whiskey in his haste. "You shouldn't be here," he mumbled, his voice barely above a whisper.

Jaxon didn't waste time. He stepped forward, closing the distance in a heartbeat, his gun aimed squarely at Marek's chest. "The Wraith," Jaxon said flatly, as if the name itself was enough to make everything else fade into the background.

Marek's face drained of color. For a brief moment, I almost felt sorry for him. Almost.

"You don't understand," Marek stammered, glancing between Jaxon and the stranger in the corner. "This is bigger than you. Bigger than me."

"Does it look like I care?" Jaxon's words were a quiet threat, the edges sharp and unforgiving. He took a slow step forward. "What did you do, Marek?"

The hooded man shifted, but not in a way that seemed defensive. More like he was waiting for the right moment to strike. His hand went to his waist, and I saw the faint glint of something metal—a blade, perhaps, or another weapon. My pulse quickened.

But Marek, to his credit, didn't crumble immediately. His eyes flicked to the man in the corner again, as though searching for reassurance, but there was nothing there. The stranger had no intention of helping him.

"You really want to know?" Marek laughed, a brittle, humorless sound. "You think this is about me? About control? It's about survival. The Wraith has a plan, and I'm just a pawn. You're all pawns."

I wasn't sure what I expected to hear, but that certainly wasn't it. The Wraith—an enigma, a ghost who made entire organizations kneel in fear—had a plan. A plan that involved me, perhaps? The thought sent a cold shiver down my spine.

Jaxon's expression hardened, his gaze narrowing, but it wasn't directed at Marek. It was at the man in the corner.

"You're telling me this… thing," he gestured sharply toward the hooded figure, "has a plan that doesn't just involve you? You think you can talk your way out of this?"

Marek opened his mouth to speak, but before he could get the words out, the stranger moved. The action was swift, a blur of motion, and suddenly, a blade was pressed against Marek's throat. It was a warning, nothing more—too clean, too calculated. But it was enough to make the air thicken with the threat of violence.

"Enough." The stranger's voice was gravelly, barely audible, but it was a command. And even in the tense quiet that followed, I could feel the weight of his words settling into the room like an unwelcome guest.

I took a slow breath, my eyes flicking between Jaxon and the stranger. We were outnumbered, and I had a gut feeling we were in way over our heads. Whatever was happening here wasn't just a fight for control. This was something darker, and we were just at the start of it.

I could hear my heart in my ears, the steady thump of it drowning out everything else as I shifted, trying to find my footing. Jaxon's gaze briefly met mine, an unspoken question hanging in the air between us. I could see it there—he was starting to wonder just how deep this rabbit hole went, and whether we could climb out once we fell in.

The tension in the room was suffocating, thick as the smoke that seemed to hang in the air. I could feel it in my chest—each breath a little harder to take, the weight of what was happening pressing down on me like the proverbial elephant. I shifted slightly, trying to make myself less of a target, but the air felt so heavy, I couldn't escape the sense that everything had already been decided. The stranger's blade still hovered against Marek's throat, but it wasn't the weapon that held all the power. It was the quiet certainty in the man's eyes. He wasn't here to negotiate. He wasn't even here to kill. He was here to remind us who was really in charge.

I had seen men like him before—silent, dangerous, moving with an ease that screamed practice. He wasn't worried about being caught, about leaving evidence. He was a shadow in the flesh, a piece of the dark puzzle that had pulled me into this mess. And just like that, I realized I wasn't in control of this situation anymore. I was the pawn.

"Do you know who I am?" The stranger's voice, low and steady, slid across the room like ice. I didn't need to hear the words to know he wasn't talking to Jaxon or me. He was talking to Marek, though the question hung in the air, as though it was meant for all of us.

Marek swallowed hard, his Adam's apple bobbing in his throat. "You're..." His eyes darted to Jaxon, as if seeking help, but Jaxon didn't budge, his expression set in stone.

The stranger tilted his head slightly, and the blade pressed closer. It wasn't a gesture of threat, but a promise. Marek's response didn't matter anymore.

"I am the one who makes the rules," the stranger continued, his words cutting through the tension like a well-placed punch. "I am the one who sees every move before it's made. I see every mistake, every weakness. And I don't need you to tell me what you think is important, Marek. I already know."

For a moment, the room was completely still. Even the dust in the air seemed to freeze, suspended in the haze of stale smoke and fear. Then, without warning, the door at the far end of the room creaked open, and a voice, soft but unmistakable, drifted in.

"I think it's time we had a real conversation, don't you?"

The voice was smooth, almost polite, like a gentleman stepping into a room that was far too small for the weight of his presence. I didn't have to turn to know who it was. The Wraith.

I felt Jaxon's body stiffen beside me, his muscles coiling in that predatory way I had learned to recognize. He was ready. But ready for what? We were outnumbered, outmaneuvered, and every exit was covered. My mind raced, trying to find a way out, but there was nothing. Not here. Not now.

The Wraith stepped into the room, his figure obscured by the shadows that clung to him like a cloak. He was taller than I'd imagined, but not imposing in the way most criminals were. There was nothing rough about him, no jagged edges that screamed power. He was the kind of dangerous you didn't notice until it was too late.

"You're late," Marek said bitterly, his voice cracking. The man had lost his bravado the moment the Wraith walked through that door, and now, all that was left was a shell of the man I'd expected him to be.

The Wraith didn't acknowledge the remark, his gaze sweeping over Marek with an air of disinterest. "Timing is everything, Marek.

Don't forget that." He spoke like he was giving a lecture, as if the man's failure was just another lesson in his endless curriculum of power.

I couldn't look away. Even with the tension so thick it felt like we were all suffocating, there was something magnetic about him—this man who had orchestrated so much destruction from the shadows. The fear in Marek's eyes, the sudden tightness of Jaxon's jaw—it all felt so small in the face of the Wraith's presence. This was the puppet master, the one who had been pulling every string.

"And you..." The Wraith's voice turned toward Jaxon, then me, but mostly Jaxon. "You've been a nuisance. I didn't expect you to come this far. Thought you'd have been gone by now."

"I don't do disappearing acts," Jaxon said, his voice steady but edged with something more. He was waiting, watching, looking for a crack, a weakness in the Wraith's impenetrable calm.

I could feel the electricity between them, the unspoken understanding that neither was willing to back down. And for a moment, I saw it. Jaxon wasn't just trying to survive this. He was calculating, running through all the possible moves in his head. He wasn't just in the game; he was playing to win.

"And yet here you are," the Wraith mused, almost to himself. "Still trying to be the hero. It's a pity. You're not even close."

The words stung more than they should have. I could tell Jaxon didn't like being taunted. But I couldn't help the way my eyes flicked back to Marek, who was now trembling under the Wraith's gaze, barely able to stand up straight. His mouth opened and closed, like he was trying to form words, but nothing came out. The man was a shell, broken by the power of someone who thrived on control.

"Tell me," the Wraith said, his voice sharp and cutting, "what do you think will happen next? You think you'll just walk out of here? That this ends with you, Jaxon? You're nothing but a cog in a machine you'll never understand."

I felt a surge of anger, sharp and fierce, rising in me. I didn't care if I was outmatched. I didn't care if I was standing in front of the very man who had engineered every moment of chaos that had led us here. "You're wrong," I said, my voice cracking slightly under the weight of it. "You think you have control, but you don't. You never did."

For a brief moment, the Wraith looked at me, his eyes narrowing, and I could feel the weight of that stare. There was nothing human in it—just a cold, calculating emptiness. And then, just as quickly, he smiled.

"Don't be foolish," he whispered. "You're already too far in. There's no going back."

And then, in an instant, everything went black.

Chapter 5: The Heart of Darkness

The rain had been falling for hours, a steady thrum against the rooftop of the dilapidated building where I crouched. I could taste the wetness in the air, sharp and metallic, like the promise of something more dangerous than the storm. Below me, New Chicago stretched out in a blur of neon and shadows, the city's veins pulsing with the hum of a thousand untold stories. The Wraith's operation was supposed to be easy—a raid, swift and silent. But nothing in this city ever went according to plan.

I could hear Jaxon moving beside me, a breath away but somehow worlds apart. He was always like that—too calm, too still, the way a predator waits for its prey to make the first move. His hand brushed mine as we crouched low, the cool touch sending an unexpected jolt through my spine. For a second, it felt like we were in sync, like we could move through the night without making a single sound. But then came the crack of a distant gunshot, followed by the rapid shuffle of footsteps in the alley below. It was enough to break the moment, to remind me of why we were here.

Jaxon's voice came through the earpiece, low and steady. "You ready?"

I didn't answer right away. I didn't have to. I knew what he meant. We'd been playing this game for months—sifting through the ashes of New Chicago, trying to uncover the true face of The Wraith. But every lead we followed, every step closer we took, only seemed to pull us deeper into a web of lies. The city's underbelly was thick with them, and there was always the nagging feeling that the more we learned, the less we actually understood.

Jaxon's presence, though, was something I could count on. Or at least, I had thought so. That trust, the one we'd been building slowly over the past few weeks, was beginning to feel fragile, like it might crack open with the wrong word, the wrong movement. I tried not to dwell on it, but the thought lingered, like smoke in the back of my mind.

"We go in on my signal," he said, his voice cutting through the static in my ear. I didn't respond. I didn't need to. I was already moving, my fingers brushing against the slick surface of the building as I slid down the side, the rain helping to mask the noise of my descent. Jaxon was behind me, his movements fluid and precise, just like I expected.

When we hit the ground, we were ghosts in the dark. The alley stretched out before us, a narrow corridor of brick and grime. The light from the neon signs flickered above, casting jagged shadows that seemed to twitch at the edges of my vision. I stayed low, moving as quietly as possible, the sounds of the city swallowed by the pounding of my own heartbeat.

The warehouse loomed ahead, its heavy steel doors cracked open just enough for us to slip inside. The air was thick with the smell of oil and sweat, a staleness that made my stomach churn. We weren't here for the goods—the drugs, the weapons, the money—that wasn't the point. We were here to find the truth. And I had a feeling we were about to find something much darker than we had ever anticipated.

Inside, the operation was running smoothly. Too smoothly. Men moved in and out, loading crates, exchanging brief words. There was nothing urgent about their movements, nothing that screamed danger. It was all too perfect. A setup.

Jaxon's eyes met mine, and I saw the same suspicion reflected back at me. We moved deeper into the building, careful to avoid detection, weaving between stacked crates and machinery that hummed softly in the shadows. My breath felt tight in my chest, every corner we turned only adding to the growing unease that twisted inside me.

And then we found it.

THE RUSE

The door at the end of the hall was barely noticeable—just another rusty door hidden behind a pile of discarded equipment. But as we approached, a cold shiver ran down my spine. There was something about it, something off. I could feel the tension in the air like static before a storm.

Jaxon was the first to reach it, his hand resting on the doorknob. His fingers twitched. I could hear his breath, shallow and steady, but I knew he was on edge. He gave me a quick glance, his eyes dark with something I couldn't place.

"You know what this is?" I whispered, my voice barely audible.

He nodded, his lips pressed into a thin line. "Let's see if it's what we think."

With a slow turn, he opened the door. Inside, the room was nothing like I expected. No high-tech computers, no maps or files, just a single chair in the center of the room. And then, the shadows moved.

A figure stood up from the chair, their silhouette tall and imposing in the dim light. It was a woman—her hair slicked back, her expression unreadable. And in that moment, I knew who she was. My stomach dropped. It couldn't be.

"I was wondering when you'd find me," she said, her voice smooth, calculated. The words sent a ripple through me, as if the ground beneath my feet had cracked open.

Jaxon's hand gripped my arm, the pressure enough to pull me back a step. "What is this?" he demanded.

But I didn't hear him. All I could hear was the pounding in my ears, drowning out everything else. The woman's gaze flickered to me, and then a smile crept onto her lips, the kind that didn't reach her eyes. I should've known.

"You think you're the only ones who've been playing the game?" she asked, her voice tinged with something darker than malice. "This city has been mine for a long time, sweetheart."

My breath caught in my throat. She was the key to everything—the Wraith's right-hand, the puppet master. And I had just walked into her trap.

I couldn't stop staring at her, the woman who had somehow eluded us for months, even though she'd been under our noses the entire time. She was calm, far too calm for someone in a room like this, surrounded by danger, by betrayal. But then again, she didn't look like someone who feared anything. Her face was like polished stone, unmoving, unreadable. Her eyes, though, those eyes... they gleamed with something sharp and knowing.

"I've been waiting for you," she repeated, her smile now stretching just enough to make it clear she found some twisted pleasure in this moment.

Jaxon's grip on my arm tightened, but I didn't move. I couldn't. There was something about her presence, the way she just stood there, like she was waiting for us to realize something we'd missed. I couldn't put my finger on it, but I knew—this was bigger than just a raid. This wasn't about capturing some lackeys or blowing up a stash of weapons. This was personal. This was the heart of everything.

"You've been pulling strings, haven't you?" I said, my voice tight with a mixture of awe and fury. "Everything—the Wraith, the chaos in the city—it's all been your doing."

The woman tilted her head, almost lazily. "Oh, sweetie, you've barely scratched the surface." Her voice was smooth, dripping with something venomous. "This city? It's been mine for longer than you think. The Wraith is just the middleman. I'm the one who orchestrated the play."

My stomach dropped. The words hit me like a slap. It made sense, in a way. The Wraith, his elusive nature, his ability to stay in the shadows—it all fit now. But I hadn't expected this. Not her. I hadn't known about her at all.

I looked at Jaxon, hoping for some kind of reassurance, some sign that he understood what was happening here, but his expression was unreadable. That was the problem. The longer I spent with Jaxon, the more I realized how little I actually knew him. His walls were higher than the ones I'd built around myself. He was good at keeping things hidden. And right now, he was hiding something from me.

I felt a flicker of something—hurt, maybe, or anger—flicker inside me. But I shoved it down. I didn't have the luxury of letting emotions get in the way, not now.

The woman's smile deepened as she watched me. "You didn't think you were going to get away with this, did you? You thought you could just waltz into my world, throw a few punches, and walk out with your precious secrets? It's cute, really."

I forced myself to step forward. "What's the endgame?" I asked, trying to regain control of the situation. "What do you want? Why drag us into this mess?"

Her eyes flickered to Jaxon before she answered. "The endgame is simple, darling. Power. Control. And, of course, survival." She looked at me again, the intensity in her gaze enough to make me take a hesitant step back. "You see, New Chicago was always a powder keg. It just needed the right person to light the match."

I glanced at Jaxon, feeling a slight unease in the pit of my stomach. I had a feeling we weren't just talking about the city anymore. We were talking about something deeper—something we hadn't even begun to uncover.

"And you thought you could use us to set it off?" Jaxon asked, his voice colder now, more measured. His posture was stiff, but there was something in his eyes that I didn't like. Something... distant. The connection we had built was slipping away like sand through my fingers, and I hated it.

"Oh, sweetheart," she cooed, glancing at him with a condescending tilt of her head. "You think you've been playing the game. But in reality, you've been dancing to my tune since the beginning."

That hit harder than I expected. I glanced at Jaxon again, but this time, there was no answer in his eyes. The silence between us stretched, thick and uncomfortable, the way an argument builds without a single word spoken.

It was like a slap in the face, but the sting was nothing compared to what was coming. I had been so careful, so diligent in keeping my past buried, hidden beneath the walls I'd constructed around myself. But now, with this woman standing in front of us, I felt every crumbling brick. I felt the secrets pushing at the surface, ready to break free. I could already hear the words in my mind, the confession that would fracture everything.

And I wasn't sure if I could stop it.

"What do you want from us?" I asked, trying to regain some semblance of control over the situation. "You've got your hands in everything, but why us? What's the point?"

The woman's gaze softened, just a fraction, and for a second, I saw something that almost looked like pity. Almost. "The point, dear, is that you're a pawn. You always have been." She stepped forward, close enough now that I could smell the faint trace of perfume, something floral and sharp. "The Wraith? A tool. Jaxon? A distraction. You?" She paused, the weight of her gaze heavy. "You're a wildcard."

I felt the floor shift beneath me. My breath caught in my throat, and for a brief moment, I was paralyzed, trapped in the space between truth and disbelief.

But that wasn't the worst part. No, the worst part was when I turned to Jaxon, expecting to see the man I had come to trust. But what I saw instead was a flicker of doubt, of something... not quite betrayal, but close. And that, I couldn't bear.

THE RUSE

"I think it's time for the truth to come out," the woman said, her voice dripping with satisfaction.

And that was when I realized—everything was about to change.

The tension in the room became unbearable. Every breath felt too loud, too shallow, as if the very air was thick with the weight of secrets we hadn't yet understood. The woman stood there, unfazed, as if she were watching a play unfold—our play. And I was too numb to do anything about it. Every instinct in me screamed to bolt, to get away before the floor crumbled beneath us, but my feet were frozen. Jaxon stood next to me, but he felt like a stranger, a shadow of the man I'd come to trust.

His eyes flickered between the woman and me, but there was something distant in them now. It wasn't confusion. It wasn't fear. It was suspicion. The kind that felt too familiar. Too real.

"I think we're past the point of games, don't you?" she said, her voice a sweet melody of malice. "You're wondering why I've been playing this little game with you two. But you should know something important—everyone's a pawn, even you." Her eyes slid back to me, and her smile sharpened. "Especially you."

The words cut through me like glass. Every part of me wanted to scream, to demand answers, to break the walls of silence that had encased us all. But I was too aware of Jaxon standing there beside me. How long had he been looking at me like that, with that expression I couldn't decipher?

"You don't even know the whole story, do you?" she continued, her eyes gleaming with an almost perverse satisfaction. "You think you're in control, don't you? All this time, you've been chasing shadows. I've been watching, manipulating every move." She paused, savoring the silence. "Including yours."

The weight of her words hung in the air like smoke, clouding my thoughts. I glanced at Jaxon again, trying to find something—anything—in his expression to tell me that he hadn't already figured it out. But there was nothing. His face was unreadable. There was a moment, just a flicker, when our gazes met, and I felt the tremor of doubt that now separated us.

"Tell me," she purred, looking between us, "What do you think will happen next? Do you honestly believe you're going to walk away from this, unscathed? Do you believe Jaxon here still trusts you?"

I swallowed hard, my chest tightening. Jaxon's face was hard now, like granite, as if the mask he wore had slipped into place just when I needed him to show me his true self. But the words still echoed in my ears, the betrayal they implied sinking deeper. She was playing us like chess pieces, and I had no idea how many moves ahead she was.

"I trusted you," Jaxon finally said, his voice low and deliberate, each word feeling like a stone dropped into the silence between us. "But now? I'm not so sure."

I felt the cold sting of those words slap me across the face. I wanted to reach out, to take his hand, to make him see that this wasn't me—that I was still the person who'd stood by him when things got dark, when we'd made our own rules. But the space between us felt like miles, and in this moment, I knew the distance wasn't something I could easily close.

The woman smirked, her eyes glinting. "Oh, that's rich," she said, almost mockingly. "The once-loyal sidekick suddenly doesn't know who to trust anymore. How predictable. How utterly... human."

I wanted to scream at her, to tear into her until she cracked open like the fragile mask she was wearing. But I couldn't. I was too busy holding myself together, pretending that none of this hurt, that everything hadn't just shattered in a heartbeat.

She leaned in a little closer, her gaze never leaving Jaxon. "Do you really think she's innocent in all of this? That she just stumbled into your little crusade and accidentally became the hero? You're both so naive."

THE RUSE

The venom in her words dripped with the weight of something ancient, something cruel. My breath caught, and I felt that prickling sensation—the one that crawls up your spine when you realize you've been cornered in a game where you didn't even know the rules.

And then, in an instant, it clicked.

I had been running from something, burying it so deep inside of me, hoping it would stay locked away forever. But it hadn't. It never did. The truth always found its way to the surface, and the cost of hiding it was about to come due.

"You have no idea what you're talking about," I said, my voice shaking, but I made myself stand tall, meeting her gaze. "You think you can control everything, that you can break us with your words. But you can't."

"Oh, darling," she purred, her voice a sickening mockery of comfort, "I've already broken you."

Jaxon looked at me then, really looked at me, and in that moment, the air between us snapped like a taut wire. The trust was gone, replaced by something darker. Something heavier.

"You should have told me," Jaxon said, his voice barely above a whisper, the weight of accusation hanging between us. "I had to find out from her?"

My stomach twisted in knots. The truth was coming, like a flood, and I didn't know how to stop it. I didn't know if I could.

Before I could respond, a loud crash echoed from behind us, followed by the sound of footsteps approaching fast. The door to the room slammed open, and in the doorway stood two men, both armed, both looking at us like we were already dead. I didn't have time to react, no time to think.

"Get down!" Jaxon shouted, his hand grabbing my arm and yanking me to the ground just as the first gunshot rang out.

Everything blurred into chaos. The room spun. Gunfire ricocheted off the walls, and in that moment, I realized something that stopped my heart.

We weren't alone anymore. And the truth, whatever it was, was about to unravel.

Chapter 6: A Dance of Deception

The music reverberates through the floor beneath my feet, as if the building itself is alive, humming with a strange, almost menacing energy. I grip the edge of my champagne flute tighter, feeling the cold glass bite into my skin as I scan the crowd. The opulence of the room, the swirls of gold and crystal, might as well be a dream, a carefully constructed illusion. Every smile here is calculated, every handshake a potential weapon. But that's exactly why I'm here.

I spot Jaxon across the room, the familiar ripple of tension running through me at the sight of him. His back is straight, shoulders squared, his expression unreadable beneath the sharp lines of his tailored suit. His eyes, dark and stormy, are focused on something—or someone—at the other end of the ballroom. It's strange, that we've managed to come this far without tipping our hand, but I can feel the weight of his gaze as if he's silently measuring the room, measuring me. He's always doing that, analyzing, assessing, even when it's not necessary.

For the first time in what feels like ages, I can't read him. And that unsettles me.

The air is thick with the scent of fresh flowers, expensive cologne, and the underlying tension of the mission. It's the kind of night where one wrong word, one misplaced glance, could send everything spiraling. My disguise—the luxurious, tailored dress that clings to every curve, the meticulously styled hair that falls in waves down my back—is supposed to make me blend in. But there's no blending in here. Not when you're surrounded by wolves dressed in silk.

I take a slow sip of my drink, savoring the bubbles, the sweet burn of it. The first rule of infiltration: never look like you're out of place. And I'm doing my best to look like I belong. But there's a nervous flutter in my stomach, an instinct that tells me to be ready. Always be ready.

As I start to cross the room, the sea of glittering gowns and sharp tuxedos parts for me—either out of politeness or the dangerous allure of someone who doesn't quite belong. Either way, the effect is the same. But it's not the people that I'm focused on tonight. It's the man I came here with.

I reach him just as he turns toward me, his lips curling into that half-smile that's equal parts dangerous and enticing. It's a look I've seen a thousand times, but tonight, under the crystal chandeliers, it feels like it's meant for me. A subtle acknowledgment that he's noticed I'm standing a little too close, that the line between us is just a shade too thin.

"You clean up well," I say, the words slipping out before I can think better of them.

He raises an eyebrow, his eyes still scanning the crowd, but I catch the hint of something—humor, maybe, or the edge of a challenge. "I could say the same about you, but I'm not sure the dress suits your usual... more practical style."

"Practical?" I let out a dry laugh. "I'm practically suffocating in this thing. I don't know how you stand it, all this pretense."

His eyes flick toward me, and for a moment, there's nothing in them but raw understanding. A fleeting moment, but enough to remind me that we're in this together. We're both outsiders in a world built on facades.

"We're not here to discuss fashion," he murmurs, leaning in just close enough to make the air around us thicken. "We're here to find The Wraith."

His voice is low, deliberate, and it makes my pulse quicken. He's right, of course. Fashion doesn't matter. Nothing matters except the mission. But the mission has a way of complicating things when you're too close to the fire. And Jaxon is like a live wire, all danger and charm wrapped up in one. He's too much—too dangerous, too unpredictable, too... distracting.

I force my thoughts back to the task at hand. "Any luck?"

He shakes his head, but I can see the flicker of doubt in his eyes. His jaw tightens, and for a split second, he looks like he's about to say something else, something that has nothing to do with The Wraith and everything to do with... us. But then he notices something across the room, his expression shifting to that of a hunter spotting his prey. I follow his gaze, and there, standing in the far corner of the room, is a figure draped in black, the silhouette unmistakable. The Wraith.

I feel the familiar jolt of adrenaline surge through my veins. It's the moment we've been waiting for. It's time to move.

We start toward the figure, keeping a careful distance, both of us blending in, our steps synchronized, like two dancers lost in a rhythm only we can hear. As we draw closer, the hairs on the back of my neck rise. There's something off. Something about the way The Wraith is positioned, the way his eyes flicker toward the door as if waiting for something.

I feel it before I hear it—the slight shift in the air. A subtle tightening in the room, the change in the music. It's too late. I turn to Jaxon, but the look in his eyes has already shifted. There's a flash of something I can't quite place, something darker, more uncertain.

"You didn't—" I begin, but the words are lost as the door slams shut behind us. The room, once alive with laughter and music, now feels like a cage.

Jaxon's hand shoots out, grabbing my wrist just as a dozen armed men spill into the room, their cold eyes scanning the crowd for any sign of resistance.

The Wraith is gone.

And now we're trapped.

The doors slam shut with a finality that sends a ripple through the crowd, freezing the air in the room. For a split second, no one moves. I can hear my heart thundering in my ears, a reminder that, for all my training, there's no controlling how quickly things can spiral out of hand. I glance over at Jaxon, whose jaw is clenched tight enough to crack stone. His grip on my wrist tightens, but his expression—unreadable as always—gives nothing away. Not even a flicker of the panic that's slowly clawing its way up my spine.

I can feel it, that suffocating pressure in the room, like a storm about to break. The air, once light and buoyant with the hum of chatter, now presses down on me, thick and dangerous. I can almost taste the fear, bitter and metallic, as the suited men—too many to count—move with synchronized precision. They don't hurry. There's no need. This is their turf, their game. And we're the intruders.

"Stay close," Jaxon mutters, his voice low, just for me. It's not a command—more of a warning. I nod, my fingers curling around the cool fabric of his sleeve as we move back, as subtly as we can, toward the farthest corner of the ballroom.

"Good evening, everyone," a voice booms over the speakers, too smooth to be real. It sends a chill through my bones. "I trust you're all enjoying the festivities? However, I must inform you that the evening's entertainment has taken a... slight detour."

I freeze, the implication hanging heavy in the air. The Wraith. His voice is everywhere and nowhere, slithering through the words like an unseen predator circling its prey.

The crowd is still. Silent. Waiting for something to happen.

Jaxon's eyes are locked on the nearest exit—too far, too obvious. He knows we can't escape without causing a scene, and neither of us is particularly keen on drawing attention. He pulls me further into the shadows, where the sharp edges of the room blur into nothingness. "We have to move, now."

I don't argue. There's no time for that. We both know what's at stake, even if he's still holding on to that faint thread of doubt, that skepticism buried deep within him. We're only as strong as the bond we've built—and lately, that bond feels a little threadbare.

THE RUSE

A flicker of movement catches my eye—a whisper of black cloth slipping through the crowd. It's subtle, barely noticeable, but my instincts flare. The Wraith's people. His operatives. They're weaving through the guests with the ease of wolves in sheep's clothing, their movements choreographed, every step designed to keep everyone in their place. And for the first time, I realize how out of place we really are here.

"They've locked the doors," I whisper, pulling Jaxon's arm so I can see his face more clearly. "We're trapped."

His lips press into a tight line. "We'll make our own exit."

I want to believe him, but the odds are stacked against us. I've been in situations like this before—cornered, outnumbered—but somehow, it always feels different when you're not in control. When you've lost the element of surprise.

"We'll need a distraction," I say, almost to myself. The words hang in the air, and Jaxon's gaze sharpens as he processes the implication. He's already calculating, already moving, even if he doesn't show it.

The next few moments feel like an eternity stretched out, the kind of silence that presses on your chest, making every breath feel too loud. Jaxon tugs on my arm, pulling me back into the main part of the room, away from the shadows, where the guests are beginning to murmur nervously. The tension is palpable, thick as smoke.

"What are you doing?" I hiss, trying to pull away, but Jaxon has already made up his mind. His fingers close around mine, and for one second, I wonder if he's leading me into a trap of his own design. But that's the problem with him—he's always five steps ahead, and I'm not sure I want to be the one who catches up.

"We need to blend in," he says, his voice cool. He's playing the game, like always. No one knows what's happening yet, not really. "We do what we do best. Get their attention. Make them think we're still part of the show."

"Part of the show?" I repeat, incredulity lacing my voice. "You've lost your mind."

But Jaxon's eyes are steely. His hand moves to his pocket, his fingers brushing the small device tucked there, and I know exactly what it is. A signal jammer. One of his favorite tricks. "We've got one shot at this," he murmurs. "If we don't move now, we'll never get out."

I swallow hard, feeling the sharp pulse of anxiety thrumming through my veins. The device is our ticket—if we can get to it without being spotted. It's a risk, an enormous risk, but it's all we have.

He slips the jammer from his pocket, his fingers grazing mine for just a moment before he presses it against his chest, hidden under the fabric of his suit.

"We make it look like we're still part of the entertainment," he says again, more firmly this time. "When the alarms go off, when the signal's cut, you move. You're faster than I am."

I open my mouth to protest, but the words die on my tongue as the first sharp notes of a piano cut through the tension. The music swells, pulling everyone's attention back into the moment. In an instant, the lights dim. The stage is set. A dancer in a gleaming silver mask emerges from the crowd, and for a breathless second, all eyes are on her. Her movement is fluid, mesmerizing, a perfect distraction.

Jaxon's hand tightens on mine, and we move, not walking, but gliding, blending into the ebb and flow of the crowd. Every step we take is calculated, every movement precise. And I hate how easy it is to fall into the rhythm of this dangerous dance.

We move together through the crowd, a seamless pair caught in the flow of bodies, but my mind is racing, desperate for a plan that won't fall apart in the next ten seconds. The piano continues to soar in the background, the haunting melody amplifying the pressure that builds with every step. It's the perfect distraction. The perfect cover. But even as we slip through the throng of guests, my eyes dart nervously between Jaxon and the growing shadows on the periphery. It feels too easy, like we're moving in sync, as if we've done this before—and maybe we have. But tonight? Tonight, there's something off. Something I can't place.

Jaxon moves like he owns the room, each step effortless, each glance calculating. He's good at this—too good. And I hate the fact that I'm starting to wonder whether I've been part of his plan all along. The thought gnaws at me like a bad taste, but I push it down. There's no room for doubt right now. No room for anything except survival.

"We're close," he murmurs under his breath, his voice barely above a whisper, the words for me alone. His hand brushes mine, a fleeting touch that sends a jolt of warmth through me. His grip on my wrist tightens, and I feel the tension in his body, the tightness of someone who's just as aware as I am that there's no going back from this.

The dance moves in tandem with the music, a choreography I've learned well over the years. A step to the left, a spin to the right. It's as if we're both caught in the same dangerous rhythm, a rhythm that was never meant to be this close. We don't make eye contact. Not yet. The room is too crowded, too dangerous, and if anyone suspects a thing, we're done.

I glance over at Jaxon, studying his sharp profile as we glide past yet another row of guests. He's calm, as usual, but there's an edge to him now, something I can't quite pin down. It's like he's waiting for something—or someone. His dark eyes flick across the crowd with practiced ease, but his fingers twitch ever so slightly around my wrist. His usual confidence is cracked, just enough for me to notice. And it unsettles me.

But the moment passes, and we slip further into the dance floor, blending with the thrumming pulse of the music. The plan is simple:

get close enough to The Wraith, get the intel we need, and get out before anyone notices we were ever here. It's a good plan. A simple plan. But as the minutes stretch on, I can feel the trap slowly closing around us, like a noose tightening inch by inch. I try to shake the thought, but it lingers, gnawing at the edges of my mind.

Then, the signal comes. A subtle flicker of movement across the room, the shadow of someone pulling their mask just slightly askew—a signal I've seen too many times to mistake. My heart skips a beat, but there's no time for hesitation.

Jaxon tugs me forward, his body pressing closer to mine, an unspoken warning that we're about to make our move. I feel the sudden heat of his breath against my ear, his voice barely audible above the orchestra.

"Now," he whispers, and just like that, we're no longer dancing. We're moving, pushing, shoving our way through the guests in a blur of silk and diamonds. It's a cacophony of confusion and chaos as people scream, as the sound of the piano screeches to a halt, replaced by the deafening wail of an alarm. The lights flicker, then cut out completely.

And in the darkness, I can feel the world change. It's no longer a ballroom; it's a battleground.

For a split second, everything is silent. The world feels like it's holding its breath. Then—shouts. People begin to panic, scattering in every direction. But Jaxon? Jaxon moves with calculated precision, like a man who knows exactly where he's going. I'm not far behind, but I can feel the pulse of the moment, the sense that everything has shifted. That we're no longer in control.

"Where's The Wraith?" I shout, my voice hoarse, but it's drowned out by the chaos around us. I try to make sense of the dark, to catch any hint of movement in the haze of shadows and flashing lights. But it's useless. We're too far in now. Too far gone.

THE RUSE

Jaxon's expression is unreadable, but the way his jaw tightens tells me everything I need to know. He's still searching. Searching for something—someone.

Then I see it.

A shadow moving in the corner, slipping past the curtain that separates the ballroom from the quieter halls beyond. It's too swift to be a guest—too deliberate. And as it vanishes into the dark, something clicks. My stomach drops.

"We've been set up," I whisper, more to myself than to Jaxon. But he hears me, and in the dim light, I see his eyes flash with something between frustration and anger.

"No," he mutters, almost to himself. "We haven't."

But I know better. This isn't the plan we discussed. This wasn't part of the deal.

Before I can react, the trap slams shut with all the subtlety of a steel door dropping. We're surrounded. From every corner, figures in black emerge, their faces masked, their eyes glinting with cold, calculating intent. I don't know how many there are—too many, all closing in too fast.

My heart races, but I don't move. Not yet.

Jaxon turns to face me, his expression hardening into something cold. "Stay close," he commands, his voice low but firm, almost soothing in the midst of the storm.

I nod, but there's no time to plan. No time to think. It's just us, caught in the net, the sounds of muffled footsteps growing louder.

And then, just as the first figure lunges toward us, a familiar voice echoes from the shadows.

"Not so fast."

I don't need to see the face to know whose voice it is.

Chapter 7: Bonds of Fire

The bunker was colder than I anticipated, the damp walls echoing each breath as though even the shadows could breathe. I sat on the hard, uneven floor, tucked into a corner where the flickering light of the single bulb cast long, jagged shadows. The scent of earth and metal hung in the air, mingling with the faint odor of old leather and sweat. Somewhere in the depths of the underground space, pipes groaned, though whether it was from the pressure of the water or something far less innocent, I couldn't say. I wasn't exactly in the mood to investigate.

My fingers traced the edge of my sleeve, the fabric worn thin from days of constant use, its seams barely holding on. Each movement of my hand seemed to amplify the silence between us, a thick tension stretching from the tip of my fingers all the way to where he stood. He was just across the room, standing with his back to the only entryway, but even the shadows couldn't conceal the dangerous air that clung to him. Everything about him had the edge of a storm waiting to break loose, from the lean muscle beneath his worn jacket to the sharpness of his jaw, set in an expression that told me he wasn't thinking about the cold, or the food, or anything else that mattered right now. He was thinking about me.

I could feel it in the way his eyes moved when they found mine. They were burning, but not with anger—not this time. No, these were the eyes of someone who had seen too much, had bled too much, and who, for the briefest moment, was on the edge of breaking all the rules. I wasn't exactly innocent, either. Our paths had crossed under the most unlikely of circumstances, and here we were, two enemies now forced into an unholy alliance by a world that had forgotten how to be fair.

It was funny how fast the lines had blurred, how the smoldering looks we'd exchanged during our first encounter had transformed into something else entirely. Something like trust, though I would never, ever say that aloud. The warmth of his body close to mine was a stark contrast to the chill in the air, and that warmth—god, it was enough to make my thoughts scatter. Not that I was about to let myself forget who he was. I had a survival instinct, and it was still very much intact.

But survival, as it turned out, wasn't as simple as I'd hoped. We were trapped here, cut off from any real escape. And while the world above us burned, we sat in this place, the weight of everything hanging between us like a live wire, ready to spark at any moment.

"You're staring again," he said, his voice low, rough—like gravel being scraped across stone.

I blinked, not realizing my eyes had lingered. My mouth worked to form a response, but the words stalled. Damn it. "Not staring. Just... watching."

He chuckled, the sound like something made of silk and danger. "You do that a lot. Watch."

"I do not," I snapped, though my pulse quickened under his gaze.

He stepped closer, just a few inches, but it felt like miles. The air between us crackled, charged, as though we were standing on the edge of something dangerous. He tilted his head, a small smirk playing on his lips. "You do," he said quietly, voice barely more than a whisper.

I couldn't hold the stare anymore. It was too much, too close, too real. Instead, I let my eyes fall to his hands, which were steady, unfazed by the growing tension. Hands that had been stained by more than just dirt and blood. Hands that could kill, I was sure.

"How many people have you killed?" The question slipped out before I could stop it, the curiosity not entirely my own. The silence that followed was thick, but I didn't dare look up.

I wasn't afraid of his answer. Not in the way I should've been.

He took his time responding, and when he did, it wasn't with the violence I expected. Instead, it was with a shrug. "Too many."

I frowned, disliking the simplicity of it. "That's it?"

"That's all you need to know."

The bluntness of his words made my chest tighten. I wanted to ask more, to dig into the mess of his past, to try and make sense of him, but I didn't. There was no point. We weren't here to talk about our pasts, we were here to survive the present.

Still, I couldn't stop the curiosity, the need to understand why someone so seemingly... detached could still stand there with his heart beating. Alive. In front of me. "You really don't feel anything about it?"

"I feel." His voice lowered even more, something dark slipping in. "But it doesn't matter."

His words left an uncomfortable silence between us. I could see the flicker of something in his eyes, a memory too ugly to speak. And for the first time since we'd met, I wondered if I had misjudged him.

"You're right," I said, forcing the words to sound lighter than they were. "It doesn't matter."

But even as I said it, the weight of his presence began to settle on me like a blanket made of iron. The air grew warmer, and I felt my heart beat a little faster, an involuntary reaction. His proximity was intoxicating, dangerous. Every muscle in my body was screaming to take a step back, but I didn't. Not even when he moved closer, just enough for me to feel the heat radiating off him.

"Why are you still here?" he asked suddenly, his voice dropping lower, like the question had been bubbling beneath the surface for some time.

I tilted my head, a sharp laugh slipping out before I could help myself. "Because I don't have anywhere else to go."

He didn't laugh with me. His expression darkened, the smirk slipping off his face as quickly as it had appeared. Instead, he studied me, his gaze growing heavier, more intense. The air between us grew thicker with every passing second, and it was almost unbearable. Almost.

"You know," he said, voice barely above a whisper, "I never thought you'd be the one to stick around."

I met his eyes then, steady and unblinking. "Maybe I'm not done yet."

The air in the bunker had grown thick with unspoken words, each of us battling the weight of our secrets. It wasn't just the oppressive walls that held us in place; it was the shared understanding of what lingered just beyond the steel door. There was no need to say it aloud. We both knew that the world outside was still a storm, and though we had found shelter, we were no safer than two candles in the wind. Still, as the hours bled into each other, the fear of what lay ahead began to settle in the corners of the room like the dust motes dancing in the dim light.

His gaze never fully left me, not once in the time we'd been here. I could feel it like a weight pressing down on my skin, making my pulse quicken despite the chill. His silence wasn't comforting. It was like the calm before the storm, a taut wire ready to snap. There were moments when I thought I might finally ask him about everything—the things he'd buried behind that smooth, unreadable exterior. But each time, the words turned to ash in my mouth. Instead, I clung to the raw urgency of our situation. There were more pressing matters, after all. Survival. Trust. And yet...

"Why did you come back for me?" I blurted it out, the question hanging between us like a dare. My breath caught in my throat before I could stop it, but the words were already out there.

He blinked slowly, his expression unreadable. "What do you think?"

I could feel the heat of his body just behind me now, close enough that I could hear the faint rasp of his breath against the silence. "I think you had no other choice," I said, trying to force a note of bravado into my voice.

A slow smile tugged at the corner of his lips, but it didn't reach his eyes. "You think too much," he said, stepping forward. The air seemed to pulse with the force of his movement, and I resisted the urge to step back.

"You still haven't answered me."

He leaned in, his face inches from mine, so close that I could feel the heat radiating off his skin, smell the faintest trace of gunpowder mixed with the lingering scent of him. It was intoxicating, disorienting. "You know, you have a real talent for asking questions at the worst possible time."

I met his gaze, holding my ground. "That's because I'm not the one pretending that nothing is happening."

His eyes darkened, his voice low, rough. "What if I'm not pretending?"

For a split second, the world stopped spinning. His breath was warm against my lips, his presence so overpowering that I could almost taste the tension in the air. I shouldn't have let it get this far. I shouldn't have let myself be this close to him. But there was something about the way he looked at me, something raw and intense, that made everything else fade away.

I shifted, trying to pull away, but he caught my wrist, the movement so quick and deliberate it almost took my breath away. His grip was firm, but not painful. Just enough to keep me in place, just enough to remind me that we were here, together, suspended in this fragile moment between the past and whatever the future might hold.

I could feel my heart pounding in my chest as he tilted his head, eyes never leaving mine. "You're afraid," he murmured, almost to himself.

THE RUSE 65

I didn't deny it. I wasn't sure what it was I was afraid of—him, this, the storm that was coming, or all of it at once—but I wasn't about to admit it to him. Instead, I tugged my wrist free, deliberately slow, but not because I wanted to escape. No, the truth was, the longer I stayed this close to him, the more impossible it became to think straight.

"You think you know me," I said, taking a step back, though my voice was far steadier than I felt. "But you don't. I'm not the person you want me to be."

He didn't react immediately. He simply stood there, watching me, as though waiting for the rest of the story. But there was no rest. Not yet, anyway. There were only moments like this, fleeting and heavy with promise, moments when it felt like everything was coming together, and yet nothing was really changing.

"I never wanted anything from you," he said finally, his voice soft but sharp. "But that doesn't mean I don't see you. Don't think I haven't noticed the way you carry yourself. The way you fight. The way you—"

His words trailed off, leaving something unsaid in the space between us, something more vulnerable than I was willing to acknowledge. And yet, his admission hung in the air, a confession without an apology.

"And yet you still think I'm the enemy," I muttered, my voice a mix of bitterness and disbelief.

"Not the enemy," he replied, his eyes never leaving mine. "But that doesn't mean we're on the same side either."

The words should have stung, should have thrown me off-balance, but somehow they didn't. Instead, they grounded me. The truth of it settled in my bones, cold and unwavering. We were two halves of something that didn't quite make sense. We were allies for survival, nothing more. And still, as much as I wanted to deny it, there was something between us, something that was harder to ignore than any of the lies we'd told each other.

I turned away, though the movement felt more like an admission of something than a rejection. I didn't trust him. I couldn't. But that didn't mean I didn't feel what I felt when he was close. There was a fire between us, one that had been kindled in the heat of our shared struggles, a fire that I couldn't snuff out no matter how hard I tried.

"What do we do now?" I asked, trying to push the weight of everything else aside.

He stood in the silence for a moment, then, finally, he spoke again, his tone almost grim. "We survive. And after that... we'll see."

The bunker felt smaller with each passing hour, its corners closing in on me, pressing me into the reality of our situation. But it wasn't just the space that was shrinking—it was the distance between us. Somehow, after all the time spent avoiding it, we had drifted into the center of something far more dangerous than I was prepared for. The barrier between enemy and ally was becoming less defined by the minute, and I wasn't sure whether to embrace it or push it away.

I was still caught in the heat of our last exchange, my thoughts spinning in circles as I paced the length of the room. Every step felt heavier, the floor cold beneath my worn boots, but the heat of his stare—constant, heavy, unyielding—was warmer than I cared to admit. It was a pressure, suffocating in its intensity, yet I couldn't seem to tear myself away from it. Not yet. Not now.

He didn't say a word as I moved across the room, the silence between us thick with unspoken things. I couldn't look at him, not yet. Not until I figured out how to stop my pulse from racing every time his eyes flicked over me, like he was reading me in ways I didn't understand. He leaned back against the wall, arms crossed, watching me with a quiet intensity that made my skin burn. When I stopped in front of him, he didn't flinch, didn't move—just stood there, waiting for me to do something. Anything.

"Do you think we're actually going to make it out of here?" My voice was a little rougher than I intended, but it didn't matter. What was left to hide?

For a long moment, he didn't respond. I could feel his gaze flickering over my face, down to my lips, back to my eyes. And then, finally, he spoke. "We'll survive. If we have to."

The calm in his words didn't ease the tightness in my chest. If anything, it made it worse. His certainty didn't match the chaos brewing just outside. The world above us was a ticking time bomb. The whispers of danger weren't distant anymore. They were right here, pressing at the seams of the bunker, threatening to tear everything apart.

I swallowed hard, my throat dry, my mind clouded with questions I was too afraid to ask. "That's it? You think we'll just... survive?"

He took a step toward me, his boots dragging against the cold concrete. "That's all anyone's doing now. Surviving."

His voice had changed, rougher, like something raw was just beneath the surface. And I wasn't sure if I should reach out to him or pull away. The air between us was thick with something unspoken, something dangerous, and for the first time since we'd met, I wasn't sure where the lines were anymore.

"You're not answering the question." I wasn't sure why I pushed, why I needed him to say more, to give me something—anything—to help me make sense of this. I had never been so unsure, so completely out of my depth.

His gaze softened for just a moment, a fleeting thing. But it was enough. Enough to remind me that there was something more to him than the man I'd first met. He wasn't just the cold, calculating stranger I had feared. There was something beneath that, something human. And that terrified me more than anything else.

He stepped closer, so close that I could feel his breath, warm and steady against the cold air. "What do you want me to say?"

I wanted him to lie. I wanted him to tell me that we would make it out, that we'd walk out of this bunker together and leave all of this behind. I wanted a future that didn't involve fear and survival. But I wasn't that naive. I wasn't that foolish. I knew what the truth was.

"What happens after?" The question left me almost breathless, as if asking it aloud would change everything.

He hesitated, just for a second, his brow furrowing slightly. But then, as if coming to some silent decision, he answered, his voice low, rough. "After... we keep going. We get out. And we do whatever it takes to stay out. No matter what."

I could feel the weight of those words, heavy with the promise of something more, something that was still too far out of reach to grasp. It was that look in his eyes—the one that had always seemed distant, unreadable—that made me wonder if this was the beginning of something that would break us both in the end.

The silence stretched between us, thick and suffocating, until I couldn't take it anymore. I reached out before I even had the chance to stop myself, my hand brushing lightly against his arm. The contact sent a shock through me, like a spark igniting in the dark.

He didn't pull away. Instead, his fingers grazed my wrist, the touch electric, as if something deep inside him was stirring. And suddenly, I was no longer thinking about escape, about survival. I was thinking about him.

"Are you scared?" The question slipped out before I could stop it. But the truth of it was simple. I didn't know what we were doing, or where this was going. All I knew was that the world outside was still broken, and I had no idea if we were strong enough to make it out alive.

He tilted his head, studying me with a strange intensity. "Not scared. Just... prepared."

Prepared. It was a word that made the air feel heavier, like the weight of everything that had happened—and everything that still might—was pressing in on us. He wasn't afraid. And that made me question whether I had the strength to face whatever came next.

And then, just as the tension between us reached its peak, the door to the bunker slammed open with a force that sent us both stumbling backward. The darkness of the outside world poured in, and the sound of boots on gravel and hushed voices filled the silence.

I didn't have time to react, didn't have time to think about what would happen next, only that everything had just changed.

We weren't alone anymore.

Chapter 8: Shadows of the Past

The room was thick with the smell of fresh paint and old regret. The kind of air that clung to you, suffocating just enough to make you remember every little mistake you'd ever made. I hadn't intended to be back here, standing on the worn wood floors of my grandmother's house, but life had a funny way of dragging you back to the places you'd thought you'd outgrown. My fingers brushed the edge of the dusty mantelpiece, the familiar creak of the floorboards beneath my boots making my stomach tighten. I hated this place. Not because it held bad memories—well, maybe a little—but because it had the power to bring out every version of me that I'd ever tried to bury. The girl who trusted too easily. The one who didn't know how to say goodbye.

A knock at the door echoed like thunder through the quiet house. I froze. It wasn't supposed to happen this way. He wasn't supposed to be here, not now. The man on the other side of that door was a ghost I had hoped would stay buried, a reminder of a life I barely recognized anymore.

I hadn't heard from Noah in years, not since we parted ways in a storm of harsh words and broken promises. He'd been my best friend once, the kind of friend who knew every secret, every scar. But we weren't children anymore. And I wasn't the girl who'd laughed at his stupid jokes or traded stolen glances over the back fence. I was something else now, something I'd never let him see.

The knock came again, louder this time, a reminder that I couldn't avoid what was coming. I glanced at the kitchen table where Jaxon sat, his long fingers wrapped around a glass of whiskey, his eyes flickering toward the door with an unreadable expression. We hadn't spoken much since I told him I needed some space, but the silence between us felt heavier than anything we'd said. There were too many unsaid things, too much air between us that neither of us was willing to breach. His jaw clenched, and I could see the muscles in his neck tighten, a silent warning that I shouldn't open that door. But I couldn't stop myself. Not this time.

I walked toward the door, each step a protest against my better judgment. I could feel Jaxon's eyes on me, sharp and watchful, but I couldn't let his presence dictate my actions. Not with Noah standing just beyond the threshold. I took a breath, pushing open the door.

And there he was.

Noah looked exactly the same, and exactly different. His hair was longer than I remembered, falling in messy waves that framed his face in a way that made him seem younger. His eyes, though, they hadn't changed. They still held that same intensity, the kind that could burn you alive if you weren't careful. He smiled when he saw me, but it was the smile of a man who knew how much damage time could do. It didn't reach his eyes.

"Jolie," he said, his voice like gravel, rough and familiar. "I knew I'd find you here."

I didn't answer right away. Part of me wanted to slam the door in his face and pretend this never happened, but another part of me—the part that knew Noah too well—knew that doing so wouldn't solve anything. I stepped aside, letting him in, and the second he crossed the threshold, it was like the air shifted. Tension crackled in the space between us, thick and electric.

"Jaxon, this is Noah," I said, my voice tight, keeping my eyes firmly on Noah as I introduced them. "Noah, this is Jaxon."

Jaxon didn't stand. He just took another long sip from his glass, his eyes never leaving Noah. It wasn't a subtle move, but then, Jaxon wasn't the subtle type. I could feel the heat of his gaze like a tangible thing, and I knew instantly that his jealousy was simmering beneath the surface. He'd been quiet for too long, but I didn't want to deal with this now. Not with Noah here.

Noah nodded at Jaxon, but it was stiff, uncomfortable. The kind of recognition that made the space between them feel even more unbearable. I saw Jaxon's muscles tense, his posture stiffening. I could feel the edge in the room, a delicate balance between the past and the present, between two men who couldn't be more different but were both claiming a part of me. I hated that they were both here.

"I didn't come here for pleasantries," Noah said, his tone curt. He didn't look at Jaxon as he spoke, his eyes fixed on me. "I came because I know something. Something that could change everything. About The Wraith. About the plans he's been making."

The words hit me like a slap, cold and sharp. The Wraith. I'd been running from that name for months, hiding from the truth of what it meant, but here it was, rearing its ugly head again. I could see the way Jaxon's grip tightened on his glass, his knuckles turning white. There was something in the way Noah said it, though, that made me question everything. His words were heavy with knowledge, but they weren't the kind of words you could just dismiss. Not when they had the power to bring everything crashing down.

"Why now?" I asked, my voice barely a whisper. I didn't want to ask, didn't want to let the truth come any closer, but it was already here. There was no escaping it.

Noah's eyes flickered to Jaxon, then back to me. "Because The Wraith isn't just a shadow in the dark. He's been planning something. Something bigger than any of us realized. And I know how to stop it."

The weight of those words pressed on my chest, suffocating me. I had to make a choice now. Between the past and the present. Between the man who had once been my closest friend and the one who had come to mean so much more. The air between us thickened, and I knew that whatever happened next would change everything.

The silence hung in the room like a dark cloud. The only sound was the slow, deliberate swirl of Jaxon's drink in his hand, the ice cubes clinking with each movement, a quiet reminder of how little he cared to break the tension. Noah hadn't moved. He stood just inside the door, his eyes fixed on me, his expression a carefully crafted mask that I could almost see through. I knew Noah better than anyone. There was a restlessness about him, an urgency that was only ever present when something was terribly wrong. And I knew that look. It had been the same when we were younger, when he'd show up at my door, half-crazy and full of secrets he could never hold onto.

"I don't trust you," Jaxon finally said, his voice sharp and thick with accusation. The words hit Noah with the force of a slap, but Noah didn't flinch. He wasn't the type to back down.

"I don't need your trust," Noah shot back, his voice as cold as Jaxon's. "I need hers."

I stood between them, the weight of their tension pressing down on my chest, threatening to crush the air out of my lungs. "This isn't about trust," I said, my voice quieter than I meant it to be. "This is about The Wraith, and I think we all know that."

Noah nodded slowly, his gaze flickering to Jaxon before returning to me. "I didn't come here to make nice," he said, his voice low, intense. "I came because there's no time left. The Wraith is moving faster than we thought. And I've seen the signs. I know what he's planning."

"You're still caught up in his games," Jaxon spat, his eyes narrowing in disbelief. "You think you're the one who gets to save the day, after all this time? You disappeared, Noah. You left her—left all of us. And now you think you can just waltz in here and be the hero?"

Noah didn't rise to the bait. He didn't even flinch. Instead, he met Jaxon's gaze, steady and unmoving, like he knew exactly how to handle this, like he'd been waiting for this moment all along. "It's not about me, Jaxon. It's about stopping what's coming. And you're either with us, or you're in the way."

Jaxon's grip on the glass tightened, his knuckles turning white, but he didn't say anything more. His jaw clenched, the muscles in his neck tensing, as though he was holding something back. Maybe it was anger, maybe it was fear—I couldn't tell. But I could feel it, the raw energy humming between us, dangerous and volatile.

I turned to Noah, needing to focus on him, needing to hear what he had to say. "What do you mean by 'what's coming'?" I asked, my voice trembling slightly despite my best efforts. The name The Wraith had haunted me for months, a shadow I couldn't outrun. Every time I thought I'd escaped, it had a way of finding me again, dragging me back to the mess I'd been too afraid to clean up.

Noah's expression softened, just for a second. I saw a flicker of something in his eyes—guilt, maybe. Or regret. "I've been watching him," he said, his tone grave. "I know what he's doing, Jolie. I know the pieces he's moving. And if we don't stop him now, we're all going to be caught in his web. There's no way out."

I swallowed hard, my heart thudding in my chest. I wanted to believe him, to trust that this wasn't just another one of his wild schemes. But the past was still fresh, still bitter in my mind, and I couldn't shake the doubt gnawing at the edges of my thoughts. "Why should I believe you?" I asked, my voice stronger than I felt. "You disappeared. You left me, Noah. And now you expect me to just take your word for it?"

He flinched at my words, but his face remained stoic, unreadable. "I know," he said, his voice soft, almost apologetic. "I don't expect you to forgive me. I don't expect you to believe me. But I'm not asking for forgiveness. I'm asking for help."

The words hung in the air, heavy with unspoken meaning. Help. I had spent so long convincing myself I didn't need him, that I could handle things on my own, that I could protect myself from The Wraith without anyone else's interference. But now, hearing Noah say it, hearing the urgency in his voice, I wasn't so sure anymore.

THE RUSE 75

Jaxon shifted behind me, the tension radiating from him like a storm on the horizon. "You really think she's going to help you?" he asked, his voice dangerously calm. "After everything you've done?"

Noah didn't answer right away. Instead, he looked at me, his eyes full of things I couldn't quite place. There was a story there, a history we both knew but never talked about. The kind of history that could destroy everything if it came to light. But I couldn't focus on that now. Not when The Wraith was still out there, watching, waiting.

"I don't know," Noah said finally, his voice quieter. "But I know that if we don't work together, none of us are going to make it out of this alive."

The words sank in like a stone in water, heavy and inevitable. I looked from Noah to Jaxon, the weight of their glares making it hard to breathe. Each of them wanted something from me, each of them had their own version of the truth. And I had to decide, right now, who I was going to trust. I could feel the pieces of my life slipping through my fingers, the past and present colliding in ways I couldn't control.

The door swung open behind me, breaking the silence, and the sound of boots on the floor was unmistakable. Another presence, another complication. The last thing I needed right now was more people, more secrets, more lies. But as the figure stepped into the room, I knew the game had changed once again.

The door creaked open behind me, and I felt the air in the room shift, a quiet disruption that made my skin prickle. The weight of it pressed on me, pulling my gaze toward the figure now filling the doorway. I hadn't expected it—hell, I hadn't even known there was anyone else in the vicinity—but there she was, standing there like she owned the space, her presence undeniable.

I didn't need to turn around to know who it was. Her scent preceded her: a combination of citrus and something softer, like vanilla. It was the smell of old secrets and whispered promises—familiar, too familiar.

"Am I interrupting something?" her voice, smooth and effortless, slid into the tension like a blade. There was no mistaking it. That tone. That practiced, teasing, everything's fine smile. It had been her signature back when we were young, before everything had fallen apart.

I knew her. Far too well. Her name was Ava, and she was the kind of person who made you question everything you thought you knew about loyalty and love. Once, she had been my closest friend. Now, she was the last person I wanted to see.

Jaxon's eyes flickered toward me, then to Ava, a muscle in his jaw twitching as if he were fighting the impulse to storm out of the room. The tension between the two of us was already so thick it felt like we could cut it with a knife, but now with Ava here, it was as if the whole house was holding its breath.

Ava took a step into the room, her heels clicking sharply on the wood floors. She barely glanced at Noah, who still stood near the door, looking like he was trying to make himself smaller. But then, Ava had a way of doing that—commanding attention without ever asking for it.

I opened my mouth to say something, but words failed me. What could I say? What did any of this mean? My life was a jigsaw puzzle and every time I thought I had it figured out, someone else appeared, throwing the pieces in the air.

"Well," Ava drawled, looking between Jaxon and Noah, a smirk curling at the edges of her lips. "Isn't this cozy? A reunion of sorts?"

I could feel Jaxon's muscles tense behind me, his fingers gripping his glass so hard I was surprised it didn't shatter. I wasn't sure which part of this was bothering him more—the fact that Noah was here, the fact that Ava had shown up like she owned the place, or the simple truth that everything I had built with him was now starting to look like a house of cards.

I turned to face her, trying to keep my voice steady, trying to make her see just how much her presence felt like a wrecking ball. "What are you doing here, Ava?"

Ava's eyes glittered as if she were enjoying every second of the drama unfolding. "Don't act so surprised. You think you're the only one who's been keeping tabs on The Wraith?"

I could feel the weight of her words sink into my bones. It was one thing to hear about The Wraith from Noah, who I knew could be reckless but also genuinely believed in the fight. It was another thing entirely to hear it from Ava, who had a knack for always being in the right place at the right time, usually when things were about to go terribly wrong.

"You know about him?" I asked, my voice tinged with disbelief.

Ava leaned against the doorframe, her posture as casual as if she were discussing the weather. But there was an edge to her now. She wasn't the girl who used to laugh and trade old secrets with me; she was someone else entirely—someone with a purpose. "Of course, I know about him. Who do you think I am?"

The words were like a slap. A part of me had always known, but to hear her admit it, just like that, made me sick to my stomach. Ava had always been too clever, too dangerous for her own good. She had a way of weaving her influence into places I didn't even know existed. But this... this was beyond anything I had ever imagined.

Jaxon's voice broke through my thoughts, low and dangerous. "You've been tracking him?"

Ava gave him a languid smile, completely unfazed. "Not tracking. Observing. There's a difference."

"Observing?" I repeated, my heart rate picking up. "What the hell is that supposed to mean?"

Ava shrugged, looking genuinely bored. "It means, Jolie, that I know exactly what The Wraith is planning. And I know why he's doing it. It's not just some petty revenge plot. No, he's after something bigger. Something none of you are prepared for."

The weight of her words hung in the air, but it wasn't until she looked at Noah that I truly understood the implications of what she was saying. Her eyes were too sharp, her gaze too knowing, as if she'd been playing a different game all along, one that none of us could see.

Noah stiffened, his eyes locking onto hers, and for the first time since I'd seen him, there was something resembling fear in his expression. "You don't know anything," he said, though his voice lacked conviction. It was a thin veneer over something darker, something more desperate.

Ava tilted her head, considering him like a scientist observing a lab rat. "Don't I, though?" she said softly. "I've been in this game longer than you think, Noah. I didn't disappear. I adapted. And now I'm here to make sure you don't screw it up."

Jaxon's temper, which had been barely contained up until now, snapped. "Don't talk to him like that."

But Ava wasn't done. She took a step forward, her eyes never leaving mine. "You should listen to me, Jolie. Because if you don't, everything you think you've built is going to crumble. The Wraith isn't after just your life. He wants you—your blood—and once he has you, none of us will be safe."

The words hung like a final warning, but before I could respond, the sound of a phone ringing shattered the fragile quiet in the room. The moment stretched, and for one sickening second, I wondered if it was too late.

But the phone was mine. And when I picked it up, the voice on the other end wasn't one I recognized.

"Jolie," the voice rasped. "You don't know me, but you're in danger. The Wraith knows where you are."

Chapter 9: The Reckoning

The storm clouds had gathered on the horizon, thick and angry, casting a suffocating shadow over the valley. I felt the weight of it all in my chest, a tightness that seemed to wrap around my ribs like a vise. The Wraith was coming, his presence rippling through the air like an unsettling whisper. There was no escaping him. No running. The only option left was to face him head-on.

But that didn't mean I wasn't terrified.

Jaxon stood next to me, his eyes scanning the jagged cliffs, his hand resting on the hilt of his sword. His posture was calm, steady, but I could see the flicker of worry in his jawline, the subtle tension in his shoulders. He wasn't immune to the threat we were about to face, and despite his best attempts to mask it, I knew. He was as afraid as I was.

I tried to push the thought aside, but it clawed at me. The fear wasn't just about The Wraith. It was about everything that had come before. Everything we had become. I had never been good at love—at really letting myself love. My past was a shroud, one that I thought I could hide beneath, that I could wear and never be seen. But as we stood there, waiting for the inevitable, I realized something else: I had been hiding from the truth of my feelings for Jaxon as much as I had been running from The Wraith.

"Are you ready?" His voice was low, just above a whisper, but it cut through the silence like a knife.

I couldn't look at him. Not yet. Because I knew what would happen if I did. The way his presence consumed me. The way his warmth made everything else feel so cold. "Ready as I'll ever be."

The words sounded hollow, even to me. They were a lie, but what else was there to say? How could I admit that the closer we came to the end, the more I was terrified of losing him? The more I realized

I couldn't live without him, not after all this time of running, of pushing him away.

"You're not alone in this," he said, his voice softer now, a reminder that even in the darkest of moments, there was still a light—he was my light. I hated the way his words made my throat tighten. It was as if I couldn't bear to admit how badly I needed him.

The first flash of movement caught my attention—like a ripple in the air. The Wraith. He was here.

There was no hesitation now. No more time for second thoughts. My instincts kicked in, and I drew my sword, feeling its cool weight in my palm. I could sense Jaxon's gaze on me, but I refused to meet it. I had to focus. I couldn't afford the distraction. Not now.

The Wraith emerged from the shadows, a tall figure draped in darkness, his eyes glowing with an eerie light. His smile was a thin, cruel thing, stretched across his face like a wound that had never healed. He didn't say anything at first. He didn't need to. His presence alone was enough to send a chill through the air. The ground beneath us seemed to tremble in anticipation.

I swallowed hard, trying to steady my breathing. This was it. This was the moment I had been running from. But no more. Not now. The Wraith didn't deserve my fear. He didn't deserve any of my power.

I glanced at Jaxon. Our eyes met for a brief second, and in that moment, I saw it—the uncertainty, the same hesitation that had been growing in me. But there was something else, too. Something deeper. A bond that had formed between us over the months, unspoken but undeniable. And as the Wraith's shadow loomed over us, I realized that no matter what happened next, I would fight with everything I had. Not just for my life, but for him. For us.

Jaxon stepped forward, his stance unwavering, his eyes never leaving mine. "We end this, together."

THE RUSE

His words were simple, but they struck a chord within me. Together. That was what mattered. Together.

The battle began with a sudden burst of energy, a clash of steel and shadow. The Wraith's movements were a blur, his strikes coming at us with a precision that left no room for error. But we fought back, our movements synchronized, as if we had done this a thousand times before. Every swing of my sword, every step I took, felt like it was in perfect rhythm with Jaxon's. It was as if we were two halves of the same whole, our destinies bound together, our fates intertwined.

Yet, despite the fury of the battle, there was something else—something I couldn't quite place. The Wraith's power wasn't just in his strength; it was in the way he made us doubt ourselves, the way he forced us to question everything we had ever believed. He was trying to break us, to drive a wedge between us.

He would fail.

I lunged, my sword flashing in the dim light, and The Wraith's laughter echoed through the valley like a warning. I could feel it then—the pressure of the moment. The weight of my own heart, tangled in knots of fear and hope. I had spent so long pretending that I didn't need anyone. That I didn't need him. But as the dust from the battle swirled around us, as the air crackled with the heat of our fury, I understood something else entirely.

Jaxon wasn't just my ally. He was the piece I had been missing. The part of me I had been too afraid to claim. And now, with everything on the line, I would fight not just for survival, but for the chance to hold onto something real, something worth fighting for.

In that moment, everything changed. The stakes had never been higher, and the cost was steep. But I was ready to pay it.

The fight blurred into a frenzy of motion, a dance of shadows and steel, each swing of my sword a desperate plea for survival. The Wraith was relentless, every strike a reminder that this wasn't just a battle for our lives—it was a battle for our very souls. His presence, dark and oppressive, filled the air like a suffocating fog. I could barely breathe, the weight of his power pressing down on me, but Jaxon was there, always there, his every movement an unspoken promise that we would make it through this. Together.

We were so close. I could feel it in my bones. The endgame was upon us, the final confrontation waiting just beyond the reach of our swords. My heart was a drumbeat, thumping in my chest, faster and faster as the moments ticked away. The Wraith was stronger than I had anticipated, his dark magic wrapping around us, tugging at our minds, trying to tear us apart. But we had something he didn't. We had each other.

"Focus," Jaxon's voice came through the chaos, low and steady, like a beacon in the storm. He was always the calm in the madness, the anchor when everything threatened to drift away. But even he couldn't mask the undercurrent of tension in his words, the fear threading through the quiet command. He was afraid. He was terrified, just as I was. We both knew that if we failed here, if we couldn't push past the fear and the pain, we would lose everything. Everything we had fought for. Everything we had become.

The Wraith's laugh echoed through the valley, a sound that grated against the edges of my sanity. "Is this really all you have left? How pitiful."

I gritted my teeth, my grip tightening on the hilt of my sword. This wasn't about me anymore. It wasn't even about The Wraith. It was about us—Jaxon and me. The tension that had always simmered beneath the surface, that unspoken thing between us, was no longer a burden. It was a fire, burning bright and fierce, threatening to consume us both.

With a sharp exhale, I lunged, aiming for the Wraith's throat, my blade slicing through the air. But he was too quick. The air around him rippled, his form twisting and flickering like smoke, and I struck nothing but empty space. For a moment, I was disoriented, a feeling I couldn't afford, but before I could recover, I felt the cold, biting grip of his magic wrap around my throat.

"You think you can defeat me?" he hissed, his voice a venomous whisper in my ear. "You are nothing."

I struggled, the power he wielded overwhelming, threatening to crush me from the inside out. My vision blurred, the edges of reality warping as he squeezed. But then, something shifted. A flicker of light in the darkness, a surge of warmth that I knew wasn't my own.

Jaxon.

He was there, by my side, his arm wrapping around me, pulling me back from the edge. "Not today," he growled, his voice low and dangerous. And then, with a force that shook the ground beneath us, he struck.

The Wraith howled in pain, a sound so raw and primal that it sent a shiver down my spine. I gasped, drawing in a breath as the pressure around my throat vanished. The Wraith staggered back, his eyes flashing with a fury that sent a cold chill through the air.

"I told you," Jaxon said, his words a fierce promise, "we're in this together."

And I realized, in that moment, how much I had been holding back. How much I had been afraid to give of myself. Jaxon wasn't just some warrior standing at my side. He was the reason I was still standing, the reason I hadn't fallen apart in the face of everything I had lost. He was the anchor I had been searching for, the one thing that made everything else make sense.

The Wraith's form shimmered, his magic crackling with a malicious energy, but I didn't care. My heart was no longer chained by fear. I wasn't running anymore.

I stepped forward, my sword raised high, and for the first time in a long while, I knew exactly who I was. The Wraith could try to tear us apart, but he would fail. He would fail because he didn't understand what we had—what we could be. He didn't understand love.

With a cry, I thrust forward, the blade biting into the Wraith's flesh, and for the briefest of moments, there was silence. A thick, suffocating silence, as if the world itself had paused to witness the end.

But The Wraith wasn't finished. Not yet.

With a scream of rage, his body flickered, turning into a blur of shadow and light, twisting in ways that defied all logic. And then, with a force that knocked me back, he sent a wave of power crashing into us, sending us sprawling across the rocky ground. My head hit the dirt with a sickening thud, and for a moment, everything spun.

Jaxon's voice reached me through the haze. "Get up. We're not done yet."

He was right. We weren't. I pushed myself up, my limbs heavy, my vision still clouded, but I couldn't stop. Not now. Not when we were this close.

The Wraith staggered toward us, his body still shifting, his power growing with every breath. But I didn't look away. I couldn't. This was it—the final stand. I was done running. I was done hiding.

"Together," Jaxon murmured, his words almost lost in the wind.

Together.

I nodded, a fierce smile tugging at the corner of my mouth as I stepped toward him, my sword raised high once more. Whatever came next, we would face it side by side. We had already conquered the darkest parts of ourselves. There was nothing left to fear.

The Wraith raised his hand, but I saw it then—the flicker of doubt in his eyes. He wasn't invincible. Not anymore.

And with one last, unified strike, we ended it.

The ground trembled beneath my feet as the last of The Wraith's shadowed form crumbled, disintegrating like dust in the wind. His scream had been raw, a sound that didn't belong to the physical world—more like the cry of a dying star, echoing across the void. It was over. At least, I thought it was. But when the silence settled in, it carried with it a new weight, one that felt heavier than the battle itself. The air felt empty, hollow, like a place that had been drained of everything real, everything alive.

Jaxon stood beside me, his chest rising and falling in steady breaths, the only sign that he was still in the same world as me. His gaze didn't meet mine immediately. He stared ahead, his face etched with something I couldn't quite name, something that wasn't relief, but rather... an acknowledgment of what we had just survived. Or perhaps what we had just lost.

"We did it," I said quietly, the words not so much a declaration as an attempt to fill the void between us, to make sense of the chaos. But even as the words left my lips, I felt them fall flat, untrue somehow.

"We did," he replied, but his voice was distant, his eyes faraway.

I shifted, suddenly uncomfortable in my own skin. The adrenaline of the fight had dulled, leaving only the raw ache of exhaustion. But the real weight of the moment had nothing to do with fatigue. It had to do with the aftermath, the part that no one prepared you for when the battle ended and the quiet began.

"Jaxon," I said, my voice small, uncertain. "What now?"

He didn't answer immediately. Instead, he turned toward me, his eyes flicking over me with an intensity that made my heart skip. I saw the conflict in them, the same turmoil I had been feeling but had refused to acknowledge. The Wraith was gone, but the question of us remained—of what we had become in this tangled mess of survival and shared moments. What was this thing between us, this thing I had spent so long denying, afraid to name?

"I don't know," he admitted, his voice low. The honesty of it stung. "I thought we'd have time to figure it out. But now... now I don't think there's time for anything except what we've already chosen. And I think we've both known that from the start."

I swallowed hard, the weight of his words settling like a stone in my gut. "You mean... you mean I've been running all this time? From what I've always wanted?"

He gave a short laugh, almost bitter. "You've been running from everything. And I've been right there, waiting. But I'm done waiting, Ava. I'm done being afraid of what might happen if we..."

His words trailed off, and I didn't know if I wanted to hear them completed. But the silence between us stretched too long, and finally, I turned to face him fully, the cold bite of the wind around us matching the storm inside my chest.

"What are you saying?" I asked, my voice trembling just a little. "That we pretend none of this matters? That we walk away from this—everything we've been through—without even acknowledging what's between us?"

Jaxon didn't answer right away. His eyes searched mine, and for a brief moment, I thought he might pull away, that maybe he'd take the easy road. But instead, he stepped closer, his hand brushing my arm, sending a spark of heat through me that made me catch my breath.

"I'm saying we don't get to keep pretending anymore," he said quietly. "The battle's over. But the war inside of us? That's something only we can fight now."

The words hung between us, and for a moment, the world around us seemed to fade. All that remained was the soft sound of our breathing, the thrum of our hearts in perfect sync. And for the first time, I didn't feel afraid. Not of him, not of us.

"I never meant to hurt you," I whispered, a tear slipping from the corner of my eye. I didn't bother to wipe it away. The moment felt too real, too raw for me to hide anything anymore.

He reached up, his thumb brushing the tear away, his eyes soft but firm. "You didn't. You just didn't know how to let yourself be loved." His voice was thick with emotion, and it made my insides twist in a way I didn't know how to untangle.

I shook my head. "I'm sorry."

His lips quirked into a half-smile. "No apologies, Ava. Not from you. Not anymore." Then, his hand moved to the back of my neck, his fingers threading into my hair as he pulled me closer, just enough to close the distance that had always separated us. "What happens next is ours to choose."

And before I could respond, before I could say anything that might tear apart the fragile thread between us, he kissed me. It wasn't urgent, but it was full of everything we had been too afraid to say out loud. It was the culmination of months—years—of pain, of longing, of missed chances. In that moment, it felt like the only thing that mattered, the only truth that could ever exist.

When we finally pulled apart, breathless and disoriented, I saw the same realization in his eyes that I was feeling inside. We were standing at the edge of something—something vast and unknown, a precipice we could either jump from or walk away from. But there was no turning back now.

The silence was broken by a distant noise—something that didn't belong, something far too familiar.

A low rumble, a growl, like something large was stirring in the shadows.

I froze, every muscle in my body tensing as the air shifted, thickening with a presence that chilled me to the bone. Jaxon's hand tightened on mine.

"Ava," he whispered, voice tight with warning. "This isn't over. Not by a long shot."

And just as the words left his lips, the ground beneath our feet began to quake, the sky above us darkening with an unnatural storm.

Something was coming.

And it was worse than we ever imagined.

Chapter 10: A Web of Lies

The night stretched endlessly, as if the world itself was trying to hold its breath. The air smelled of rain, of something heavy and damp that had yet to fall. In the stillness of the room, Jaxon and I stood in silence, the weight of our words pulling at the edges of the atmosphere. His chest rose and fell in steady rhythm, but I could feel the tension between us, thick and suffocating. The heated exchange we'd just had still lingered, a cloud of fractured trust that neither of us seemed able to shake. My fingers twitched at my side, longing for the cool, comforting weight of my knife. But it wasn't the blade I needed right now. It was answers.

I tried to focus on the task at hand, the one thing that had kept me going when everything else felt like it was about to collapse under the pressure. The Wraith. The elusive criminal kingpin who'd cast a long, dark shadow over every inch of our lives. His influence stretched far and wide, touching every corner of the city like a disease, rotting everything it touched. I had spent months—years, really—tracking down the fragments of his operation, piecing together the puzzle with the kind of obsessive determination that only a person with nothing to lose could summon. And now, I was closer than ever to finally tearing down the web of lies he'd spun.

But something was off.

I could feel it in the way the pieces shifted when I turned them over in my mind, like I was looking at a mirror with a crack down the middle, each side fractured and incomplete. A nagging suspicion wormed its way under my skin, making my pulse quicken. The Wraith had always been a step ahead of me, always a shadow just beyond my reach. But what if it wasn't just him pulling the strings? What if someone else, someone close to me, was playing their own game? The thought hit me like a sucker punch to the gut, leaving me breathless.

Jaxon, standing at the other side of the room, hadn't moved since the argument began. I could see the muscles in his jaw flexing, the tension in his body so palpable I could practically hear it creaking. He was angry, no doubt about it, and who could blame him? I had just dropped a bombshell—accusing him, in not so many words, of being a part of this mess. His eyes, usually so calm, were now stormy, their usual warmth replaced by something sharper. I wanted to reach out, to explain myself, to take back the words that had come out of my mouth in the heat of the moment. But I knew better.

I knew what we were really fighting for, and it wasn't just our fractured relationship—it was survival.

"Do you think I would lie to you about this?" he finally spoke, his voice low, controlled. Too controlled.

I let out a breath I didn't realize I'd been holding. The silence had been suffocating, and now that the words were in the open, they didn't seem to make anything easier.

"I don't know what to think anymore, Jax." I dropped my head into my hands, rubbing my temples. The weight of it all was too much. The lies. The betrayals. The dead bodies piling up like a morbid reminder that nothing, not even love, was sacred in this world. "I just—" I stopped myself, my voice breaking under the strain. I couldn't finish the sentence. Because deep down, a part of me already knew the answer. And it scared me more than anything else ever could.

"You think I'm the one who's been feeding information to the Wraith?" His tone sharpened, the accusation hanging in the air like a blade poised to strike.

"I don't know, Jaxon," I whispered, my voice thick with frustration. "I don't know what to think anymore. All the clues keep leading back to someone close to us. Someone who knows everything. Who can anticipate our every move."

There was a moment of silence between us, the kind that made the space between our bodies feel like a yawning chasm. And then, something shifted in his gaze. The hardness in his eyes melted just slightly, replaced by something softer, but no less dangerous.

"Who do you suspect?" His voice was quiet now, dangerous in a different way.

I hesitated. The name that had been echoing in my mind like a drumbeat was one I never wanted to say aloud. But I couldn't ignore it anymore. The pieces all pointed to one person. Someone I never thought I'd have to question.

"Lena," I finally said, the name slipping out like a confession. "It's her."

The air between us seemed to freeze. Lena had always been one of us—part of our tight-knit crew, our ally in this never-ending fight against the Wraith's empire. But what if she wasn't who she said she was? What if she was playing both sides, working against us from the inside? The thought made my stomach turn, and the fear that had been growing inside me turned into something sharper, colder.

"You're wrong," Jaxon said firmly, but there was a flicker of doubt in his eyes. It was so brief, so subtle, but I caught it. And in that moment, I realized that I wasn't the only one questioning everything.

The world felt like it was tilting on its axis, and for the first time, I wasn't sure where I stood. The lines between truth and lies had blurred beyond recognition, and I wasn't sure if I could trust anyone—least of all myself.

The tension in the room was a living, breathing thing, wrapping itself around me in tight coils. It was suffocating, relentless, and there wasn't a single place to hide from it. The soft, melodic hum of the overhead lights did nothing to quell the anxiety that gnawed at my insides, the feeling that if I took one wrong step, it would all come crashing down.

THE RUSE

Jaxon's gaze never left me. He stood in the doorway like a silent sentinel, blocking out the faint light from the hall behind him, his body a dark silhouette against the faded wallpaper. I could almost hear the thoughts spinning in his head, a whirl of confusion, anger, and—if I was being honest—hurt. And that hurt? It was mirrored in me. I hadn't wanted to go this far, but there were too many shadows to ignore, too many secrets to bury beneath the surface.

"I didn't think you'd accuse me like this." His voice was a tight thread, each word carefully measured.

I didn't know what to say to that. There was no easy way out of this mess, no simple solution that would make everything go back to the way it was. "It's not just you, Jax. It's all of us. Lena's been playing both sides for God knows how long. Don't you see it? She's too perfect, too involved. I've seen her with my own eyes, Jaxon, slipping in and out of places she shouldn't be."

His eyes softened, but there was something else there now—something darker, like a storm waiting to break. "And what makes you think she'd betray us? She's one of us. She's—"

"Exactly," I cut in, my voice more desperate than I wanted it to sound. "She is one of us. That's what makes her the perfect double agent. She knows our every move, every weakness. Hell, she probably knows me better than I know myself at this point. You can't tell me that doesn't seem off."

Jaxon's jaw clenched, and for a moment, I thought he might lash out, might finally say what he'd been holding back since we started down this path. But instead, he just nodded. Not in agreement, but in resignation. "I'm not saying you're wrong. I'm just saying that if we're going to make accusations like that, we need proof. Concrete proof. Not just suspicions."

I wanted to scream, to throw my hands up in frustration. Proof. It was always about proof. I'd spent months chasing ghosts, picking apart every crumb of information I could find, and now I was supposed to bring hard evidence to the table, something that would silence all doubts? The reality of the situation hit me square in the chest. I didn't have proof. Not yet.

"Fine," I muttered, crossing the room in a few long strides, my boots clicking sharply against the hardwood floor. I could feel the pulse of my own heartbeat in my throat, each beat a reminder of how close I was to the edge of something dangerous. "But we're running out of time. The Wraith is always two steps ahead. And we're sitting here, playing guessing games about who's stabbing us in the back. This isn't a game, Jax. It's our lives."

For a moment, the room was quiet, save for the soft ticking of a clock somewhere in the distance. The silence between us felt thicker now, heavier, as if the very walls were closing in, and I couldn't tell if that was because of the secrets I was holding or the ones I was uncovering about the people I'd trusted most.

"I know," Jaxon said finally, his voice softer, less sure. "But we can't just start throwing blame around without knowing what we're dealing with."

I turned to face him, my eyes searching his. I was tired. Tired of pretending everything was fine, tired of pretending like this was just another job to get done. This was personal. More personal than anything I'd ever known. "You don't get it, do you?" I asked, my voice low, almost a whisper. "I'm not just worried about the Wraith anymore. I'm worried about who's betraying us from within. Who's been lying to us this entire time."

He stepped forward, slowly, cautiously. The space between us had never seemed so vast, despite our proximity. I could see the conflict playing across his face, the battle between the man I knew and the one who was being forced to confront the possibility that everything was a lie.

"You're right," he finally said, and his voice cracked just slightly, a betrayal of his otherwise composed demeanor. "I don't get it. Not entirely. But I'm trying, okay? I'm trying to understand."

I swallowed the lump in my throat, nodding as I blinked back the sudden rush of emotion that threatened to choke me. "We don't have much time. The Wraith is making his move. If we don't figure this out—"

The sound of footsteps approaching stopped me cold. Jaxon's body tensed, and I caught a glimpse of him reaching for something hidden beneath his jacket. A gun, most likely, though I wasn't sure what good it would do us if the real threat was already inside.

The door creaked open, and in stepped Lena.

I froze, my entire body going still, every muscle locking in place. She didn't look like a traitor. She didn't look like the person who'd sold us out. She looked exactly as she always had—smiling, effortlessly charming, like the woman who had become my closest confidante in a world that demanded we trust no one.

But I knew better now.

Her smile didn't reach her eyes. It never did, not anymore.

"I hope I'm not interrupting," she said, her voice smooth, almost too smooth. "You two have been having quite the conversation."

Jaxon didn't respond. He just stood there, eyes narrowed, watching her carefully. I could feel the weight of her presence in the room, like a quiet storm waiting to break.

For a moment, I thought the air would crackle with the tension between us. But then, Lena spoke again, and this time, I could hear something else in her voice—a hint of something that wasn't just a friendly invitation to chat. Something darker.

"You should know," she said slowly, "I'm not here to explain myself. You won't believe me anyway."

Lena's words hung in the air like a warning. Her smile, the one that had always been as warm and inviting as a sunny afternoon, now felt like a mask. Beneath it, there was something darker, colder—something she had been hiding, something that I had known all along, but was now unwilling to face. My pulse quickened, and the heat of the moment seemed to rise, as though the room itself was holding its breath, waiting for the inevitable storm to break.

Jaxon, standing beside me, hadn't moved a muscle, his expression unreadable. He was always good at this—masking his emotions. But I saw it, the faintest twitch in his eye. The same doubt that I had felt earlier was crawling up his spine now, creeping into the corners of his thoughts. It was impossible to ignore, not with Lena standing in front of us, her posture poised and casual, as if this was just another day, another mission. But everything inside me screamed that it wasn't. It never was.

"You don't have to explain yourself to me, Lena," I said, forcing my voice to stay steady, to hide the tremor of uncertainty. "But you'll have to explain to him. To Jaxon. If you plan on walking out of here tonight."

She tilted her head, an amused glint flickering in her eyes. "I don't need to explain anything to either of you." The words were sharp, cutting through the tension like a knife. "I didn't want to get involved in this mess. But someone had to do it."

I could feel the weight of her gaze on me, like she was looking right through me, seeing the cracks in my armor. My instinct screamed at me to act, to confront her, but I forced myself to stay still. The last thing I wanted was to make a mistake now.

"I'm tired of the games, Lena," Jaxon said finally, his voice low but full of a restrained fury. "If you think we don't know what you've been up to, you're wrong. This isn't a game anymore. People are dying. Our lives—my life—are at risk because of the choices you've made."

Lena stepped forward, closing the gap between us with deliberate slowness. Her eyes never left Jaxon's, but I could see the flicker of something—uncertainty, maybe, or regret. But it was gone too quickly, masked by her practiced indifference.

"People die every day, Jaxon. You should know that by now," she said, her voice steady, as though she was speaking to a child. "But if you're looking for a reason, a justification for what I've done, maybe you should look a little closer to home."

I felt the ground beneath me shift, the words sinking in like stones dropped in the water. "What does that mean?" I demanded, a chill creeping up my spine.

She gave a soft, humorless laugh. "Don't act like you haven't figured it out. You've been piecing it all together, haven't you? All the little inconsistencies. All the little lies we've told ourselves. But here's the truth, sweetheart—you're the one who's been played."

My breath caught in my throat, and for a moment, the room felt too small, too suffocating. The walls pressed in, as though they were closing me in. I could hear the pounding of my heart in my ears, drowning out everything else. I tried to steady myself, tried to make sense of the words she had just said. But I couldn't. I couldn't make sense of anything anymore.

"You've been lying to me," I whispered, more to myself than to her.

Lena's smile widened, a slow, predatory curve of her lips that made my blood run cold. "Not exactly, darling. I've just been... strategic with the truth."

I could feel Jaxon tense beside me, his hand moving ever so slightly toward his gun, but I caught his wrist before he could make a move.

"No," I said, my voice suddenly firm. "Don't do it."

He looked at me, confusion written all over his face. "What are you talking about? She's the one who—"

"I know," I cut him off, trying to catch my breath. "But it's not about her anymore. It's about who she's been working for. Who she's really been working for."

Lena's eyes flickered toward the door, then back to us, her expression unreadable. "If you think this ends with me, you're wrong. The Wraith is only part of the problem. The real game is about to begin, and you're not ready for it."

I took a step back, a sinking feeling in my stomach. "Who are you working for, Lena?" I asked, my voice quiet, barely above a whisper. But she heard me.

She smirked. "Do you really think I'm the biggest threat here? You've been so focused on the Wraith, you've missed the bigger picture. All of you have."

I glanced at Jaxon, but his face was pale, his expression shifting from anger to something much darker. Fear.

"You're not telling us everything," he said, his voice tight. "Who else is pulling the strings?"

Lena's gaze flickered to the window, to the rain that had begun to patter against the glass. For a moment, she seemed lost in thought, like she was weighing something in her mind. Then she turned back to us, her gaze steady. "It's too late to stop it now," she said, her voice colder than I'd ever heard it before. "There's nothing you can do. The Wraith was just the beginning."

And then, before either of us could respond, the sound of a door slamming open echoed through the room, followed by the unmistakable hiss of a silenced gunshot.

Everything happened in an instant.

Chapter 11: Bound by Blood

The air between us crackled with tension, heavy with unspoken words. Jaxon stood across the room, his broad frame outlined in the pale light filtering through the blinds, casting shadows on the walls like specters of the past. The silence was thick, suffocating, as if it had a weight of its own. I tried to steady my breath, but it was hard with the storm of emotions churning inside me, threatening to spill over at any moment.

I had always thought I knew him. The quiet strength in his eyes, the way he would touch the small of my back when things got tough, the way he smiled, half-smirk, half-mischief. But all of that—every single part of him—felt like a lie now. His family's history, the ties that bound him to The Wraith, had carved deep gashes in the fabric of everything I thought I knew about us.

"You don't understand," Jaxon said, his voice low, controlled, but there was an edge to it—a crack that betrayed his calm exterior. "I never wanted this life. It's not mine. It's not who I am anymore."

I wanted to believe him. I wanted to reach across the room and touch him, remind him of the man he had become in the time we'd spent together. But there was a fear in me now, gnawing at the edges of my resolve. What if the truth was darker than I could ever imagine? What if, like the blood that flowed through his veins, this dark legacy was inescapable?

"You can't just erase your past, Jaxon." My voice came out sharper than I intended, and I regretted it the moment the words left my mouth. "You can't pretend it doesn't exist. The Wraith... the people he's hurt, the lives he's ruined. You're tied to that. Whether you like it or not."

His eyes flickered with something—regret, maybe. It was hard to tell. But before he could respond, I cut him off.

"Don't say it's not your fault. Don't tell me you didn't have a choice in all this. You didn't walk away from him, from that world. You didn't say no when you had the chance."

Jaxon's jaw tightened, his hands balling into fists at his sides. I could see the internal struggle warring inside him, the conflict between the man he wanted to be and the blood that pulled him back into the darkness. It was like watching a battle between light and shadow, one that could tear him apart if he wasn't careful.

"I didn't have a choice," he muttered, his voice almost breaking. "You don't understand what it's like... to be born into this, to have no way out."

I shook my head, stepping closer to him, though every inch of me screamed to turn and run. My heart was racing, and the tightness in my chest made it hard to breathe. But I couldn't leave—not yet. Not when I still loved him, despite everything.

"You're not that man anymore," I whispered, reaching for him, my fingers trembling. "I don't know who you were before, but I know who you are now."

His eyes softened for a moment, but then the doubt came flooding back, crashing through the cracks. He took a step back, almost imperceptibly, but it felt like a canyon had opened between us.

"But what if I'm wrong? What if everything I think I know about myself... about us... is just another lie?" His words were like a knife, sharp and cutting through the fragile space that had once felt like home.

I couldn't answer him, because I didn't know the truth either. I didn't know if I could ever trust him the way I had before, or if the shadows of his past would swallow us whole. But I knew one thing for sure: I couldn't walk away, not without fighting for him. For us.

THE RUSE

"You're not your father, Jaxon," I said, my voice steadier now, despite the storm inside. "You don't have to be. You can choose a different path."

He looked at me, his gaze unwavering, as though searching for something in my eyes. "Can I? Or am I already too far gone?"

I didn't have the answer. But I wanted to be the reason he fought. I wanted to be the one who reminded him that love, however fractured it may seem, was still worth fighting for.

The weight of his family's legacy hung between us like an invisible chain, unspoken but undeniable. The Wraith's influence was a shadow that couldn't be outrun, no matter how fast we ran. His blood, dark and tainted, was a part of him, whether he liked it or not. But there was still light in him. I'd seen it. And if I could just reach him, if I could just help him see that he didn't have to be bound to a past that wasn't his to claim, then maybe—just maybe—we could find a way out of this mess together.

But the road ahead was uncertain. There were too many forces beyond our control, too many enemies circling, waiting for us to make a mistake. And with every passing second, I felt the weight of their presence, creeping closer, drawing us into a web of danger we might not survive.

I reached out again, this time with more purpose, more resolve. "I don't know what the future holds, Jaxon. But I know this—whatever happens, we face it together. I'm not leaving you. Not now. Not ever."

His gaze softened, and for a moment, I thought I saw a flicker of hope in his eyes, a spark that had been buried beneath years of secrets and lies. But as quickly as it appeared, it was gone, replaced by that familiar wall he had built around himself.

"Then you'll hate me too," he murmured. "When you find out what I'm really capable of."

I didn't know what I expected when I first stepped into this tangled mess of a life, but it certainly wasn't this. Maybe it was naïve to believe that love could somehow rewrite the chapters of history. That the past could be swept under the rug, ignored long enough to fade into oblivion. But that was before Jaxon, before the quiet force of him settled into my world and spun everything I thought I knew about myself into a knot I couldn't untangle.

I took a breath and closed the distance between us, the air thick with the tension between words neither of us was ready to speak. His gaze flickered over me, sharp as ever, like he was waiting for something—permission, a decision, maybe even a hint of the fear that had to be lurking behind my eyes. It was hard to mask it, even with the walls I'd spent years building around myself.

His fingers twitched at his side, but I wasn't sure whether he was trying to fight the instinct to reach out or if it was something else entirely, like the last tether of control snapping in half. He looked so different in that moment, not the man who made me laugh in the middle of a bad day, not the man who held me like he wanted to keep me safe. But the weight of his family's secrets, the legacy of blood and betrayal, had changed him. Or maybe it hadn't. Maybe it was always there, buried beneath the surface.

"I won't hate you," I said, though the words tasted like ash on my tongue. "But I don't know if I can trust you anymore."

It was an honest admission, and one I regretted the second it left my mouth. Trust was a delicate thing, fragile enough that I had to fight to keep it intact in the face of everything falling apart around us. But honesty—brutal, ugly honesty—had become the only currency we had left to spend. So I pressed on, my voice soft but firm.

"You say you're not like him, but you can't just erase what's inside you. The Wraith isn't just some villain in your past; he's in your blood. He's in your bones." I took another step closer, but this time there was no reaching for him. No instinct to close the gap between us. I wasn't sure I even wanted to.

Jaxon's face tightened, the sharp angles of his jaw setting hard, and I saw it—the darkness that had been simmering beneath the surface. It wasn't the first time I'd seen it, but this time it was different. It wasn't just the shadows of his past—it was the weight of his choices, the gravity pulling him back toward a life he couldn't escape.

"You think I don't know that?" he rasped, his voice like gravel scraping against stone. "You think I don't wake up every damn day with the knowledge that I'm—" He stopped, his mouth pressed into a thin line as if the words he wanted to say were too heavy to lift.

I didn't know what to say. I didn't know what to do. There were so many things I wanted to scream at him, questions I wanted to throw in his face, but I kept my mouth shut because there was something else there, something softer underneath the anger that flared in his eyes. And that terrified me more than anything else. The vulnerability that he tried so hard to hide from the world—and from me—was slipping through the cracks now. I could see it, feel it, and I hated how much it made me want to reach out and offer him something to hold onto.

But I couldn't, not when the truth about his family had cut so deep. I wasn't sure if I could be the one to pull him back from the edge. And I wasn't sure I wanted to be. I had my own scars, my own history I was trying to outrun. The last thing I needed was to be dragged into the abyss with him.

"I don't want to be him," Jaxon said, his voice rough, raw. "I never did. But the things I've done... they're not something I can just undo." He exhaled slowly, shaking his head. "The Wraith is still out there, pulling strings, making things happen. And I'm tangled up in all of it."

I swallowed hard, my throat tight. "But you don't have to be. You don't have to stay in the cage he built for you."

He laughed then, but it was bitter, empty. "You think it's that easy? You think I haven't tried to walk away from all of this? I've been trying to break free from him my whole life. But every time I take a step forward, it feels like he drags me right back. There's no escape, not really."

The truth hung between us, a suffocating weight, and I felt the full force of it, like a tidal wave that I couldn't outrun. It wasn't just about me anymore, about the choices I'd made or the love I thought I could hold onto. It was about forces bigger than us, bigger than anything we could fight. The Wraith's shadow stretched long, and it was closing in on us.

I could see it now, the road he had walked down, the decisions he had made—whether he wanted to admit them or not. Every choice had led him here, to this moment where the lines between right and wrong blurred until they became indistinguishable. It was a path carved with blood and betrayal, and I could feel myself being dragged into it, even as I tried to fight against it.

But I wasn't sure I could fight him anymore. Or the pull of his past.

I took another step back, the weight of my decision crushing me under its force. "Maybe it's not about whether you can escape," I said, my voice barely above a whisper. "Maybe it's about whether you're willing to fight for something else. Something better."

He didn't answer me right away. Instead, he looked at me—really looked at me—as if seeing me for the first time. There was something unreadable in his eyes, something I couldn't quite grasp, but I knew one thing for sure: whatever it was, it had nothing to do with the man I thought he was. Not anymore.

"Maybe," he said, his voice barely a murmur, as if he didn't believe it himself. "Maybe you're right."

The silence between us stretched out like an ocean, vast and impossibly deep. I watched Jaxon, standing so still that he seemed to blend with the shadows in the room, a man half-lost to a past he could never outrun. I wanted to reach for him, to remind him that I believed in the man he was becoming. But the ghosts of his family, the memories of blood spilled and deals made in the dark corners of the world, felt too close. It was hard to tell where his past ended and his present began, and I wasn't sure which one would win in the end.

"You're not who they say you are," I said, the words coming out softer than I intended. They were as much for me as they were for him, a fragile declaration that I wasn't ready to back away from, not yet. "You're not your father."

Jaxon's lips pressed into a tight line, but there was something in his eyes—a flicker of pain, of guilt—that made my heart ache. He didn't answer right away, as if the weight of those words was something he hadn't heard in years, maybe never. It wasn't the first time someone had told him he wasn't The Wraith, but it was the first time someone who mattered had said it.

"I don't know what you want me to say," he muttered, his voice tight. "I can't undo what's already been done. And if you think I can just walk away from all of it, you're wrong."

I couldn't keep still any longer. My hands, cold and clammy, trembled at my sides, but I forced myself to stand tall. "I never asked you to undo it, Jaxon. I just want to know that you're not going to let it destroy you."

He laughed, but it wasn't a sound of joy. It was hollow, bitter. "You don't get it. This isn't something you walk away from. Not when your blood is tied to it. Not when you've made the kinds of decisions I have."

I wasn't ready to give up, even if every word he spoke was like a slap in the face. "But you can make different choices now. You have a chance to change. To fight for something else."

Jaxon's gaze softened, but there was a sadness there now, a resignation that twisted something deep inside of me. "I can't promise you that. I can't promise anything anymore."

It felt like a door had slammed shut between us, but I couldn't walk away from it. I couldn't just leave him there, surrounded by the ghosts of his past, waiting for him to figure it out alone. Maybe it was foolish. Maybe it was naive to think that love could heal this kind of wound. But it was the only thing I had left to offer.

"I don't need promises, Jaxon," I said, my voice quieter now, but steady. "I just need to know you're willing to try."

For a long moment, he didn't say anything. His eyes were distant, as if he were looking at something far beyond the walls of the room, a place I couldn't follow. But then, just when I thought I might break, he finally spoke.

"I'm trying," he whispered, almost to himself. "But it's not enough. It'll never be enough."

I wanted to argue, to tell him that wasn't true, but before I could, the sound of a door slamming open echoed through the house. I froze, my heart leaping into my throat. Jaxon's body went rigid, his eyes flickering toward the doorway with a kind of terror that made my blood run cold.

The door slammed shut again, and then there was the unmistakable sound of footsteps—slow, deliberate—coming toward us.

"We don't have time for this," a voice growled, sharp and commanding. I didn't recognize it, but the weight of it made my stomach drop. "The Wraith's people are closing in. We've got to move. Now."

Jaxon's face drained of color, his body tense as if he were caught in a vice. "How did they find us?"

"Does it matter?" the voice snapped back, rough with urgency. "We have minutes, maybe less. If we don't go now, they'll have us all in the crosshairs."

I looked at Jaxon, and for the first time, I saw the full depth of the fear in his eyes. It wasn't for himself. It wasn't for the past that haunted him. It was for me. The fear that, somehow, this wasn't just his battle anymore—it was mine, too.

Before I could say anything, he was at my side, grabbing my arm with a force that was both protective and desperate. "We don't have time to argue," he said, his voice low, almost pleading. "You need to trust me, and you need to trust them. We're not safe here anymore."

The panic in his voice sent a jolt through me, snapping my body into motion before my mind could fully process what was happening. I didn't understand. I didn't understand how we'd gone from a quiet confrontation to this, to the looming threat of enemies who seemed to come from nowhere.

I wanted to ask what he meant, who he was talking about, but there was no time. His hand tightened around mine, pulling me toward the back door. And for the first time since I'd met him, I felt the weight of his decisions, of the people he was tied to, pulling us both deeper into the darkness.

The world outside was dark, cold, and the night felt alive with danger. My pulse pounded in my ears, but all I could hear was the sound of Jaxon's breathing, shallow and fast.

And then, just as we reached the edge of the yard, I heard the unmistakable sound of a gunshot echoing in the distance.

Jaxon froze. I froze. And then we both heard it: the rustling of leaves, the crack of twigs breaking under heavy boots.

We were surrounded.

"Run," Jaxon said, his voice barely above a whisper. But the urgency in it made my legs move before I could think, before I could question whether we had a chance at all.

And as I ran, hand in hand with the man I thought I knew, I realized with a sinking feeling that the truth—our truth—had only just begun to unravel.

Chapter 12: The Edge of Betrayal

I never imagined that stepping into the world of high-stakes danger would feel so much like stepping into quicksand. The more I moved, the more I sank. I thought I was prepared for everything—masks, codes, half-truths—but I hadn't accounted for the way the air would tighten around me. Or for how close I'd get to Jaxon.

The plan had seemed simple enough at the time. Let myself be caught in the web of The Wraith's operation, play the part of an informant who's tired of being in the shadows, someone with critical information for the right price. What could go wrong, right? Except for everything. I hadn't anticipated how deeply the lines would blur between the role I was playing and who I was becoming in the process. In all the espionage novels I'd read, there was always some moment of clarity—the hero would snap out of it, right at the critical moment. But there's no clarity when you're knee-deep in a game where the stakes are life and death, and the rules keep changing on you.

I stood at the edge of the rooftop, feeling the cool bite of the wind on my face, staring down at the city that had become my prison. Jaxon was somewhere below, waiting. His patience was unnerving. In another life, we might've made sense together—a twisted, dangerous kind of sense—but now? Now I wasn't so sure.

"Don't overthink it," Jaxon had said earlier, his voice calm but laced with something I couldn't quite place. I hated the way he always sounded so sure of himself, as if the world bent to his will. I was the opposite. Every step I took felt like a misstep, and yet, I couldn't stop myself from moving forward. He had orchestrated everything—my role, my place in this game—and while I trusted him in the way one trusts a loaded gun, I couldn't quite shake the unease that gnawed at my insides. It was the same feeling I had when

I walked into a room full of people wearing too much perfume. Overpowering, suffocating.

But Jaxon was my partner in this, for better or worse. He had made that clear, but he wasn't one to share. Not really. And in a world where every truth was a carefully constructed lie, it felt like the only thing I could trust was the tension that hummed between us, sharp and relentless.

The night we were supposed to make our move, everything went wrong. I had been positioned exactly where I needed to be, acting the part of someone who was losing her nerve—too eager to please, too desperate for the approval of people who wouldn't hesitate to tear me apart if I so much as blinked wrong. The message had been clear: give us the information, or you won't make it through the night.

My phone buzzed, the vibration an odd comfort in the midst of everything. It was a text from Jaxon: Stay focused. Simple, direct, his usual tone. But I knew him well enough to sense the undercurrent of tension, the way the words never fully captured the weight of what he wasn't saying.

I glanced over my shoulder, eyes narrowing as I caught sight of two men approaching. The Wraith's men. As they came closer, my heart picked up its rhythm, like a drumbeat in a dark alley. I swallowed, forcing my pulse to calm. I had rehearsed this part in my head a thousand times. But there's a difference between playing pretend and having your life on the line.

"Is she the one?" one of them asked, his voice low, but with an edge that sliced through the silence. I didn't move, didn't give them the satisfaction of flinching.

I nodded, once, slowly. "I have what you need."

"Good," the second man said, his tone colder, more menacing. "Let's see how long you last."

And then, just like that, I was no longer in control.

THE RUSE 109

I didn't know how long I stood there, the words floating in the air, my mind a haze of conflicting thoughts. The city lights blurred behind me, and for a moment, I felt weightless, as if I was suspended in time, caught between two worlds I didn't belong to. The one where I could still walk away, where I was still in control—and the one where I was so far in that there was no escape.

The ground beneath me shifted, and I realized too late that I was being pushed forward, taken somewhere I didn't want to go. Panic rose in my throat, but I kept my face neutral, the practiced mask I wore slipping into place like a second skin. But I could feel the sweat, the cold panic crawling up my spine, threatening to shatter the fragile illusion I'd worked so hard to create.

That's when it happened. A sharp crack of a gunshot. The world seemed to stop for a breath before chaos erupted. The air was thick with the scent of gunpowder and something far more dangerous: betrayal.

Jaxon's voice sliced through the noise like a rope fraying in the wind. "Run. Now."

But it wasn't just a command. It was a warning.

I didn't hesitate. I couldn't. The sound of my feet pounding against the concrete echoed in the distance, but I couldn't outrun the truth—something had gone terribly wrong, and I was in far deeper than I ever intended to be.

Behind me, I heard another gunshot, but I didn't turn. Didn't dare to look. Not until I reached the door and slammed it shut behind me. Only then did I realize what I had done—what we had done. The trap had been set, and I had walked straight into it, fully aware that trust, once broken, would never be fully mended.

The sound of the door slamming behind me didn't come close to matching the roar inside my chest. It wasn't fear, not in the way I expected it to feel. It was the sharp, acid edge of betrayal, carving a permanent scar into my thoughts. It had happened—whatever it was. The thing I had been trying to outrun, to control, had been set in motion, and I was standing right in the middle of it.

Jaxon's voice echoed in my ears like an aftershock, the urgency of it crashing over me, but I couldn't move. My body was frozen in place, caught somewhere between the adrenaline of the chase and the sinking realization that I had just stepped too far into a world I couldn't escape from. There was no "out" anymore.

And then, I heard the telltale sound of footsteps, too heavy to be just my own, too familiar to be anyone else's.

"Don't just stand there." Jaxon's voice was strained, like it was laced with the same tension that crackled through the air around us. I turned, but he wasn't there. He was still somewhere, out of sight, his tone snapping through the silence like a whip.

"I didn't know you could make a grand exit," I managed, half-exasperated, half-relieved to hear the familiar snap in his voice. It was like a lifeline in the chaos—somehow, his presence was both a comfort and a reminder of everything I had to lose.

"You're not exactly the best at listening," he muttered, appearing from the shadows just in time to make me wish I'd stayed frozen. He was breathing harder than usual, his jaw clenched in that way that always made me want to scream at him—and kiss him, which only added to the delightful confusion I'd been stewing in.

He reached out, one hand brushing the edge of my shoulder, the touch so soft it could've been a trick of the light. But it wasn't. He was here, really here, pulling me further into the dark abyss that was his world. "You shouldn't have done that," he said, and even though the words were clipped, there was something else lurking in the undertone—concern, maybe, but it was the sort that didn't belong in a place like this.

"And you shouldn't have trusted me," I snapped back before I could stop myself. "This wasn't your plan, Jaxon. Not really."

He shook his head, a brief flicker of amusement flashing across his face. "That's rich, coming from someone who just waltzed into the lion's den dressed as dinner."

I couldn't help it. I rolled my eyes. "Do I look like I'm having a good time?"

He didn't answer right away, his gaze moving over me, like he was checking for cracks. I hated that he could do that so easily—pull me apart, stitch me back together, then pull me apart again. I wasn't his puzzle, damn it. He'd been clear about what we were, what we were doing, and yet here I was, tangled up in his world, trying to make sense of a game I had no business playing.

The soft hum of a car engine in the distance was a reminder that the world was still spinning, that the night wasn't over, and whatever game we were playing had only just begun.

"I never thought it would be easy," I said, lowering my voice. The words came out harder than I expected. I didn't like showing weakness in front of him—not like this. "But I didn't think it would feel like this either. Like I'm standing at the edge, about to fall off a cliff, and you're the one who's holding the rope. Except, what if you're the one who's gonna let me go?"

His eyes darkened. "You really think I'd do that?"

I met his gaze without flinching. "Would you?"

For a long moment, he said nothing. Just stood there, his face unreadable, his posture stiff, like a man who knew the weight of every choice he made. And then he exhaled, like he was releasing a breath he didn't realize he'd been holding. "I wouldn't do that, but you're already too far in. Too deep to be a safe bet for anyone."

I took a step back, the words stinging more than I wanted to admit. The truth hurt, but it was the kind of truth you can't run from—no matter how hard you try.

"So what now?" I asked, forcing the question through my throat. "We wait for the storm to hit?"

The corners of his lips twitched. "You sound like you're ready to give up."

I shook my head. "I'm not ready for anything anymore. I'm just trying to figure out what's real and what's a lie."

He stepped closer, closer than he'd been all night, and the distance between us closed with a crackle of tension. "You should know by now, nothing here is real. It's all smoke and mirrors, sweetheart."

"Right," I muttered. "Like your charming personality."

He smirked, a flash of something dangerous in his eyes. "You really think you've got me figured out, don't you?"

"Not really. But I'm getting there." I bit my lip. "Getting there... and regretting it."

Jaxon's expression faltered, just for a second, before he masked it again. "You know, you're making this a hell of a lot harder than it needs to be."

I arched an eyebrow. "You've never liked easy, Jaxon. I've watched you tear apart perfectly good plans just for the thrill of making them more complicated."

"Complicated is better than boring," he said, his voice low and dangerous. "I thought you'd figured that out by now."

I opened my mouth to retort, but before I could, the soft shuffle of footsteps echoed down the hall. Too soft to be anyone we knew, too heavy to be casual.

Jaxon's hand shot out, grabbing mine with a force that surprised me. He tugged me toward the nearest doorway, and we both slipped into the shadows, the cool walls pressing against my back as we waited.

The footsteps grew louder. Closer.

And just when I thought I could catch my breath, the door swung open with a force that made my heart stop.

THE RUSE

Jaxon's grip tightened around my wrist. "No turning back now," he whispered.

The world outside the narrow room seemed far away, almost dreamlike in its stillness. It was the kind of quiet that wasn't natural, the kind that hinted at something dangerous lurking just out of sight, a silent breath before a storm. I stood frozen, my back pressed to the cool metal of the door, my breath shallow as the footsteps neared. My pulse drummed in my ears, every beat a reminder of what was at stake.

Jaxon's fingers were still locked around my wrist, a grip that could have been reassuring if it weren't so tense, so tight. He didn't need to say anything; I could feel it in the way his entire body seemed coiled, like a spring ready to snap. His silence was a statement in itself, one that I didn't want to hear but couldn't escape from. His proximity felt like a force field, one that both protected and trapped me, keeping me tethered to a world I no longer understood.

The door creaked again, this time with more force, a warning of what was to come. My hand, of its own accord, tightened around the edge of the shelf next to me, and I cursed myself for not being able to keep my composure. I wasn't supposed to be nervous. I wasn't supposed to have any doubts.

"Stay quiet," Jaxon murmured, his lips brushing against my ear. His voice was low, a hushed command that carried more weight than anything else he'd said tonight. It was the kind of voice that didn't allow room for argument. Not that I would've argued.

The footsteps stopped just outside the door. A long silence stretched out between us, like the world was holding its breath. I could practically feel the person standing on the other side of the door, waiting, watching, and I wondered if they could hear my heartbeat, the loud, frantic rhythm that threatened to give us away. My mind raced, conjuring images of what could be waiting out there—threats, weapons, a hundred different ways for this to go wrong.

And then, as though on cue, the door swung open.

The figure in the doorway was shrouded in darkness, their silhouette barely visible in the dim light from the hallway. But I didn't need to see their face to know they weren't here to offer us a cup of tea and a polite conversation. The tension in the air thickened, crackling with the electricity of too many unsaid things.

"Get away from her," Jaxon's voice was like a growl, low and fierce. But I could see the hesitation in him, the brief flicker of uncertainty in his gaze. He wasn't the kind of man to show weakness, yet in that split second, I saw it. It was subtle, but it was there—we're in trouble.

I didn't have time to ask questions. The figure in the doorway shifted, and suddenly, they were moving toward us with purpose. I took a step back, instinctively pressing closer to Jaxon, who didn't flinch. His eyes never left the newcomer, assessing, calculating. But the longer I stared at the figure, the more I felt like something wasn't right. I could see the shape of them clearly now—too tall, too familiar. The voice, though muffled by the distance, was unmistakable.

"Jaxon, let her go."

The words came out like a whisper, but they hit harder than any punch.

I froze. My heart stumbled in my chest, a cold wave sweeping over me. I wasn't sure if I heard it correctly. Or if I wanted to hear it at all.

"Lena?" Jaxon's voice cracked, the name escaping him with a rough edge. His face went pale, and his hand loosened slightly around mine.

The woman in front of us stepped fully into the light then, and I realized just how badly I had miscalculated. It wasn't just someone from the enemy's camp. No, this was someone far more dangerous, someone whose betrayal cut deeper than anything we could have expected.

Her eyes locked with mine, and I felt the weight of her gaze. She was wearing the same look I had seen on Jaxon countless times—the cold, calculating look of someone who didn't care who they had to destroy to get what they wanted. The look of someone who wasn't afraid to make hard choices.

"I told you I'd make you regret this, Jaxon," she said, her voice soft but edged with venom. "I told you, and now look where we are."

I looked between them, feeling the weight of the moment press down on me. I wanted to scream, to demand answers, but the knot in my stomach kept me quiet. This wasn't just a betrayal. It was a masterstroke—one that had been playing out behind closed doors for longer than I had realized.

"You're working with them?" I asked, my voice barely more than a whisper, but the shock in my words echoed louder than any shout.

Lena didn't even blink. "I'm doing what's necessary," she replied with that same chilling calm. "You should have never gotten involved in this, Jaxon. You should have known better."

I wanted to scream. I wanted to demand that she explain herself, that she give me some shred of reason, of clarity, but my throat felt tight. My mind was racing, spinning in a dozen different directions, trying to process this new reality. She was the mole. The one we'd been searching for. The one who had been feeding information to The Wraith, the one who had made it all possible.

And she had been right under our noses this entire time.

Jaxon's jaw was clenched, his face pale, his eyes flashing with a mixture of fury and something darker. He looked between me and Lena, his mind working faster than I could follow. But all I could do was stand there, trapped in the middle of it.

"Do it," Lena said, the command sharp and final. "Or I will."

A flicker of movement caught my eye—Jaxon's hand was moving toward his belt. And for a terrifying moment, I thought he was going to do something drastic. But when he reached for the gun, it wasn't for the woman who stood before us. It was for me.

I didn't have time to scream. The sharp click of the gun's safety was the only warning I got before everything went dark.

Chapter 13: Into the Abyss

The city had always been alive, but tonight, New Chicago felt more like a living thing itself—breathing, pulsating, its heartbeat quickening as we wound deeper into its veins. The streets twisted underfoot, alleyways narrowing until they felt like claustrophobic tunnels, each shadow cast by crumbling walls hiding something darker than just the night. Every corner we turned seemed to pull us further into the labyrinth, and with each step, I couldn't help but wonder if we would ever find our way out again.

My boots clicked against the damp pavement, the sound of them almost unnerving in the stillness that surrounded us. The air was thick with tension, the smell of rust, oil, and something more acrid hanging heavy, coating the back of my throat. My fingers gripped the hilt of my knife, more out of habit than necessity, but my other hand was wrapped firmly around Jaxon's wrist. His touch grounded me, anchoring me in this chaotic sea of uncertainty. It was strange, how in the midst of this madness, his presence felt like the only thing I could rely on.

His breath came quick beside me, steady but strained. He hadn't said much since we entered the Wraith's territory, and I hadn't pushed him. Words weren't necessary when our world was reduced to the raw reality of survival. Every step we took felt like we were moving further from sanity, plunging deeper into the abyss that the Wraith ruled. There was something in his silence, though, something heavy, like a storm about to break. I didn't know whether to be grateful for the quiet or terrified by it.

We came to a stop at the mouth of another alley. The flickering neon sign above us buzzed, casting the street in an eerie glow, its light dancing off the jagged graffiti that marred the walls. My eyes scanned the shadows, every creak of a door or shift in the night making my pulse spike. Jaxon leaned in, his voice a low murmur in my ear.

"Stay close," he whispered, his breath warm against my skin. "They're here."

I felt my stomach tighten. The Wraiths, with their sharp eyes and sharper blades, were notorious for hunting in packs. They thrived on fear, fed on weakness, and when they sensed it... well, you were as good as dead.

I took a slow breath, steadying myself. There was no room for fear now. We had made it this far, and there was no turning back. Not that I would. Not when the only thing standing between the Wraiths and the rest of New Chicago was us.

Jaxon's grip tightened on my wrist as we moved forward, my feet barely making a sound as we glided through the alley, the only noise the pounding of my heart in my chest. We reached a small clearing, where a broken-down market stall sat abandoned, the remnants of shattered glass glistening like diamonds on the cracked pavement. The air here felt different—chilled, as though the temperature had dropped several degrees without warning.

"Do you hear that?" I asked, my voice barely above a whisper.

He nodded, his eyes narrowing as he scanned the area. A rustling sound came from the far corner, followed by the soft scrape of boots on concrete. They were close. Too close.

Without warning, Jaxon shoved me behind the stall, his hand pressing firmly against my back to keep me hidden. My pulse raced as I peered around the edge, my breath catching in my throat as I saw them. Four of them, their faces obscured by the hoods of their dark cloaks, moving with a predatory grace. The Wraiths. I could almost taste their bloodlust in the air.

"Stay low," Jaxon murmured.

I nodded, barely breathing as I crouched, my back pressed against the cold stone of the stall. The Wraiths' footsteps grew louder, closer. One of them—a tall figure, even taller than Jaxon—paused, his head tilting as if he could smell us. For a moment, time seemed to stop, the world held in a breathless silence. I dared not move, not even an inch.

Then, just as suddenly, the Wraiths were gone, disappearing into the shadows as quickly as they had come.

I exhaled, the rush of air making me dizzy. My hands shook as I gripped the edge of the stall, leaning against it for support.

"They're gone," I whispered, more to myself than to Jaxon.

Jaxon stood up, his gaze flicking toward the direction the Wraiths had vanished. His expression was unreadable, a mask of cold calculation. But there was something in his eyes—something dark. Fear, maybe, but also determination.

"Not for long," he said, his voice steady but with an edge that sent a chill down my spine.

I didn't have to ask what he meant. The Wraiths were still out there, waiting for the perfect moment to strike. But this time, it wasn't just them hunting us. We were hunting them too.

I glanced at Jaxon, his sharp profile lit by the dim neon, and for the briefest of moments, something softer flickered in his eyes. I didn't know if it was fear or relief, but it was there. Just for a second, before he shut it down, locking it away behind the steel walls he'd built around himself.

I wanted to say something, but the words stuck in my throat. Instead, I stepped closer, my hand brushing against his, and he didn't pull away. I could feel the heat of him, the tension between us crackling, and for a fleeting instant, I wondered if we were both just drowning in this madness, pretending that we could still find air to breathe.

Before I could say anything, he broke the silence, his voice low but firm. "We need to keep moving."

And just like that, the moment was gone, swallowed whole by the abyss we were tumbling toward.

The alleyway curved sharply, its corners jagged like broken teeth, and I could hear the low hum of distant engines echoing from beyond the high-rise buildings. It was the sound of New Chicago—a city that never slept, its pulse steady beneath the chaos, a rhythm we couldn't escape even if we tried. The further we moved into the Wraiths' turf, the heavier the air became, thick with the scent of smoke and metal, as if the very ground itself was soaked with secrets, waiting to swallow us whole.

I kept my head low, my footsteps silent as I followed Jaxon through the murky gloom. His every movement was calculated, precise, like a dancer gliding through a dangerous waltz. I envied that certainty in him—his ability to stay calm, to stay cool when everything around us was nothing short of a ticking time bomb. I was the one who fidgeted, who jumped at shadows, but Jaxon? He was the storm's eye, a perfect center of control in a world that seemed to have gone mad.

"How far?" I asked, my voice barely more than a whisper, though the silence pressed in on us like a weight.

"Not much farther," Jaxon replied, his voice low but steady. "Stay sharp."

I nodded, though the knot in my stomach tightened at the thought of what waited for us ahead. The Wraiths didn't just control territory—they owned fear itself. They thrived on it, wrapped it around their necks like a necklace, and I wasn't sure if we could make it through without becoming part of that collection.

The city's pulse quickened as we entered a more familiar stretch of alleyway—one where the walls were lined with makeshift market stalls, their tattered awnings hanging like ghosts in the fog. Old news clippings fluttered in the wind, stuck to the metal surfaces of abandoned carts, their headlines a cruel reminder of how much had been lost in this war against the Wraiths. One headline caught my eye as we passed: Vigilantes Stand Tall Against The Wraiths. The paper was yellowing, its ink running with time, but the words still hit hard, and I couldn't help but think how naive it all seemed now. We weren't standing tall anymore. We were stumbling, trying to keep our footing in a world that was too far gone to save.

Jaxon stopped abruptly, holding up a hand to silence me. He cocked his head, his expression unreadable.

I froze, my hand instinctively reaching for the dagger at my side, but Jaxon shook his head slightly. "It's not them," he muttered, eyes scanning the dimly lit street ahead. His gaze was sharp, cutting through the dark like a blade, and it wasn't long before he lowered his hand. "But someone's following us."

I stiffened, my heart picking up speed as I pivoted to look over my shoulder, squinting through the dark. I didn't see anything, but that didn't mean they weren't there. We were always being watched now.

I swallowed, trying to force my breath into something that resembled calm. "How do we shake them?" I asked, trying to keep the panic from my voice.

Jaxon's lips curled into something that was almost a smile, though there was little amusement in it. "We don't," he said with an easy confidence that didn't match the situation. "But we can make them regret it."

I didn't ask for details. I didn't want to know. We kept moving, the alley narrowing even further, forcing us into the sort of close quarters where every noise felt like a siren. A scuffle sounded in the distance, too muffled to make sense of, but enough to heighten my sense of urgency. We had to get out of this maze before whatever shadow followed us finally pounced.

We reached a series of metal doors, their surfaces battered by years of neglect. Jaxon knocked twice—quick, deliberate—and after a tense pause, the door creaked open to reveal a dimly lit room filled with shadows and murmurs. Inside, the walls were lined with old crates and dusty machinery, remnants of some long-forgotten past. The scent of metal and stale air hit me immediately, a sharp contrast to the damp, sticky air outside.

A man stepped forward from the shadows, his face half-hidden beneath the brim of a cap. His eyes were cold, calculating. "Thought you were dead," he said, his voice a rasp, though there was a familiarity to it that gnawed at me.

Jaxon didn't blink, his posture straightening. "Not yet. And I'd appreciate it if you kept it that way."

The man didn't respond immediately, his gaze flicking from Jaxon to me, his lips pressing together in a tight line. "You're not welcome here, you know that, right?" he said, his tone more matter-of-fact than threatening. "The Wraiths don't take kindly to intruders."

"I'm not here for the Wraiths," Jaxon replied smoothly, his voice like honey, masking something sharp beneath it. "I'm here for you."

The man didn't flinch, but his hand twitched toward the gun strapped to his hip. It was a subtle movement, almost imperceptible, but I saw it. I took a half step back, my hand resting on the dagger at my side, ready for whatever came next.

"You're in my territory now," the man said, his lips curling into a grim smile. "You know the rules."

"Rules?" I snorted, louder than I intended. "Rules don't apply when you're already on the wrong side of them."

Jaxon shot me a warning glance, but I could see the flicker of amusement in his eyes. The man stiffened, the muscles in his jaw tightening. The tension in the room was thick, suffocating, but neither of us flinched.

"We're not here to play games," Jaxon continued, his voice suddenly cold, the warmth gone like a breath that had never been. "Tell me where I can find them. And maybe, just maybe, I'll let you walk out of here."

THE RUSE

The man's eyes narrowed. There was no room for negotiation, not when Jaxon spoke like that. But I couldn't help but wonder if this was all just a game—a dangerous game that neither of us knew how to play, but both of us were too far gone to turn back now.

The man hesitated, then let out a long, slow breath. "Fine. But you're not going to like it."

The man's smirk deepened, a knowing glint in his eyes as he motioned for us to follow him deeper into the room. The air felt colder, the silence pressing in on us like a weight, and I could sense Jaxon's irritation, though he did his best to mask it. The walls seemed to close in around us with every step. The man wasn't wrong—this wasn't exactly a place anyone should want to be, but here we were. There was no turning back now.

The dim overhead light flickered like a heartbeat, casting strange shadows against the grimy floor. Every step I took felt like it might be my last, and I could feel the tightness in my chest growing with each breath. Jaxon's hand brushed against mine briefly, a silent reminder that I wasn't in this alone. I clung to it, as if his touch could somehow shield me from whatever was coming. I was acutely aware of how easily the air could turn sharp, like the calm before a storm.

The man led us to a small, cluttered desk that looked like it hadn't been touched in years. Papers were strewn about in chaotic piles, some yellowed with age, others drenched in what could have been blood or rust or both. The man leaned over the desk, rifling through the clutter as he spoke.

"I don't know if you're brave or stupid, but either way, it's your funeral," he muttered. He paused for a moment, eyeing Jaxon like he was trying to decide whether he was still a threat. "I wouldn't go poking around where you're headed. The Wraiths don't appreciate intruders. But since you're persistent"—he threw us a glance that could have been an apology or a warning—"I'll tell you what you want to know. Just know, it won't be easy. Nothing in this city is easy."

Jaxon's expression didn't change. He leaned against the wall, his arms crossed, eyes fixed on the man without a flicker of emotion. "Get on with it," he said quietly, but the low, firm tone in his voice made it clear that he wasn't interested in any more games.

The man exhaled a long breath, then grabbed a battered map from the cluttered desk and spread it out in front of us. The paper was old and worn, the edges curling like the dead leaves scattered in the alleyways outside. "The Wraiths have their headquarters in the old power plant near the river," he said, his voice softening as though he was giving us a priceless piece of knowledge. "The place is a fortress, but it's not just the Wraiths you need to worry about. They've made... alliances. There's more at play here than you realize."

I studied the map, my mind racing as I traced the lines with my fingers, trying to make sense of the labyrinth ahead. "And these alliances," I asked, my voice colder than I intended, "what are we really walking into?"

The man paused, his gaze flicking from the map to Jaxon and then back to me. There was something in his eyes—something that shifted like a shadow. "You don't want to know," he muttered, then stood up abruptly, as though the weight of his words had suddenly become too much for him to bear. "Just get in, get what you need, and get out. Don't go poking around. The less you know, the better."

I felt the stirrings of unease in the pit of my stomach. There were layers to this—things beneath the surface I wasn't seeing, things Jaxon was clearly aware of but wasn't sharing. "You think it's that simple, huh?" I asked, a bitter laugh escaping my lips as I caught Jaxon's eyes. "Get in, get out? This is the Wraiths we're talking about. There's no 'simple' with them. You don't just waltz in, steal a few secrets, and walk out. That's how you end up in a shallow grave somewhere in this city."

THE RUSE

Jaxon's gaze flickered briefly to the man before he fixed his attention back on me. "Don't get ahead of yourself," he murmured. "We'll handle it."

I wasn't so sure. I'd been with Jaxon long enough to know that his calm confidence was often a front for the storm brewing just beneath the surface. We were both terrified of what lay ahead, but neither of us dared to admit it. The Wraiths had their claws in everything—New Chicago was their kingdom, and we were nothing more than insects scurrying across their floor.

The man didn't seem to care about our hesitation, or perhaps he was too eager to be rid of us. "If you're still alive when this is over, come back here," he said gruffly, shoving the map toward us. "I'll have something more for you. But until then, good luck. You're going to need it."

He turned away, his figure retreating back into the shadows, and we were left alone in the cramped, oppressive room. The map was heavy in my hands, and I could feel the weight of the decision settling in my chest. There was no turning back.

Jaxon's voice broke the silence, low and purposeful. "Let's move."

We didn't waste time arguing. There was no time to waste. The moment I stepped out of the room, the hairs on the back of my neck stood up. It wasn't just the danger pressing in on us—it was something else, something I couldn't quite put my finger on. A sense of being watched, followed, even though the alleyway was empty. The city felt like a trap, and we were caught in its jaws.

We walked in silence, the map clutched tightly in my hands. My pulse quickened as we neared the outskirts of the Wraith's territory. The tall, crumbling buildings loomed ahead, their windows dark and hollow like empty eyes. There was no sound except for the distant hum of the city. The further we went, the more the streets seemed to close in on us, as if the walls themselves were conspiring to keep us from escaping.

A sudden crash echoed from behind us, and without thinking, I spun around, my hand instinctively reaching for the knife at my side.

I froze.

A figure emerged from the shadows, moving too quickly to be anything but deliberate.

And then I heard the voice, low and dangerously familiar.

"Going somewhere?"

My heart stopped.

Chapter 14: The Tides of Fate

The air was thick with the smell of damp stone and rust, an acrid scent that clung to my clothes like the touch of a ghost. The deeper we ventured, the more the shadows seemed to grow hungry, swallowing every trace of light that we tried to summon. My pulse quickened with each step, not from fear—no, that had long since become a dull hum in my chest—but from the dread of what awaited us ahead. I glanced at Oliver, his dark eyes focused ahead, his hand steady on the hilt of the knife at his side. The faintest flicker of uncertainty passed through me, but I swallowed it down. We were too close now. I couldn't afford to hesitate.

"Are you sure about this?" I asked, my voice barely above a whisper.

Oliver didn't flinch, didn't even look at me. His gaze remained fixed on the winding tunnels ahead, their sharp turns threatening to swallow us whole. "The Wraith's down here, and he won't be alone. But we're going to find him. We're going to stop him."

I almost smiled at his certainty. He had no idea what this place was doing to us. How could he? He had never felt it, the weight of everything we had already lost, the years we had spent chasing ghosts and shadows. This—this was more than just about bringing someone to justice. This was about redemption, about proving that we weren't fools for believing we could fight a force as insidious as fate itself.

I felt the icy grip of the tunnels closing in around me, pressing against my chest like the walls were trying to suffocate me. The silence was deafening, the kind of quiet that made you feel like you were underwater, the world muffled and distant. Each echo of our footsteps seemed too loud, too brash. I tried to ignore the creeping sensation that the walls were moving, that the very earth was shifting beneath us, preparing to swallow us whole. But I couldn't shake the feeling. Not this time.

Oliver's hand brushed mine, just for a moment. A fleeting connection, but one that made my heart stutter in my chest. I glanced up at him, meeting his gaze for the briefest second. There was something there—something unspoken, a bond that tied us together in ways I hadn't been able to name. Maybe it was desperation, maybe it was something deeper. I couldn't tell. But as his eyes met mine, there was no doubt in my mind that we were more than just allies now. We were... something else.

He turned a corner sharply, the flickering torchlight casting strange, dancing shadows across the stone walls. The temperature dropped even further, if that was possible, and I pulled my jacket tighter around my shoulders.

"I don't like this," I muttered.

Oliver didn't respond, but I could tell from the set of his jaw that he didn't like it either. The Wraith had been nothing but a shadow to us until now—an elusive figure that danced just out of reach, leading us through a maze of lies and dead ends. But now... now we were in his territory. And the air seemed to hum with the promise of violence, thick and suffocating, like a storm about to break.

We turned another corner, and there it was. The door—or what passed for one in this place. A thick, iron-bound slab that looked more like a tombstone than an entrance. It stood half-open, a crack just wide enough for us to slip through. My breath caught as we approached, and I felt something stir deep inside me, a pulse of energy that I couldn't quite name. It was the same feeling I got when I knew we were on the verge of something big—something dangerous.

"Ready?" Oliver asked, his voice low and steady.

I nodded, my hands trembling despite myself. "As ready as I'll ever be."

The door creaked as we pushed it open, and I half expected it to sound like the cry of a dying animal. But it didn't. Instead, there was silence, and then—footsteps. Slow, deliberate, like someone taking their time to savor the moment.

"Welcome," a voice rasped from the darkness ahead, smooth like velvet but laced with something darker, something far more dangerous.

I froze, my heart hammering in my chest. The Wraith. He was here.

"Did you really think you could catch me?" the voice continued, an unsettling mix of amusement and venom. "You're too late."

The words slithered into my mind like poison, and I felt the weight of his presence pressing down on us, wrapping around us like a suffocating cloud.

Oliver's grip on his knife tightened, and I reached for my gun. "We're not here to catch you," I said, my voice steely. "We're here to end this."

There was a pause, then a soft chuckle. "End it? You think you can end this? You think I'm the one who's been playing games? You're the pawns here. You've always been."

I couldn't see him yet, but I could feel him—his eyes on us, like a predator sizing up its prey. The tension in the air was palpable, and I could almost hear my heart beating in time with the ticking clock of fate.

Oliver stepped forward, his face hard with resolve. "We've been playing your game long enough, Wraith. The only thing left is for you to lose."

Another laugh, this one colder, more calculated. "You don't understand, do you? The game was never mine. It's always been yours. You've just been too blind to see it."

I didn't have time to process his words. The shadows stirred, and I knew we were about to face whatever horror the Wraith had prepared for us. Whatever trap lay waiting in the darkness.

The shadows closed in around us, thick and suffocating, but I refused to let the fear win. Oliver's presence at my side was steady, a grounding force in the chaotic unknown. The Wraith's voice had dissipated into the dark, but the weight of his words lingered, creeping through the walls, curling around my thoughts like the tendrils of some toxic vine.

"Don't let it get to you," Oliver said, his voice low, but with the slightest trace of warmth. He must have noticed the tightness in my shoulders, the way my hands had started to shake. "He's just trying to mess with our heads."

I met his eyes, his steady gaze offering more comfort than I could have expected. It was strange, how in the middle of all this—this vast underground labyrinth, the echo of the Wraith's taunts, the uncertainty pressing in from all sides—Oliver's mere presence made the storm in my chest quiet, if only for a second.

"We know what we're doing," I said, even though I wasn't entirely sure I believed it.

There was a flicker of something in Oliver's expression—a brief flash of doubt, quickly masked. He opened his mouth to say something, but we both froze at the sound of the footsteps.

Heavy. Measured. Deliberate.

Someone—or something—was coming toward us.

Without a word, we moved in sync, ducking into the nearest alcove, a narrow gap between two jagged stone walls that felt more like the gaping maw of a monster than a hiding place. I could hear Oliver's breath, steady, controlled, like he wasn't standing on the edge of a precipice, like he hadn't just heard the Wraith's taunt. I hated how well he wore the mask of calm. It made me feel all the more like the frantic one. But then again, maybe that was the trick of it all. Maybe that's what the Wraith had planned for us: get us to doubt ourselves, to doubt everything we were fighting for.

THE RUSE

The footsteps drew closer, their rhythmic thud growing louder, as if whatever was coming could feel us hiding, feel us holding our breath. My heart raced, and I couldn't stop it. There was no sound but that slow, deliberate march and the frantic beat of my pulse. I barely dared to breathe.

Then the footsteps stopped. My stomach lurched. Had they found us? Were we too late? My grip tightened on the gun at my side, my knuckles whitening, but Oliver, ever the steady one, made a small gesture with his hand, a barely perceptible sign to stay quiet.

The silence stretched on, longer than I could bear. My skin crawled, the air growing heavier with each passing second. A drip of water echoed somewhere in the distance, reminding me that we were still in the heart of something ancient, something that knew no mercy.

I shifted slightly, trying to ease the tension in my muscles, but that was enough. A flicker of movement caught the corner of my eye. A figure, barely more than a silhouette against the dim light, slipping into the alcove opposite us. The Wraith.

I tensed, instinctively reaching for Oliver's arm, but he was already ahead of me, the knife in his hand a silent threat. He was ready.

The figure's back was to us, and for a brief moment, I felt an odd sense of control—an illusion, of course, but one I desperately clung to. This was our moment. This was our time. We could do this. We could—

And then the figure spoke.

"Don't bother," the voice rasped, a twisted smile curling its edges. "You're not the first to try. And you certainly won't be the last."

The words sent a chill down my spine, though I couldn't figure out why. I knew that voice. I'd heard it before. I'd just never expected to hear it from the Wraith.

The figure turned slowly, deliberately, and I barely stifled the gasp that almost escaped me. It wasn't the Wraith at all. Not exactly. Standing there, in the same sickly shadows, was someone I hadn't expected to see in this place, in this moment—my sister.

"Maya?" My voice came out in a strangled whisper. The shock hit me like a punch to the gut.

Her smile was all teeth, a grin that didn't reach her eyes. "Did you really think you could win, Elle?" she asked, tilting her head. The soft gleam of her knife caught the faint light, and I swallowed hard. This wasn't possible. Maya had been gone for years. There was no way—

"Why are you here?" I choked out. "You—you're dead. I watched you—"

"Yes, well," she interrupted, her smile turning into something darker, "you must have missed the memo. It's funny, really. You thought you were the only one playing the game."

I took a step back, the weight of her words pressing down on me. Oliver was next to me in an instant, his hand on my arm, grounding me in the present. "Who the hell are you?" he demanded, voice sharp. But Maya just laughed.

"Who am I?" She tilted her head again, a soft, cruel laugh escaping her lips. "I think that's the wrong question, darling." Her gaze flicked to me, and for a moment, I saw a flicker of something—something old and familiar in her eyes. A shadow of the sister I once knew, before all of this—before the Wraith, before the lies, before the darkness. "The real question is, who are you?"

I opened my mouth to respond, but nothing came out. My mind spun, caught between the memories of a life that was supposed to be long gone and the present—this twisted, dark version of it. The pieces didn't fit.

THE RUSE

"You always were the weak one," Maya whispered, eyes narrowing as she took a step toward us. "Always trying to save everyone. To fix everything."

Her words stung, cutting deep, and I fought the rush of emotion, the bitter twist of confusion, fear, and anger that threatened to overwhelm me.

"Get out of our way," Oliver said, his voice steely and dangerous. But Maya's smile only widened.

"We'll see," she said, stepping back, her form disappearing into the shadows. "We'll see how long you can keep running."

The air in the cavern thickened as Maya disappeared back into the shadows. Her last words clung to the space between us like smoke, curling around my mind, refusing to let go. I had barely processed what had just happened, still fighting the instinct to reach out, to somehow bring her back from wherever it was she had gone. But this was no longer my sister. Not the girl I had known. Not the one who had shared my secrets, my fears, my laughter. That girl was long gone, replaced by... whatever this was.

"Elle," Oliver's voice cut through the stillness, pulling me back to the present. He was standing close, too close, his breath warm against my skin, his hand steady on my arm. "What do we do now?"

I should have had an answer. But all I could do was shake my head. My mind was a mess, tangled in the wreckage of everything Maya had just thrown at me. She wasn't dead. She wasn't gone. But what had she become? What was the Wraith doing to her?

I could feel the weight of Oliver's gaze on me, but it wasn't pity, not like I half-expected. It was something different—something almost... understanding. He didn't need me to explain. He saw it, the broken pieces of me that were scattered in a thousand directions. "You know we can't leave without knowing what's going on, right?"

I swallowed hard. "Yeah, I know."

He nodded once, taking a step forward, though his eyes never left mine. "Then let's finish this."

The words hung between us, heavy with promise. This was no longer just about The Wraith, no longer about finding and stopping him. This was personal now. The Wraith had crossed a line I couldn't even begin to fathom. The game he was playing wasn't just a game anymore. He had made it too real.

"Stay close," Oliver murmured as he took the lead, the knife still in his hand, though the sharp gleam of it seemed almost unnecessary in the dark. "Whatever happens, don't let your guard down."

I nodded, though I wasn't sure how much guard I had left to give. Maya's voice echoed in my mind, and the more I tried to push it away, the more it stayed. The Wraith wasn't the only enemy here. The real battle was happening inside me.

We moved deeper into the cavern, the path twisting and turning, like some grotesque mockery of a maze. The stone underfoot was slick with dampness, the air thick with the scent of earth and decay. It was impossible to tell how far we had gone or how much further we had to travel. Time felt irrelevant down here, as if the hours had stopped and we were all just trapped in the same endless moment, spiraling toward something we couldn't see, something we couldn't avoid.

Then, just as the silence threatened to become unbearable, a light flickered ahead. A faint, almost imperceptible glow that seemed to pulse, like the heartbeat of the lair itself. I stopped, my breath catching. There was something familiar about that light. Something I couldn't place.

Oliver stopped beside me, his eyes narrowing as he scanned the darkness ahead. "Do you see that?"

I nodded, unable to look away from the growing light. "It's... it's him," I whispered, though I wasn't sure if I was talking about the Wraith or something far worse.

As if in answer, the light flared brighter, casting long shadows against the jagged walls. And there, standing at the center of it all, was the figure we had been hunting. The Wraith.

Except it wasn't just him anymore. Around him, encircling him like a halo, were dozens—no, hundreds—of figures. But they weren't human. Not entirely. Their faces were distorted, twisted by some unseen force, like they were trapped between life and death, between here and somewhere far darker. They were his creations, his army.

The Wraith turned, his pale eyes locking onto mine as if he had been waiting for this moment. "So, you've come," he said, his voice dripping with malice, the words curling in the air like smoke.

I stepped forward, the sudden rush of adrenaline pushing back the fear. "You're going to pay for everything you've done. All the lives you've ruined."

He smirked, a slow, sadistic smile that made my stomach churn. "Oh, but you still don't understand, do you? You were never meant to stop me. You were meant to serve me."

"Serve you?" I spat the words out, my heart hammering in my chest. "You're insane."

His laugh echoed through the cavern, a low, hollow sound that reverberated in my bones. "Insane? Or perhaps I'm the only one who sees things clearly. You think you have a choice in all of this. You think you can just walk away and live your life. But you were never free, Elle. You were always mine."

I didn't know how to respond to that. The words were too cruel, too true. The Wraith had been pulling the strings long before I'd realized it. But I couldn't let him have the satisfaction of seeing me broken. Not now. Not when I was so close.

Oliver stepped forward, his body a shield between me and the Wraith. His knife gleamed in the strange, sickly light, a reminder of everything that had led us here. "We won't let you do this," he said, his voice tight but determined.

The Wraith's smile faltered, just for a second. "You really think you can stop me?" He turned his gaze to the army behind him, his minions shifting in unison, their eyes glinting with malice. "You're too late."

A cold chill ran down my spine as the figures moved, swarming toward us with unnatural speed. My pulse spiked, and the world seemed to slow. This was it. This was where it all ended. Or began.

But just as I opened my mouth to shout a warning, something moved behind us. Something far larger, far more menacing than anything I had seen before. My breath caught in my throat as a shadow swept over us.

And then, the ground shook.

The cavern rumbled beneath our feet, and for one heart-stopping moment, I thought the whole world was collapsing around us. But it wasn't the earth that was breaking—it was something else. Something far worse.

The Wraith's smile widened. "You've made a mistake," he said, his voice barely audible over the growing tremors. "You should have stayed in the dark."

And then, the wall of shadow descended on us, too fast to escape.

Chapter 15: Shattered Illusions

It was the kind of night that made you think the universe was playing a cruel joke. The sky was a bruised purple, clouds low and thick, the moon hidden like it too was embarrassed to witness what was happening beneath it. I stood in the shadows of the alleyway, my breath caught in the tightness of my chest, the cold seeping through my jacket, mingling with the tension that had knotted my insides into something unrecognizable.

Jaxon was beside me, or rather, just slightly in front of me, his posture rigid, like he was bracing for the impact of something far worse than the inevitable. I could feel his pulse thrumming in the silence, his sharp inhale cutting through the night air like a knife. We were both pretending, in some twisted way, that we hadn't already pieced it all together. That we hadn't already learned the truth about who had been feeding information to the enemy all along. But as we stepped closer to the rendezvous point, the reality of it settled in like a weight on my chest that I couldn't shrug off.

The streets were empty, save for the distant hum of the city, but my mind was loud with the sound of betrayal, of whispered conversations and secret glances. I couldn't shake the image of her—Evelyn—standing at the center of this mess, her smile so convincing, her presence so assured. She had been the one we trusted, the one who had walked beside us, who had shared our victories, our defeats. And now? Now she was the one who had played us all for fools.

Jaxon stopped short, his hand flying out to grip my arm. His fingers were cold against my skin, a sharp contrast to the heat that pulsed beneath the surface. I could feel his anxiety, the way his muscles tightened as though he was trying to hold himself together, trying to maintain some semblance of control. "You okay?" he asked, though his voice was thin, like he didn't believe it himself.

I swallowed hard, my throat dry, and nodded. "I will be." But my words felt hollow, like I was lying to both him and myself. The truth was, I wasn't sure of anything anymore. Evelyn had been our ally, our friend. I had never once questioned her loyalty, not even when the whispers had started, when the rumors had curled into my thoughts like smoke. She had been the calm in the storm, the steady presence I could always count on. But now? Now she was a stranger, someone I didn't recognize, someone whose motives were darker than the night that pressed in around us.

"Just stay close," Jaxon murmured, his hand falling away from my arm. His voice was rough, and I could hear the raw edges of his pain in it, the unspoken question that hung between us. How could we have been so blind?

The alleyway ahead of us opened up to a small courtyard, the kind that felt abandoned even on the rare occasions when people passed through. The flickering streetlamp cast long shadows over the cracked pavement, and the faint smell of old cigarette smoke lingered in the air. I couldn't tell if it was just the place or if it was me—the world seemed different now, warped by the knowledge that we had been played. That the very person we'd trusted had been working against us from the start.

I stiffened when I saw her, standing near the far end of the courtyard, her back to us, the silhouette of her figure outlined by the dim light. Her dark hair tumbled over her shoulders in the way that had always made her seem untouchable, even when she was right beside us. It took every ounce of my willpower not to rush forward, not to demand answers before my mind could catch up with the reality of the situation.

Jaxon moved to step forward, but I caught his arm, stopping him. He turned to me, his face a mix of confusion and something else—something deeper, something I couldn't name. "We have to face her," he said, and I knew he was right, but I wasn't sure I was ready. Not yet. Not with the pieces of my trust scattered at my feet.

"We face her," I said softly, my words like shards of glass, "but we don't have to be alone in it."

His eyes searched mine, something flickering there that made my heart ache. "I never was," he replied, and though his words were simple, they carried a weight that felt like it could break us both in that moment.

We walked toward Evelyn slowly, the sound of our footsteps muffled by the cracked stone beneath us. When we were just a few feet away, she turned, her lips curling into the smile that had once made her seem like someone who would always have your back. Now, it felt like a mask, one she wore to hide the truth behind her eyes.

"Hello," she said, the word too light, too casual. "I wasn't sure you'd show."

I swallowed, trying to find the right words, but all that came out was a shaky breath. "Why, Evelyn?" The question was simple, but it felt like it had the power to unravel everything. "Why did you do it?"

Her smile faltered, just for a moment, but that was enough. The crack in her mask was all I needed to see.

"Because I had to," she said, her voice cold, the warmth of our past friendship absent from it now. "It was never about you. It was about survival."

And just like that, the illusion shattered.

Her words hung in the air like a lingering perfume, sweet and sickly all at once. "It was never about you. It was about survival." The calmness with which she spoke made my stomach twist. It was as though she was discussing a casual dinner, not the wreckage she had just unleashed into our lives.

I could feel the ground beneath me shift, the world narrowing into a pinprick of confusion and hurt. "Survival?" The word slipped from my lips before I could stop it, and I hated how weak it sounded. I wasn't even sure I wanted to know what she meant. Part of me wanted to run, to bury myself somewhere far from this conversation. But I couldn't. The questions screamed in my head, demanding answers that wouldn't come without the mess of confrontation.

Jaxon stepped forward, his jaw set in a grim line, eyes cold and narrowed. I knew that look, the one he got when the world refused to make sense, when the people he trusted became strangers. "You've been playing us the whole time," he said, his voice tight with disbelief. There was no anger in it, just a flatness that was more dangerous than any shout.

Evelyn's eyes flickered, a quick flash of something—guilt? Regret? Maybe a hint of it, but it disappeared too quickly to be sure. "I did what I had to do," she repeated, almost absently, as if explaining herself to someone who wasn't listening. "You know how this world works. You know how things go when you're caught between two sides."

I wanted to scream, to hurl the weight of my betrayal back at her like a weapon, but I didn't. Instead, I forced my voice to remain steady, though the tremor in it betrayed me. "This wasn't survival. This was treason. We trusted you."

The words struck her, I saw it in the way her shoulders slumped ever so slightly. But there was no apology in her eyes. Just cold calculation. "I was never the friend you thought I was," she said, her tone colder now. "I made choices that had nothing to do with you. Nothing to do with any of you." She gave a sharp laugh that made my skin crawl. "None of us are innocent, are we?"

I took a step back, the air around me thick and suffocating. It wasn't just her betrayal that left me reeling. It was the realization that I'd never truly known her. That everything we had shared—the late nights, the quiet confessions, the laughter between battles—had been nothing but a lie wrapped in silk.

Jaxon's face hardened. "So, that's it? You just walk away from everything? From us?"

Evelyn's gaze softened for a fraction of a second before her mask slid back into place. "It's not like that. It never was. You think you've had it hard? Try living in my shoes for just one day." She looked up at the sky as if seeking some kind of salvation, some higher purpose. "You have no idea what I've given up."

Her words stung like a slap, the venom in them cutting deeper than any physical wound could. I wanted to scream, to tell her how much we had sacrificed too, how much we had put on the line, how much we had trusted her. But it wouldn't matter. It never would.

Jaxon turned away, his hands balling into fists at his sides. I could see the way he fought to keep his composure, the way he kept himself from breaking apart. For a moment, I hated him for it. I hated that he could still look at her with something that resembled pity. He had always been the stronger one between us, the one who could mask the pain, the one who could pretend it was all okay. But there was no pretending now.

"Is that it, then?" I asked, my voice quieter now, the anger turning to something colder. "We're just part of some game for you?"

"No," Evelyn said sharply, and this time, there was a flash of something more human in her eyes. She stepped closer, her gaze flicking from Jaxon to me, her expression almost apologetic. "But I didn't have a choice. You don't understand the position I was in. They were going to kill me, Jaxon. They were going to kill all of us if I didn't do what they said."

I closed my eyes, trying to block out the image of her face, trying to ignore the way the weight of her words pressed into my chest. It wasn't just that she had betrayed us—it was the way she had done it. The way she had made herself the victim, the martyr in this twisted little play she had scripted. I wasn't sure what hurt more: that she had lied to us, or that I had believed her.

When I opened my eyes, Jaxon was looking at me. He was searching for something in my face, his expression unreadable. His brow furrowed as if he was waiting for me to say something, to make some kind of decision. But I didn't know what to say. How could I? There was no fix for this. No solution that would make it all go away.

I had trusted her. I had let her in, had let her see the things I kept hidden from everyone else. And now it all felt like it was slipping through my fingers, vanishing into the dark night.

Jaxon took a breath, his voice low but steady. "You can't just expect us to let this go. You don't get to walk away from this, Evelyn. Not after everything."

Evelyn's lips pressed together, her jaw clenching. She wasn't done. I could tell she was calculating her next move, weighing her options as if the world still belonged to her, as if we were still the pawns she had manipulated so easily. But I could feel the balance shift now, feel the power slipping out of her grasp. She had underestimated us. Underestimated me.

"I never asked you to forgive me," she said, her voice surprisingly soft. "But I'm telling you, this is the only way it could have gone. I had no choice."

"Then why did you bother?" Jaxon asked, his voice sharp, cutting through the air like a blade. "Why bother pretending?"

And in that moment, I understood. It wasn't just survival she had been after. It was control. Control over us, over our trust, over everything we thought we knew. And that was the most dangerous thing of all.

The tension in the air was thick, and the weight of her words seemed to press down on us from all directions. Evelyn's smile had long since disappeared, replaced by something harder, something colder. Her eyes were calculating, like she was measuring the distance between us and deciding just how far she could push before we would break. And I hated that I could feel the tiniest thread of doubt in me, the way her words made me question everything I thought I knew about loyalty.

Jaxon's fists clenched at his sides, the veins standing out along his forearms. "You act like this is all just a game," he spat, his voice sharp with barely controlled fury. "But we're not your toys. We're people, Evelyn. You can't just—"

"Enough!" Her voice rang out, cutting him off, but there was a tremor in it now, a crack in her composure. The mask was slipping, and I couldn't help but watch with a strange sort of satisfaction. She wasn't the unshakable force I had once believed her to be. She was just as fragile as the rest of us, her armor cracked and battered, revealing the desperation beneath.

"I didn't want this," she said, her voice much softer now, almost pleading. "I didn't want to hurt anyone. I just... I didn't have a choice." Her eyes flickered between Jaxon and me, as if looking for some glimmer of understanding, some sign that we could still see her as the friend she had once been. "You don't know what it's like to have everything you've ever worked for threatened. To be cornered by people who will stop at nothing to get what they want."

I wanted to feel something for her, some trace of the bond we'd shared, but all I felt was a quiet, simmering rage. How could she expect me to care, to forgive, when she had been playing us all along? The years of trust we had built, the moments that had made us family, meant nothing to her. In the end, it had all been a game of survival, her survival, at our expense.

"What exactly are you asking for, Evelyn?" I asked, my voice colder than I intended, but I couldn't bring myself to care. "Do you want our forgiveness? Do you think this is something we can just move past?"

Her lips trembled, and for a moment, I saw a flicker of something in her eyes—regret, perhaps. But it was gone just as quickly as it came. "I'm not asking for forgiveness," she said, the words steady, though the desperation in her eyes told a different story. "I'm asking for you to understand. This is bigger than you, bigger than all of us. If I hadn't done what I did—if I hadn't helped them—everything we've worked for would have been destroyed."

I glanced at Jaxon, searching his face for any sign of where his mind was. I knew the man in front of me, knew the way he thought, the way he'd weigh every word, every action. But right now, there was nothing but a hard, unreadable mask on his face. I could feel the distance between us growing, the chasm widening with every word she spoke. This was no longer about what Evelyn had done. It was about how much we had been broken in the process.

"Do you even hear yourself?" Jaxon's voice was hoarse, and his words were like daggers, each one landing with precision. "You didn't save us. You didn't save anyone. You sold us out, Evelyn. You sold your soul."

Her expression shifted, and I could see the deflection, the way she hardened under the weight of his words. "I didn't have a choice," she said again, more vehemently this time. "I would have died if I hadn't. They were going to kill me. Kill all of us."

The last thread of my patience snapped. "I don't care anymore," I said, my voice cutting through the tension. "You don't get to justify this. You don't get to rewrite history just because you're scared." The words came out in a rush, fueled by a fury I couldn't hide, couldn't control. "We're not your scapegoats. We're not your pawns in this sick little game you've been playing."

Jaxon's hand shot out, grabbing me by the arm before I could say anything more. "Don't," he muttered, his voice thick with warning. "Don't make this worse than it already is."

But it was too late. The damage had been done. Evelyn had already crossed the line, and I could feel the anger bubbling up inside me, threatening to spill over. I wanted to shout at her, to make her

THE RUSE

feel the full weight of the betrayal, but the words caught in my throat. What was the point? There was nothing left to say.

Evelyn took a step back, eyes darting between us, calculating, like she was waiting for something. Maybe she was waiting for us to back down, to give her another chance, to offer her some kind of redemption she didn't deserve. But that wasn't going to happen. Not now, not after everything she had done.

"I'm not going to beg," she said, her voice hard now, that same coldness returning. "But you need to know something. It's not over. They're still out there. And they're going to come after us. All of us."

I frowned, my gut twisting at the sudden shift in her demeanor. "What are you talking about?"

"They're not done yet," she continued, her voice low, urgent. "The people I was working with—they know who you are. They know everything. And they won't stop until they get what they want."

I took a step forward, the ground beneath me feeling unsteady, as if everything I thought I knew was shifting. "What exactly are you saying?" My voice was quiet now, a thread of uncertainty curling its way through me.

Evelyn's eyes flickered with something—fear? Maybe. But the words she spoke next sent a chill down my spine. "I'm saying that you're already too late."

And in that moment, I heard something—something distant but unmistakable—a rustle, a faint footfall coming from behind us.

Chapter 16: A Heart Divided

The air in the room was thick with a silence that pressed against my chest, squeezing until it was hard to breathe. Every corner seemed to echo with the weight of everything unsaid, of everything that had broken between us. Jaxon sat across from me, eyes shadowed, the sharp lines of his face softened by something I couldn't quite place. Regret? Sorrow? Anger? It was hard to tell. It didn't matter. I knew that whatever it was, it wasn't enough to heal the rift that had opened between us.

"I never thought it would come to this," Jaxon muttered, his voice low, like it had been torn from him. He scrubbed a hand through his hair, mussing it more than it already was, the dark waves tumbling across his forehead.

I glanced at him, my hands tightly clasped in my lap. The tremble that ran through my fingers was a reflection of the nervous heat building in my chest. The kind of heat that made me want to tear everything down—destroy the walls we'd spent so long building, and all the mess we'd gotten tangled in. But I couldn't.

"Neither did I," I replied, the words slipping out before I could stop them. The sting in my voice was a reminder of all the betrayals I had suffered, and how deeply it had marked me. How it wasn't just him I was afraid of losing, but the pieces of myself I feared I'd never get back.

The silence stretched, broken only by the hum of the fridge in the kitchen, the distant buzz of the ceiling fan. It was too hot in here, too heavy. I could feel the tension like a living thing, pressing down on my shoulders, my chest, until it was all I could think about.

Jaxon shifted, his eyes meeting mine with a quiet intensity that made my pulse race. I knew he was looking for something—an answer, maybe, or some indication that I wasn't about to walk out the door. But I had nothing to offer, not anymore.

"I can't fix this for you, Jaxon," I said finally, my voice thick with a mixture of guilt and frustration. "I can't pretend like I don't know what you're capable of. What you've done."

The words were like knives, but they needed to be said. I needed to say them before I let myself get swallowed by the warmth of his eyes or the comfort of his presence. He had a way of drawing me in, of making everything feel like it would be okay if I just let go and gave in. But I had already let go too many times, and the pieces of me I'd lost were never coming back.

"You're right," he murmured, his eyes darkening. "I've made mistakes. But I'm not that person anymore. I swear to you, I'm not."

I almost believed him. Almost. But the way the shadows moved in his eyes told a different story—one I wasn't sure I was ready to hear. The man in front of me wasn't just Jaxon. He was the reflection of everything I had tried to escape, and I couldn't pretend that wasn't terrifying.

"You don't get it," I said, shaking my head. "It's not just about what you've done. It's about who you were... who you still are in some ways. I can't let myself get caught in that again, Jaxon. I can't. I've been burned too many times."

The hurt that flickered in his eyes made my chest ache. The regret, the apology that he couldn't seem to voice—it all hovered between us, like a heavy fog, thick and suffocating.

"I don't know how to fix this, but I'll try," Jaxon said, his voice rough, but with a fierce determination that made my heart beat faster. "You deserve that much. You deserve me at my best. I don't care how long it takes."

I could see the sincerity in his eyes, but it didn't erase the fact that the darkness of our shared past still clung to him like a second skin. That history was a part of him, woven into the very fabric of who he was. And no amount of promises could change the way it made me feel.

The tension in the room reached a breaking point, and I knew I had to say something to break the silence that threatened to swallow us whole.

"I'm not perfect either," I said, my voice soft, almost hesitant. "I've got scars of my own, ones I never wanted to show anyone. But you need to understand... this isn't just about you. It's about me too."

Jaxon's gaze shifted, curiosity flickering in his eyes. He opened his mouth to speak, but I held up a hand, stopping him.

"I'm not telling you this for you to fix," I continued, my throat tight. "I'm telling you because I need you to see me. The real me, not just the version of me you want to save. I don't need saving, Jaxon. I just need someone to understand."

There was a rawness in my voice that I didn't expect, but it felt like the first time in a long while that I wasn't holding back. I could feel my pulse quicken as I faced the truth that had been gnawing at me for so long. My past wasn't something I could hide anymore.

Jaxon looked at me for a long time, his expression unreadable. Then, finally, he nodded slowly.

"I can't promise I'll understand it all," he said, his voice quiet, almost reverent. "But I'm willing to try."

I almost wanted to laugh—bitter, sharp. Try? That was all either of us could do.

The kitchen was still—the kind of stillness that felt too heavy, like the room had forgotten how to breathe. Outside, the storm was beginning to gather, a low rumble of thunder punctuating the tension hanging in the air between us. I could feel it in my bones, the electric charge of unspoken words, the weight of everything I hadn't said yet. Jaxon, sitting at the small dining table, seemed to sense it too. His eyes traced the surface of the table, his fingers resting lightly on the wood as though the space between us was something solid, something to hold on to.

I wasn't sure what to do with the truth I'd just handed him. It was raw, unrefined—a mess of moments from my past I'd spent years hiding. And now, I could practically feel it all lingering between us, like a ghost. The room grew colder, but not from the storm outside. It was something deeper—something heavier.

"I'm not asking for redemption," I said suddenly, breaking the silence that had fallen over us. "I'm not asking you to fix me. I'm asking you to see me. To understand that some things don't just... disappear."

Jaxon didn't move. Didn't speak. He was the kind of person who held silence like a secret weapon, waiting to see how much you could take before you broke. But there was no breaking here. Not yet. Not with him.

"Sometimes," I continued, my voice a little shakier now, "I think I've spent more time hiding from myself than from anyone else." I paused, the words tumbling out before I could catch them. "I used to think if I stayed in the shadows, if I stayed quiet long enough, people would forget who I really was. What I used to be."

His gaze flickered up to meet mine. It wasn't pity, not like I had expected. Just quiet understanding. And it unsettled me more than anything. I wasn't used to being seen like that. Not in the way he was looking at me—like I wasn't something to be fixed or even saved. Just someone worth listening to.

"You don't have to tell me everything," Jaxon said, his voice low and steady. "But I'll listen."

I shook my head. "It's not about what I have to say. It's about what I haven't said. The stuff I keep buried down because it's easier that way."

"Is it?" His tone was sharp now, something flickering in his eyes that made my pulse hitch. "Is it really easier?"

The question hung between us, daring me to answer. I wanted to lie. To tell him that burying the past had been the only way to survive, the only way to stay intact. But I could feel the walls inside me, the ones I'd built brick by brick, starting to crumble. It wasn't easy. Not anymore.

I took a slow breath, trying to center myself, to find the calm that seemed so elusive these days. "I don't want to be that person anymore, Jaxon," I said, the words slipping out, raw and unfiltered. "I don't want to be the one who runs from everything that's hard. But I don't know if I can be the person you want me to be. The person who doesn't flinch when you get too close."

For a long moment, he didn't respond. His face was unreadable, his thoughts hidden behind a wall that made it hard to tell where he stood. But his eyes? His eyes were open, watching me in a way that made me feel like I was standing on the edge of something—something I wasn't sure I was ready to face.

The silence between us stretched long enough to make my skin prickle. Then, with a sudden movement, he stood, crossing the room with a quiet grace that made my breath catch. I didn't know what to expect when he reached for me. A touch? A kiss? Or something more, something I couldn't yet understand.

Instead, he stood in front of me, close enough that I could feel the heat radiating off his body. And still, he said nothing. But when his hands gently cupped my face, my heart stuttered, then thudded faster in my chest. His thumb brushed across my cheek, and the contact was enough to shatter the fragile walls I had tried so hard to hold up.

"Tell me what you need," he whispered, his voice like a caress. "I'm not asking you to be perfect. Hell, I'm not perfect. But I need to know if you're still in this. I need to know if I'm fighting for something real."

I closed my eyes for a moment, letting the words sink in. I could feel the weight of them, the truth in his voice. He wasn't asking for anything impossible. Just a piece of me. And for some reason, that seemed more terrifying than anything else.

The storm outside had reached its peak, the wind howling and rattling the windows, but inside, there was only the stillness between us. The storm in my chest felt louder than the one outside, and I wasn't sure I could weather it. I wasn't sure if I was ready to.

But I knew one thing for certain: whatever this was, this messy, imperfect thing between us, it mattered more than anything I had ever felt before. Even if it meant tearing down the last of my defenses, even if it meant facing the truth of what had happened and what might come next, I couldn't walk away. Not now.

"I'm still here," I whispered, opening my eyes to meet his gaze. "I'm here. I don't know how to do this. I don't know what's going to happen, but I'm not walking away. I just... I need you to know that."

And for the first time in a long while, I believed it. Even with the threat of The Wraith lurking in the shadows, even with the storm that raged inside me, I knew that we were worth fighting for.

There was a moment, just after I spoke, when everything seemed to pause. The room held its breath, the storm outside echoing our shared silence, as if the universe was waiting for something. What, exactly, I didn't know, but the anticipation was so thick, I could taste it. Jaxon didn't speak at first, but his fingers remained at my face, warm and steady as he held me in place, not forcing anything but offering the calm I didn't know I needed.

"I need you to understand," I said, my voice smaller than I wanted it to be, a little more fragile than I'd intended. "This isn't just about us. This is about everything I've fought to protect. Every piece of me that's still worth holding onto."

His expression shifted, a soft, hesitant understanding playing across his features. He didn't pull away, not yet, but there was a heaviness in his gaze—a realization of what we were about to confront. What I was about to ask of him.

"I know," he replied quietly, his thumb brushing against my skin, almost absent-mindedly. "But you can't keep hiding, not from me. Not anymore."

I closed my eyes, letting his words sink in, and for a second, I wished I could pull back. Shield myself. Pretend that this wasn't the moment we'd reached, the precipice where everything that had been buried would have to surface. But I couldn't.

The Wraith, that ghost of a man or whatever he was, wasn't just a threat to us—he was a threat to everything. To the future, to any hope of peace, and most of all, to me. And if we didn't deal with it now, then it would be a part of us forever, festering in the shadows, consuming us bit by bit.

"I'm not asking for your protection," I said, finally opening my eyes and meeting his gaze. "I'm asking for your trust. Just as much as I'm giving you mine."

Jaxon's lips pressed into a thin line, his eyes narrowing slightly as he took in the weight of my words. The silence stretched again, long enough that I felt like I might unravel right there. But when he finally spoke, his voice was low, edged with something I couldn't quite place—determination or maybe something darker.

"Trust doesn't come easy," he said, almost as if he were speaking to himself more than to me. "Not for me, and I'm guessing not for you, either."

I felt a sharp pang at the truth of his words. My trust had always been a fragile thing. Something I gave away too freely and too often, only to watch it shatter in the hands of those I thought I could rely on.

"I'm not asking for everything all at once," I said, my voice steadier now. "But we need to move forward, Jaxon. Together. The Wraith isn't going to wait for us to get our act together. And we're running out of time."

THE RUSE

His jaw tightened, and for a moment, I thought he might argue. But instead, he stepped back, just enough to give me space, his eyes never leaving mine.

"You're right," he said, his voice almost a whisper, as if the weight of everything we had left to do had just hit him. "We can't keep pretending that this is all going to work out on its own."

There it was—that moment. The one where everything changes. Where the past, no matter how much we wish it were different, doesn't get to dictate the future anymore. We were on the cusp of something else now. Something we couldn't undo.

But just as I thought we were reaching some kind of understanding, the ground beneath us seemed to shift.

A sharp noise—a sound I couldn't place—cut through the stillness. It was low at first, like the wind had picked up outside, rattling the windowpanes. But no, this was different. It wasn't the wind.

"Do you hear that?" I asked, my voice tight as the hairs on the back of my neck stood up.

Jaxon froze. His gaze snapped to the door, the same sudden tension running through his body.

The house had always felt like a safe haven. A place where we could close the door on the world outside and breathe, just for a little while. But now, it felt suffocating. The walls too close, the air too thick. I could feel it—he was close. The Wraith. I didn't need to look to know that we were no longer alone.

Jaxon didn't hesitate. He moved swiftly, pulling me to the side with a surprising strength, his hand gripping my arm to steady me as he reached for the knife he kept on the counter. His movements were calm, too calm, considering what was about to unfold.

"Stay here," he said, his voice sharp, and for the first time in what felt like forever, I obeyed without questioning. I stepped back into the shadow of the kitchen, my heart hammering in my chest, every instinct telling me to run. But I didn't. I couldn't.

The noise grew louder, now unmistakably a sound of something dragging across the floor. A slow, deliberate scrape. The Wraith was here.

Jaxon moved to the door, his body tense, poised like a coiled spring, ready to snap into action at the slightest provocation. His gaze flickered back to me, and for a second, I saw the raw fear in his eyes. Fear not of death or pain, but of losing me—losing us.

I couldn't breathe. Couldn't think. Only watch as the seconds stretched on, each one heavier than the last. And then, without a warning, the door to the kitchen exploded open.

I didn't see him at first—just a shadow, long and thin, his figure twisting unnaturally in the dim light. The air around him seemed to warp, like the space itself didn't want to hold him.

Then his voice came, a low rasp that sent chills crawling down my spine.

"Did you think you could outrun me forever?"

Chapter 17: The Dance of Deceit

The gala was a symphony of opulence and danger, every gold-painted surface reflecting the dim light, making the room pulse with a hypnotic glow. I could feel the buzz of luxury, each footstep on the polished marble echoing through the grand hall as a thousand whispers danced in the air. The orchestra's strings swelled in a delicate waltz that was half-melody, half-warning, and I had to suppress the instinct to tug at my collar as the weight of the night's true purpose threatened to crush my lungs.

The guests milled about, their laughter clinking like fine crystal, but underneath it, there was a distinct thrum of power. An undercurrent of menace that only a select few seemed to understand—those of us in the know. Jaxon and I were among them, but you'd never guess by looking at us. We were cloaked in deception like the best of them, our masks pristine and our smiles flawless. But beneath the surface, there was a crackling tension, an undeniable pull between us that felt more dangerous than the plot we had come to set in motion.

The scent of roses and expensive perfume clung to the air, mingling with the faint tang of cigar smoke. I swallowed hard, trying to ignore the tightness in my chest as I stood next to a gilded pillar, pretending to be nothing more than an exquisite ornament in this room of false perfection. The dress, a glittering affair of midnight blue, clung to my form in all the right places. My hair was swept up in delicate curls, held together by a clasp of silver that caught the light every time I moved. The mask I wore was a thing of beauty—intricate and delicate, the feathers brushed against my cheek like a soft caress—but it concealed the nerves crawling beneath my skin.

Jaxon, across the room, was a vision of calculated elegance. His tuxedo fit him like a second skin, his jaw sharp and unyielding beneath the silver mask he wore. He stood with a glass of champagne in hand, looking every inch the charming rogue he was. The kind of man who could make anyone believe they were the only person in the room with just a look. And he knew it. He used it. He had to, tonight, to mask what we really were—two thieves, two players in a deadly game, two souls tied together in ways neither of us had ever planned.

I watched him, not for the first time that night, wondering how I ever ended up here. He glanced back at me, a subtle shift of his gaze that sent a bolt of heat through me, quick and unexpected. That tension, that pull—it had been there from the moment we'd first crossed paths, and even now, amidst the glittering lies and the high-stakes game we were playing, it had only deepened. His eyes, dark and intense, flicked over my form, and I knew—just knew—he was thinking about the same thing I was.

"Stop looking at me like that," I muttered under my breath, adjusting the delicate chain of pearls around my neck, though it wasn't to hide my discomfort. It was more to anchor myself in this world of smoke and mirrors. To remind myself that I wasn't truly a part of it.

"Like what?" Jaxon's voice slid into my ear, a low whisper that made my pulse hitch. I hadn't even noticed him approach until he was standing just a breath away. He smelled of cedarwood and danger, a heady mix that made my heart skip a beat.

"Like you're going to steal the last breath from my lungs," I said, a wry smile pulling at the corners of my mouth despite myself. His chuckle was dark, rich, and entirely dangerous.

"Wouldn't dream of it," he replied, but there was a flicker of something in his eyes—something wild. "Unless it's part of the plan."

I glanced toward the grand staircase, where the crime lord himself had just made his entrance, the crowd parting like the sea before him. He was a man whose presence alone could command

THE RUSE 157

entire armies, his suit too tailored, his shoes too polished, and his smile too perfect. The Wraith. A man shrouded in rumors, veiled in whispers, a kingpin of unimaginable power. Tonight, we were here for him, playing our part in the most dangerous of dances. The truth was, I didn't know if we were going to walk out of this alive. But I couldn't turn back now.

I reached out, fingers brushing Jaxon's. A simple touch, nothing to anyone else in the room, but to me, it was a lifeline. "Stay close," I whispered, as if the words could bind us together, as if the heat of my touch could steady him.

His grip tightened, the briefest of pauses before he answered, "I never planned to go anywhere."

The crowd surged, and we moved together like clockwork. He was an extension of me, and I of him, as we wove through the guests with practiced ease. Each word we spoke was another lie, another thread woven into the web of deception we had carefully constructed. The Wraith's eyes skimmed over us once, but only for a fraction of a second—just enough to make me wonder if he could see past our masks.

The tension between Jaxon and me thickened, and I knew we were walking on the edge of a knife. One wrong move, one misplaced word, and this whole facade would come crashing down. And yet, as we moved through the throng, I couldn't help but think: if I let myself get too caught up in this moment, too lost in the dangerous allure of what we were, I might never leave this place the same. Maybe I didn't want to.

The atmosphere around us thickened like the humidity before a storm. Every step we took felt heavier, the ground beneath us a little less stable, the music just a touch too loud, as if the universe were daring us to make a misstep. I tried to focus on the weight of my heels, the smooth glide of my hand over Jaxon's arm as we moved, but my mind kept returning to the whispers that rippled through the crowd, the hidden conversations, the subtle shifts in posture that spoke of far more danger than anyone was willing to acknowledge.

Jaxon's fingers brushed against mine, a fleeting connection that sent an electric shock up my spine. It was just enough to remind me that I wasn't alone in this moment, that despite the tight mask of composure I had forced on, I could still feel him, still hear the sharp edge in his voice when he spoke, the way he always managed to stay one step ahead even when the world seemed to be closing in.

I glanced at him again, meeting his eyes for the briefest moment. There was something in them—something unreadable and fierce. Was it regret? Or was it the same wild thrill I felt, that desperate pull of adrenaline and fear coiling in the pit of my stomach? Whatever it was, it was enough to make me question whether we'd be able to get out of this alive, whether we'd make it out together.

"Enjoying the show?" Jaxon's voice slid into my ear, warm and inviting. He didn't need to raise his voice to be heard. The quiet, intense way he spoke only drew more attention, the subtle hint of danger hanging in his every word.

I chuckled softly, the sound a little too sharp in the heavy air. "If this is the show, I'm ready for the intermission."

He smiled—dangerous, slow, the kind of smile that made you want to believe the world could still be a place of lightness, even as the shadows stretched longer. "Patience, sweetheart. It's coming."

I knew exactly what he meant. The Wraith was here, and he wasn't just a figurehead. He was a predator, a dangerous mind who knew how to make enemies vanish, how to twist the lives of those who dared to stand in his way. Tonight, we were bait, and we had one goal: draw him out. But with every passing second, every glance I shared with Jaxon, the lines between the mission and something much more personal started to blur. Was I still playing a part? Or had I already become lost in this dance, in the heat between us that felt far too real for this charade?

THE RUSE

A murmur rippled through the crowd as the Wraith made his way toward the center of the room. He wasn't a man you could ignore—he commanded attention with every move, the crowd parting for him as though they'd been taught the choreography from birth. He didn't walk; he glided, his every movement smooth, calculated, like a serpent coiled and ready to strike.

It wasn't the elegance that unsettled me, though; it was the way the room seemed to shift when he entered. People straightened. Smiles grew tighter. And for those few moments, no one spoke too loudly, as though the very act of raising one's voice could draw his ire.

I stiffened. The plan was simple: get close to him, keep the conversation flowing, and find a way to pull the strings tight enough to get him to show his hand. I was used to danger, used to the unpredictability of a world that didn't always play by the rules, but the Wraith... he was something else. Something dark and cold.

"Do you think he knows?" I asked Jaxon, trying to keep my voice steady, though I knew the question hung in the air like an accusation.

Jaxon's smile didn't waver, but the tension in his shoulders was unmistakable. "If he does, we're already dead."

I stifled a laugh, the grim humor of the statement not lost on me. My heart hammered in my chest as I watched him move, his sharp eyes scanning the crowd with the precision of a hawk. It would take more than a casual conversation to draw him out. It would take something far more risky—and I wasn't entirely sure I was ready for it.

As if reading my thoughts, Jaxon leaned closer, his breath warm against my skin. "You know, you're going to have to get closer. A little more... personal."

I raised an eyebrow. "Personal?"

"Yes," he said, his voice a low purr. "No one pays attention to casual encounters. It's the whispers in the dark corners, the secrets exchanged in shadows. He won't move unless he feels the heat. You're going to have to make him believe you're part of the game."

I stared at him for a long moment. His words twisted in my mind, but there was no denying the truth in them. The Wraith would never show his hand unless he thought the risk was worth it. And we were playing a dangerous game, one where the stakes were higher than I'd ever imagined. But we didn't have a choice. The truth was, the only way out was through him.

I straightened, taking a deep breath as I turned toward the Wraith. He was looking right at me now, his gaze sharp and calculating, as though he could already see through my mask and into my very soul. I felt the pulse of the room slow, the entire world narrowing until it was just the two of us, locked in this silent challenge.

Jaxon's hand brushed against my back, his fingers a warm whisper against my skin. "You've got this," he said, the words a promise—or perhaps a warning. Either way, it didn't matter. The moment had come. It was time to walk into the lion's den.

I took a step forward, and the room seemed to hold its breath with me.

The heat of the moment clung to me like a second skin, the weight of the Wraith's gaze pressing on my chest as I approached. My steps were measured, my heart racing, but I didn't let it show. This was what I was here for, after all. The whole plan had led up to this moment—the point of no return. A silent dare, my hand trembling ever so slightly as I lifted the glass of champagne to my lips.

And then, his voice. Low, smooth, like velvet and smoke. "I didn't expect to see you here."

I didn't flinch, didn't let the sudden pulse of panic invade my composure. I turned toward him, the Wraith himself standing just a few feet away, his figure framed by the soft glow of the chandelier overhead. He was even more imposing up close. The tailored suit,

THE RUSE

dark and perfect, stretched across his shoulders like a second skin. His eyes—cold, calculating, and dangerous—seemed to slice through me, making it clear he had already sized me up.

"I could say the same about you," I replied, the words sliding out with practiced ease. My voice didn't waver, even though everything inside me screamed to run.

The Wraith's smile was tight, something akin to amusement dancing in his eyes, but it didn't quite reach his lips. "I'm not sure I believe that," he said. "You're not the type to belong here, not really. And yet, here you are."

He wasn't wrong. I didn't belong in a place like this, but I didn't have the luxury of doubt. I had a job to do, and nothing—not even the thickening sense of danger in the air—was going to stop me now.

"Well, you're right about one thing," I said, stepping just a little closer, feeling the heat radiate off his body, the danger coiling around us like a living thing. "But I've found that sometimes you have to pretend to be someone you're not to get what you want."

The Wraith's gaze flicked over my shoulder briefly, his attention momentarily distracted by something—or someone—behind me. I took advantage of the opening, letting my fingers brush against the glass of the champagne flute, my skin prickling with the faintest rush of excitement.

"You're bold, I'll give you that," he said, his voice low again, drawing my attention back to him. "I've learned that boldness gets people killed."

A small, almost imperceptible laugh escaped me. "Then I must be living dangerously."

For a heartbeat, the air between us felt charged with something far more volatile than just the words we spoke. His eyes narrowed, as if weighing me in some way, trying to decide just how much truth lay beneath my mask. How much of this was part of the plan, and how much of it was real?

I could feel Jaxon watching from across the room, but the distance between us seemed too great now, the tension between him and me too tangled to unravel. I had to trust that he would keep his cool—that he wouldn't jump in, not yet. Not until we were ready.

The Wraith's lips curled into a smile that didn't touch his eyes. "Perhaps," he murmured, taking a slow step toward me. "But what do you want, exactly?"

I had prepared for this. Every conversation had been rehearsed, every step carefully planned. But standing here now, so close to the man who could destroy everything with a simple flick of his hand, my mind scrambled for the right words. I couldn't afford to look like I was stalling. I had to appear as if I belonged, as if this moment was part of a larger, dangerous game, and I was playing it well.

"I want to see just how far this can go," I said finally, my voice steady. "I want to see what you're really capable of."

The Wraith's gaze darkened, a flash of something unreadable flickering across his face. "Is that so?"

"I'm not the only one with secrets," I said, stepping even closer now, until I could feel the heat of his body mingling with mine. "But I don't mind sharing mine. If you're willing to share yours."

He didn't answer right away. Instead, his gaze swept over me again, more slowly this time, as if he were trying to peel back the layers, searching for any hint of weakness. It was an unnerving feeling—being examined like that, as if I were just a puzzle to be solved. But I stood firm, every inch of me locked into place, even as my pulse quickened. I could feel Jaxon's presence behind me, though he hadn't yet moved.

"I'm curious," the Wraith finally said, his voice soft but threaded with warning. "Do you really think you can play this game, or are you just here for the thrill?"

His words struck something inside me, something I hadn't expected. For a moment, I faltered—just a brief second, but enough for the air to grow even heavier. Did I think I could win this? Or had I just gotten swept up in the rush of it all, in the madness of this twisted tango?

"Maybe it's both," I said finally, my voice tight but steady. "You don't get to where you are by being cautious. And you certainly don't get far by being afraid to take risks."

The Wraith's gaze flicked to the side again, his lips twitching as if he were deciding whether to respond. But something else caught his attention. A flicker in the crowd, a sudden shift in the air that made his gaze snap to the doorway at the far end of the room.

Without warning, the Wraith's expression changed. The mask of amusement slipped, and a sharp, dangerous edge took its place. "It seems our little game is about to get more interesting," he murmured, barely loud enough for me to hear.

I turned my head, following his gaze just in time to see a figure slip into the room—tall, dark, and unmistakably dangerous. My heart stopped. It wasn't just anyone. It was a man we hadn't expected to see, not here, not tonight.

Jaxon stiffened behind me, and I felt the subtle shift in the air, the dangerous undercurrent beneath his calm demeanor.

The game had changed, and I had no idea whether we were ready for what came next.

Chapter 18: The Last Stand

The night had started with the usual glitter, the kind that blurs the line between reality and fantasy. The chandeliers overhead refracted the light in a thousand dazzling pieces, each one casting a shimmering glow across the marble floors. Laughter spilled from groups of well-dressed elites, their whispered secrets as smooth as the velvet dresses and tailored suits they wore. I had hoped for a night of nothing more than subtle intrigue, the kind that leaves a taste of mischief on the tongue. Instead, it was the kind of evening where the air crackled with the kind of tension that made you feel like your every breath could be the last.

I stood near the grand staircase, a glass of champagne in my hand, watching Jaxon across the room. The way his eyes scanned the crowd told me that he hadn't come for the party either. We were both just playing parts, our minds tethered to a different game. His jaw was clenched, but I knew it wasn't out of irritation; it was the look of someone who had spent years in the shadows, knowing the exact moment when everything was about to fall apart.

And then, just like that, it did.

The Wraith, dressed in midnight black, his face hidden beneath a sleek mask, moved through the crowd like a predator among prey. The moment he stepped into the room, everything shifted. The air grew heavy, the light dimmed as if the very energy of the night had been sucked away, and every laugh, every conversation faltered. My pulse quickened. I didn't need to look at Jaxon to know he'd seen it too.

A crackling tension sliced through the room. Conversations halted. A cold dread slithered into my stomach, twisting it like a knife.

The Wraith stopped in the center of the ballroom, his voice smooth, yet sharp enough to cut through the silence. "How quaint," he said, his tone a mockery of civility. "A room full of fragile dreams and secrets ready to crumble."

I took a slow breath, feeling the weight of the moment settling over me. This wasn't just a gala anymore. This wasn't about elegance or grace—it was about survival. And we had only one option: fight.

Jaxon's eyes met mine, the connection like an electric jolt. Without a word, we moved toward each other. The crowd parted around us, but I could feel the tension building, like a storm ready to break. The Wraith didn't flinch as we approached. He just tilted his head, studying us with a dark amusement that made my skin crawl.

"You think you can stop me?" he asked, a sinister laugh following the words.

I didn't answer right away. Instead, I lifted my chin, the weight of everything—every sacrifice, every inch of pain—settling over me. My breath steadied, and I realized in that instant that I wasn't afraid anymore. The Wraith had done his worst. He had shattered my world before. And here we were, the two of us, standing on the edge of everything.

Jaxon's voice cut through the tension. "We don't need to stop you," he said, his words calm but deadly. "We just need to make sure you don't win."

I took another step forward, positioning myself at his side, the warmth of his presence seeping into me like a lifeline. There was no plan. No more tricks up our sleeves. This would be raw. This would be everything we had left.

The Wraith's smile stretched wider, a dangerous thing. "How quaint," he repeated, almost as if to himself. "The lovers. So predictable."

I raised an eyebrow, unable to resist. "You haven't learned, have you? You can't break us."

And just like that, chaos erupted. The air seemed to ignite around us, a barrage of noise and movement, as the gala devolved into something far darker. The Wraith's men spilled into the room like a flood, their presence a palpable weight, and suddenly, the delicate dance of the night was replaced by the sharp tang of fear and desperation.

Jaxon's arm brushed mine as we shifted into position, our bodies instinctively moving together, back to back. The chaos was deafening, but all I could hear was the sound of his breath, steady and controlled. My pulse synced with his, the rhythm of survival, of determination, and maybe something else—something deeper. Something that only made the stakes higher.

"We fight together," Jaxon murmured under his breath, just loud enough for me to hear.

I nodded, feeling a strange calm wash over me as the first wave of the Wraith's men charged. The noise, the chaos—it didn't matter anymore. We had come here with a purpose, and now it was time to finish what we had started. The metallic tang of blood, the sharp sounds of fists meeting flesh, and the heat of adrenaline pulsing in every vein—this was the moment.

With every movement, every strike, I could feel the weight of our love anchoring me, propelling me forward. It wasn't just a refuge; it was the very force that pushed me to fight harder, to fight smarter. We weren't just fighting for survival anymore. We were fighting for everything we had built, for every promise we had made to each other. And for the future that was still waiting—if we could just get through this.

The Wraith wasn't just another enemy. He was the embodiment of everything we had lost, everything that had been taken from us. But he didn't know what we had left—what we had together. And that, in the end, would be what broke him.

The sound of Jaxon's voice, low and urgent, reached me through the haze of the battle. "Don't stop. Keep moving."

I didn't need to be told twice. The world around me narrowed, and everything that had come before faded away. There was only us. Only this moment.

And then, in the heart of the storm, when everything seemed lost, I realized something crucial: love wasn't a weakness. It was the fiercest weapon we had. And together, we would stand.

The air was thick with the sting of sweat and the acrid scent of gunpowder, mingling with the sharp tang of champagne that had been spilled across the floor. I could feel the weight of each breath as the world around me fractured, and in that jagged space, Jaxon's presence was the only thing tethering me to sanity. Our bodies moved with a fluidity that was born of a bond forged in fire, each strike, each turn, calculated and precise. There was no room for hesitation, no time to second-guess.

A man lunged at me, his hand reaching for the knife at his belt, but I was already in motion, twisting beneath his arm and driving my elbow into his ribs with a satisfying crack. The shock of impact reverberated through my bones, and before he could even stagger back, I had my foot planted firmly in his chest, pushing him to the ground. My heart hammered, but there was no room for panic. Just action.

"Not bad for a girl in heels," I muttered under my breath, barely even registering the sarcasm that slipped from my lips. My mind was a machine, all instinct, all movement.

I didn't have to look at Jaxon to know he was right there, every move as sharp and calculated as my own. His presence was a steady hum at my back, a reminder that no matter how chaotic this battle was, we were in this together. We had always been in this together.

The Wraith was still somewhere in the thick of it all, his laugh ringing out above the fray like some twisted symphony. But it was his voice, the cadence of it that gave him away—smooth, almost too smooth, slipping through the noise like oil over water. His figure was a blur, his black silhouette cutting through the confusion, always just out of reach.

But we knew better now. We knew his tricks.

"I've always admired how easily you two slip into the shadows," the Wraith's voice taunted, sending a ripple through the crowd. His words were meant to get under our skin, to make us question our resolve, but I didn't flinch. Instead, I pushed harder, driving my fist into another man's gut, watching him crumple to the ground as if I had all the time in the world.

"You don't get it, do you?" I called out to the Wraith, my voice carrying over the rumble of bodies colliding. "You think you're the only one who knows darkness? I've lived it. Bled in it. It's not as glamorous as you think."

The response was a chuckle, a hollow sound that somehow made the pit of my stomach clench. "You don't know what you're dealing with, girl," he sneered, but his words were laced with something like... doubt?

I shot a glance over my shoulder. Jaxon's eyes met mine, burning with the same fierce determination I felt, and for the briefest of moments, we were the only two people in the world. The rest—every fight, every blow—faded to background noise. It was just us, standing at the edge of something terrible, something beautiful, holding each other up in the face of a battle that had nothing to do with winning. This was about surviving, about holding on to the one thing that still mattered.

"Don't make me regret that," Jaxon muttered, a hint of amusement playing in his voice, though his focus never wavered. His hand found mine for a split second, his grip tight and reassuring. "Let's end this."

I nodded, turning my attention back to the battlefield. The Wraith's voice came again, closer now, his words sharp enough to cut through the noise.

"I know everything about you," he said, his tone dripping with satisfaction. "Every secret you've buried. Every lie you've told. Your love, your rebellion, it's all built on nothing. You're just one mistake away from losing everything."

His words hit me like a cold gust of wind, but there was something hollow about them, as if they were meant to unsettle me but lacked the weight to truly reach. The Wraith may have known secrets about me, but he didn't know everything. Not the way I had come to understand myself—flawed, yes, but stronger for it.

I could feel the heat of anger rising, but it was controlled now, focused. The battlefield was no longer chaos. It was an extension of me. Every movement was precise, each strike calculated. And every time my body collided with another, the realization hit me harder: I wasn't just fighting for survival. I was fighting for us.

Jaxon moved at my side, a blur of controlled violence, his every move purposeful. His hand grabbed mine again, pulling me toward him as another wave of enemies advanced. We were in perfect sync now, and it felt like the whole room bent to our rhythm. The Wraith had underestimated us both, thinking we were just lovers caught in a storm. But we weren't just that. We were survivors, and more importantly, we were a team.

The Wraith emerged from the shadows then, stepping into the open. He was almost... regal in his posture, like a king surveying his broken kingdom. There was no trace of the man who had once been human—only the monster that had consumed him, the mask that had overtaken everything beneath it.

His eyes locked onto mine, and for a moment, I saw something there—something raw, something dangerous. It was fear.

"You're not as strong as you think," he sneered, stepping closer, his voice barely above a whisper.

"Funny," I said, my voice hard as stone, "I was about to say the same thing to you."

Before he could respond, I lunged, my movements swift and precise. But he was faster, always faster. He countered with a sharp twist, knocking me back, but I recovered instantly, never breaking my stride. He may have been the ghost in the room, the one who whispered in the dark, but we were no longer afraid of the dark.

In the chaos, with everything crashing around us, it wasn't fear that drove us anymore. It was something much stronger. It was love—the kind of love that doesn't just warm you, but burns through everything that tries to tear you apart.

And as we moved, side by side, I realized that this was our last stand, not against him, but for us. We weren't fighting just to survive. We were fighting for the future we had yet to build.

The world spun wildly as we moved in a blur of combat, the sharp scent of blood mixing with the perfume of desperation. I felt the pressure of every footstep, every blow as it landed, each impact a reminder of how far we'd come and how much we still had to lose. The chaos around me seemed distant now, a low hum under the roar of my heartbeat. My focus had narrowed, the only thing real now was the dance of survival between Jaxon and me—two bodies moving in perfect synchrony.

The Wraith's laugh echoed through the hall again, this time sharper, more unsettling. He was toying with us, I knew that much. But it no longer mattered. The fear that had once rooted me in place had become fuel, and with every punch, every kick, it was all I could do to hold on to the clarity of purpose that kept me grounded. There was no more room for doubt.

A man rushed at me from the side, a blur of fists and anger, but before he could make contact, Jaxon's hand shot out, grabbing him by the throat and slamming him into a nearby pillar. I didn't even pause, my foot meeting the next attacker's chest with a satisfying crunch. The sounds of battle were distant now, a symphony of chaos that only served to amplify the tightness in my chest—the raw, undeniable intensity of it all.

Through the fog of adrenaline, I could feel the shift. The Wraith was no longer just a threat. He was a symbol, a force, an embodiment of everything we had fought against. His presence loomed larger with each passing second, his twisted grin never faltering, even as his men fell around us like broken dolls.

And then, just as quickly as it had started, the onslaught paused.

The Wraith stepped forward, his eyes glinting with something that could almost have been admiration. It was an unsettling contrast to the violence he'd wrought. He was no longer hiding in the shadows, but standing tall in the center of it all, as though the destruction around us was little more than a calculated mess.

"You really think you can win this?" His voice was a velvet rasp, smooth and deadly. He tilted his head, eyes scanning the room with a detached amusement. "All your efforts, all your sacrifices, they've led you here. To nothing."

The words dripped like poison, each one an arrow aimed at the heart. I felt the sting, but it was fleeting.

"We're still here," I said, my voice cutting through the tension with an edge I hadn't realized was there. "And you're still losing."

His eyes narrowed, a flash of irritation crossing his features before he masked it with that smile—the kind that promised pain.

"You always think that, don't you?" He stepped closer, his boots clicking softly against the marble floor. "But the truth is, you've never been in control. Not really. You're just waiting for your little fairy tale to fall apart."

The air thickened with his words, the suffocating weight of them pressing down on me. But then Jaxon was there, a quiet fury in his stance as he placed his hand on my arm, pulling me just enough out of reach of the Wraith's venomous gaze. The touch was a reminder, an anchor.

"Enough talk," Jaxon muttered, his voice low but unyielding. "Let's finish this."

Before the Wraith could respond, Jaxon lunged, and the battle began again, faster, fiercer. I moved with him, our movements meshing, anticipating each other's every turn. The room felt too small for the magnitude of what we were up against, but we didn't hesitate. We couldn't.

The Wraith's men charged again, but this time they weren't prepared for the intensity we brought. I dodged, ducked, and struck, each move more brutal than the last. The adrenaline was a blur, the edge of my vision narrowing into a tunnel of action. But even amidst the fury, I felt something deep inside me that surged with unexpected clarity.

Jaxon's voice was in my ear, his tone fierce and steady. "He's not the only one who knows how to destroy. Remember that."

It hit me then. The Wraith had underestimated us. He thought we were just two people caught up in something bigger than ourselves. He thought we were pawns. But we were more than that. This wasn't just about survival anymore. It was about reclaiming everything he had stolen and everything we had worked so hard to protect.

I moved with a renewed sense of purpose, every blow a step closer to our final stand. The Wraith was growing more desperate, his movements erratic as he pushed his men harder, faster, with less thought. I could see the cracks beginning to form. He wasn't invincible. Not when we had each other.

A moment of hesitation—just a second—and that was all it took.

In that split second, the Wraith misjudged his reach, his hand swiping through the air just as I ducked beneath it. With a swift motion, I closed the distance, bringing my knee up into his ribs.

His breath wheezed out, and I heard the sickening sound of a bone breaking under the pressure.

For a moment, there was silence. A brief pause where the world seemed to hold its breath.

And then, everything exploded.

The Wraith's fury poured into the room, his movements no longer graceful, but reckless. He spun, his hands reaching for the gun at his side. Time seemed to slow as he drew it, the cold barrel of it aimed straight at me.

I didn't even think. I dove forward, pushing myself into the line of fire, and felt the world tilt on its axis as the shot rang out. The sound of it reverberated in my chest, and I felt my breath catch in my throat.

But the shot wasn't for me.

It was for Jaxon.

I saw it happen in slow motion, the trajectory of the bullet, the fear in Jaxon's eyes just before the impact.

The world shifted. Time froze. And then everything—everything—went dark.

Chapter 19: Rising from the Ashes

The remnants of the fire lingered in the air like a bitter aftertaste, sharp and metallic, a reminder of what had been. Jaxon stood beside me, his hand brushing lightly against mine, the weight of what we had just survived still settling in the pit of my stomach. I could see the devastation all around us—splintered wood from the once proud walls of the estate, remnants of charred trees twisting into the sky like skeletal fingers. The wind carried the smoke in thick, choking waves, but beneath it, there was something new, something hopeful.

It was strange, this feeling of peace after all the madness. I kept thinking I should feel more, maybe dread or even fear. But instead, it was as if we had shed something too heavy, something we'd been carrying without realizing the burden, and we were standing now on the edge of a new world, one that we had to build from the ground up.

Jaxon's fingers tightened around mine, his gaze scanning the horizon. His eyes, those ever-dark eyes, now held a softness that hadn't been there before, a warmth. I wondered if he was feeling it too—the strange, impossible hope that rose from the ashes. His face, once etched with lines of worry and pain, now carried a quiet resolve, like a man who had learned to stop fighting against the current and had finally found a way to swim with it.

"I thought we'd lost everything," I said, my voice rough from the smoke and the silence that had fallen after the battle. "But somehow, we haven't."

Jaxon gave me a crooked smile, a flash of that sharp, irresistible charm. "Not everything," he agreed, his thumb brushing the back of my hand in the kind of touch that made my heart stutter, even now. "We have each other. And we'll rebuild." His voice was firm, steady—assured in a way that felt new, even to me.

THE RUSE

I took a deep breath, the air still thick with the remnants of smoke, but also the scent of earth and growth beneath it. It was as if the world itself was healing, the land responding to the hope we were beginning to cultivate, even in this charred, broken place. The destruction hadn't just been physical; it had carved into our lives, our hearts, the very fabric of what we believed to be true about ourselves and each other. Yet, somehow, in this devastation, there was room for something new.

"We can do this," I whispered, more to myself than to him. The doubt that used to cloud my every decision, every step I took, seemed to have been replaced with something else. A certainty I hadn't known I was capable of. It was terrifying and exhilarating at the same time.

"You don't have to do it alone," Jaxon said, his voice low, yet filled with a promise. He stepped closer, the warmth of his body wrapping around me like a protective shield. "We're in this together."

The wind picked up, swirling around us, tugging at my hair and sending a few loose ashes dancing through the air. For a moment, I thought of the past, of all the struggles we'd endured, the secrets we'd kept, and the pain we'd caused each other. But just as quickly, the past faded, slipping away like the fog lifting with the dawn. The future stretched before us now, wide and uncertain, but filled with a kind of beauty I hadn't expected to find.

We walked together through the wreckage, side by side, our steps light despite the weight of what had happened. The world around us was in ruins, but somehow, we weren't. Our hearts beat in unison, and it was enough to carry us forward, to turn the rubble into something more. Something worth fighting for.

We reached the edge of the estate, where the trees had once lined the perimeter, their branches reaching like old friends toward the sky. Now, the space between us and the vast expanse beyond felt both daunting and promising. I could hear the distant call of birds, their song like a lullaby after the storm. The land was waking, slowly but surely, and so were we.

Jaxon stopped, his hand still holding mine, and looked out across the horizon. "We've come this far. We won't let it all go to waste." His voice was steady, but there was a vulnerability there too, something raw. He wasn't just speaking about the land, or even the physical rebuilding ahead. He was speaking about us. About this new life we had to craft from everything we had endured.

I squeezed his hand, grounding myself in the feel of him. I didn't know exactly what the future held, but I knew that together, we would shape it into something worth living for. We would build a life where trust wasn't just a word, but a promise that neither of us could break. We would forge a love that wasn't just born from passion, but from the ashes of everything we had survived.

The sun broke through the clouds, spilling gold across the broken earth, casting long shadows as it sank lower in the sky. The day was winding down, but I didn't feel the exhaustion that should have come with everything we'd just been through. No, instead, there was an energy within me, something lighter, brighter, like the first fresh breath after a storm.

"We have a future now," I said, almost in disbelief. "I can't believe it. After everything…"

Jaxon looked at me, his eyes softening, and for a moment, the weight of the past seemed to disappear entirely. "Believe it," he said quietly. "We're just getting started."

And with that, we took our first step forward, together.

The evening sun dipped lower, casting long, stretching shadows over the charred remnants of our former lives. The air was still heavy, as though holding its breath in the wake of everything that had happened. I could feel the weight of Jaxon's presence beside me, the quiet strength of his hand in mine grounding me as the world around us seemed to hold a fragile balance between what had been and what could be.

It was strange how quickly the world could shift. Just days ago, we'd been mired in uncertainty, buried under the weight of our past mistakes and the looming threat of The Wraith. Now, here we were, standing on the precipice of something new, something so unfamiliar that I couldn't quite place it, but I was learning to welcome it with open arms.

Jaxon's eyes, dark and steady as always, met mine, and for the first time in what felt like forever, there was no hidden agenda, no guarded secrets between us. He was all open, all light, and I had to admit, it was disorienting in the most beautiful way. He opened his mouth, as if to say something, then paused, his gaze flicking to the horizon.

"I think... I think I owe you an apology," he said, his voice low, almost uncertain.

I raised an eyebrow, not sure if I'd heard him correctly. "An apology? For what?"

Jaxon exhaled slowly, a wry smile tugging at the corner of his lips. "For all the things I couldn't say before. For making you feel like you were alone in all of this. For making you carry more than your share of the burden." He paused, his jaw tightening, his eyes distant for a fraction of a second before they locked back onto mine. "I'm sorry for not trusting you with the truth sooner."

My heart clenched at his words. I hadn't expected this—hadn't thought that he, of all people, would be the one to offer such vulnerability. Jaxon was many things, but humble wasn't usually one of them. But in this moment, I saw the man he had become, not just in the chaos of our past but in the quiet aftermath, too. The cracks in his armor had been exposed, and rather than retreat into himself, he was letting me in.

"You don't owe me an apology," I said softly, my voice a little shaky despite my best efforts to keep it steady. "We've both been carrying our own burdens, haven't we? I'm not the only one with regrets."

Jaxon chuckled, but it wasn't the sharp, easy laughter I was used to hearing from him. It was tinged with something softer, something real. "I think we've both spent far too much time trying to fix the wrong things," he said, his eyes drifting over the remnants of the estate. "Like this." He waved a hand toward the ruins. "I thought that this place, this life, was the problem. But it wasn't. The real issue was inside us, wasn't it?"

I nodded, the words catching in my throat. It was true. We'd both been running from our own demons, trying to outrun the pain of the past instead of confronting it head-on. But now, with the threat of The Wraith finally gone, with the dust settling, we could finally see the truth of it all. And it was terrifying, but also liberating.

A silence fell between us, comfortable for once, the kind of silence that said more than words ever could. The ground beneath our feet felt solid, not just from the earth but from something deeper—something that had been forged through every hardship, every heartbreak, every sacrifice.

I took a deep breath, inhaling the crisp evening air, the coolness of the night beginning to creep in, mixing with the warmth of the day that had clung to the earth. "So, what now?" I asked, turning toward him. "What do we do with all this?" I waved a hand at the wreckage surrounding us, the smoldering remnants of a life we could no longer claim.

Jaxon didn't hesitate. "We rebuild. Together."

It wasn't the grand declaration I'd expected, but somehow, it was everything I needed. Together. There it was again, that word. It had become the anchor we both needed to hold on to, a promise we hadn't fully understood until now.

The thought of rebuilding was daunting. The estate, the land, everything was in ruins, and there was no clear road to recovery. But as I looked at Jaxon, I realized that wasn't the point. The point was that we had the chance to try. To start fresh. To create something that wasn't burdened by the weight of the past, but rather something that could be defined by who we were now, by who we had the potential to become.

I gave him a sideways smile, the kind that was half-teasing, half-sincere. "Well, when you say 'together,' you're not just talking about us, right? Because there's no way we're doing this alone."

He grinned, his usual cocky self returning for just a moment. "Oh, trust me, we've got help. A whole army of misfits at our disposal."

I laughed, the sound catching me by surprise. It felt so natural, so right, to laugh like that again. To share this moment of levity, of normalcy, after everything we'd been through. It was like the final pieces of our puzzle were falling into place.

"We'll need more than an army," I replied, my voice full of mock seriousness. "We'll need a whole team of miracle workers."

Jaxon raised an eyebrow, that mischievous glint back in his eyes. "Good thing I know a few people who specialize in miracles."

I rolled my eyes, but the warmth in my chest spread, and for the first time in what felt like forever, I allowed myself to believe in the possibility of it all. We had both been scarred by the past, shaped by the fire of everything we'd endured, but that didn't mean we couldn't rise from it. Together, we could build something worth fighting for—something new, something beautiful. And maybe, just maybe, we would find the kind of love we'd always dreamed of, even if it wasn't the love we'd imagined. It was ours. And that was enough.

The air smelled different now. No longer heavy with the acrid stench of smoke and fire, it had taken on the sharp tang of saltwater from the nearby sea, mingling with the earthiness of the land that had been scorched and then washed clean by the rain. We had crossed the threshold, stepping away from the devastation and into something new, though I wasn't entirely sure what that "something new" was just yet. All I knew was that the weight of everything we had survived was still pressing on my chest. It wasn't gone. It never could be. But we were moving forward, and that in itself felt like a victory.

Jaxon's presence beside me was like a steady pulse, a reminder that we were no longer alone in this. The breeze shifted, tousling his dark hair, and for a moment, he looked as if he could have been carved from stone—strong, determined, and unshakable. But there was a softness in the way he looked at me now, a tenderness that had been earned over time, through the hardest of trials.

"What are you thinking?" he asked, his voice low, almost like a whisper between us and the world that had yet to be reassembled.

I turned my head to meet his gaze, not surprised by the question. I knew him too well now. He always wanted to know what was swirling inside my mind, the chaos I couldn't contain. It wasn't that he was nosy—he just needed to understand. Needed to know that, somehow, we were on the same page. Even now, after all we had been through, there was still a distance between us, but it was a distance I was learning to close, one step at a time.

"I was thinking about how different everything feels now," I replied, my voice a little breathless. "How... open it all is." I waved a hand to gesture toward the landscape—the broken grounds, the wreckage of everything that had once felt so permanent. "It's like everything we thought we knew is just... gone. Like we can do anything."

"Do you want to do anything?" he asked, turning toward me fully now, his eyes intense, searching.

I chewed on my lower lip for a moment, considering. There was so much that needed fixing—so much we had to rebuild. The estate, the town, the lives we had neglected in the name of survival. But all of that paled in comparison to what we needed to fix within ourselves. There were pieces of me that had been shattered by betrayal, by grief, and I knew that the only way forward was to rebuild those pieces, to stitch them back together with time, trust, and love.

"I want to try," I said quietly, my eyes softening as I looked at him. "I want to see what it's like, building something together. No more running. No more secrets."

He nodded slowly, his expression unreadable for a moment. Then, as if deciding something, his lips curved upward into that familiar half-smile—the one that always managed to make my pulse race. "That's all I needed to hear."

For a heartbeat, there was nothing but the sound of the wind between us, the soft rustling of leaves in the distance. It was peaceful, and yet I knew it wouldn't last. There was still so much to be done, so many pieces to pick up and carry forward. And as I stood there, next to Jaxon, watching the world begin to heal around us, I couldn't ignore the unease crawling at the back of my mind. The danger hadn't disappeared, not completely. The Wraith was gone, yes, but there were other shadows still lurking, waiting for their turn to strike.

"So," Jaxon began, his voice low, steady, "what's the first step?"

I inhaled deeply, considering the question. The weight of it pressed on me, but it wasn't the terrifying kind of weight that would crush me. No, this was the weight of responsibility, of possibility. We had a chance now, a real one, to build a future where we could breathe easy, where the nightmares of our past didn't reach out to steal our peace. But where did we start?

"We start with trust," I said finally, my voice firm, though it was laced with vulnerability. "We trust each other to be honest, even when it's hard. Even when it hurts. And we trust ourselves to handle whatever comes next."

Jaxon's eyes flickered with something—maybe surprise, maybe understanding—and then he nodded slowly. "Trust. I can do that."

But as I looked out at the horizon, something caught my eye. A flicker of movement in the distance—too quick, too deliberate to be just the wind. My heart skipped a beat. I wasn't sure why, but a sense of dread started to coil in my gut. The silence between us felt suddenly heavy, thick with unspoken words. Something was wrong. Something was coming.

"What's wrong?" Jaxon asked, his voice sharp, his gaze following mine.

I didn't answer immediately. Instead, I took a few hesitant steps forward, narrowing my eyes toward the distant treeline where the shadows seemed to shift, as though they were alive. My breath caught in my throat as the figure appeared again—flickering in and out of the trees like a shadow playing tricks on the light. It wasn't human, at least not in the way I recognized.

I turned back to Jaxon, my pulse quickening. "We're not alone."

Jaxon's expression shifted, his body tense with the instinctive awareness that something was amiss. "How far?"

I swallowed, my throat dry. "Too close."

Without another word, he moved toward me, stepping into a defensive stance that I knew he didn't take lightly. And then, just as the first rustle of movement reached my ears again, the figure stepped fully into view, and I froze.

It was someone I didn't recognize.

And the worst part? They were smiling.

Chapter 20: Reflections in the Dark

The silence in the ruined gala hall is almost suffocating, a thick, oppressive thing that hangs in the air, tangled with the stench of smoke and the faint scent of something metallic—blood, perhaps, or just the remnants of a battle too recent to fade into memory. I find myself standing in front of a shattered mirror, the jagged edges framing not just my reflection but the pieces of who I've been, who I am, and the fractured pieces of who I wish I could be. The cracks split my face in a thousand different directions—each shard showing a version of me, warped, broken, and far too familiar.

I lean in closer, my fingers brushing against the cold, sharp edges of the glass. A shard digs into my skin, but I barely register the sting. The pain doesn't matter right now. My reflection flickers, my heart beats in my ears, and I wonder how long it will take for me to disappear entirely into the shards, to lose myself so completely that I'll never find my way back. Every moment of doubt, every scar and mistake I've buried deep, rises to the surface, and the mirror doesn't shy away from showing them to me.

A noise behind me pulls me from my thoughts, and I glance over my shoulder, only to find Jaxon standing there, watching me with a quiet intensity. His clothes are torn, his face smeared with dirt and sweat, his eyes dark with the weight of what we've just been through. I should be angry with him. We've been through enough together to merit a storm of emotions—anger, frustration, maybe even betrayal—but instead, all I feel is a sense of unease. A trembling thread of vulnerability that I'm not sure I want to untangle. His presence feels like a balm, soothing yet sharp all at once.

"I didn't expect it to end like this," I say, my voice barely above a whisper, as though the words themselves are fragile enough to shatter like the mirror. I don't look at him as I speak, don't want to see the pity or the uncertainty that might be there. The silence stretches, thickening, wrapping around us like a noose. I'm afraid if I speak too loudly, if I break this delicate calm, I might break something inside of me as well.

Jaxon steps closer, his boots echoing softly on the floor, each step a reminder that he's here, that he's always here, whether I want him to be or not. His fingers brush against my arm, a small, tentative gesture that almost feels like an apology, even though I haven't asked for one. I glance up at him then, and his eyes lock with mine—steady, unwavering, full of a depth I don't fully understand. There's something in his gaze that makes the room feel smaller, and yet, for some inexplicable reason, I want to shrink even further, to disappear entirely into the shadows of this broken hall.

"I didn't expect this either," he murmurs, his voice a low rasp, like the aftermath of a storm. "But we're here now."

There's something about the way he says it, the raw honesty behind the words, that makes my chest tighten. It's as though he's carrying something heavy, something just as jagged and painful as what I've been trying to hide from him. My heart picks up pace, my breath shallow, but I don't speak. The words are stuck, lodged somewhere deep inside me, trapped by the weight of everything I haven't said.

I turn my attention back to the mirror, unable to hold his gaze for too long. My reflection, fractured and distorted, is a reminder of everything I've tried to avoid. The person I was before all of this, the person I thought I could be—strong, confident, fearless. But somewhere along the way, I've lost that person, and I'm not sure if I can find her again. I'm afraid to look too closely at the woman in the glass, because I know the truth now. I don't know who she is anymore. I don't know who I am.

The silence stretches again, long and fragile. Jaxon doesn't push me. He stands there, close enough that I can feel the heat of his body, but not so close that I feel suffocated by it. He knows, somehow,

THE RUSE 185

that I need space to breathe, to think, even if I'm not sure what I'm thinking about. His presence is a steadying force, even when I don't want it to be. Even when I don't want him to be.

"You're still you," Jaxon says, and his voice, though quiet, carries an unshakable certainty. "I don't know who you think you've become, but I see you. The real you."

I don't say anything at first. Part of me wants to argue with him, to tear his words apart because they don't match the truth I've spent years building around myself. But another part of me—one that's softer, more vulnerable—wants to believe him. Wants to believe that the person I've become is still worth something, still worthy of love, of trust. That maybe, just maybe, I haven't ruined everything beyond repair.

I turn to face him then, meeting his gaze head-on. For a moment, I'm struck by how much he's changed too. The sharp edges of his character, once so easy to read, now seem like an enigma. He's not the man I thought I knew. But then again, neither am I.

"I don't know if I can do this," I confess, my voice barely above a whisper. The words hang between us, heavy with the weight of everything unspoken. I don't know if I can keep pretending to be someone I'm not. If I can keep hiding from him, from myself.

Jaxon steps forward, closing the distance between us. His hand reaches out, hesitating for just a moment before gently cupping my face. The gesture is so simple, so tender, but it feels like a promise—a promise that maybe we don't have to fix everything right away. Maybe we can take it slow, piece by piece, and rebuild from the rubble we've left behind.

"We'll figure it out," he says softly, his thumb tracing the curve of my cheek. His voice is steady, reassuring, but there's an undertone of something raw, something real. "Together."

And in that moment, as the shards of the mirror lie shattered at our feet, I realize that maybe, just maybe, vulnerability isn't something to be afraid of. Maybe it's the only thing left that can save us.

Jaxon's hand still lingers on my face, his thumb brushing absentmindedly across my skin, but the touch feels different now. Softer. The weight of his palm grounding me, tethering me to the present, like he's waiting for me to make a decision, to choose whether I'm going to step into this uncertainty with him or run in the other direction, as I've always done. My breath catches, and I realize that the decision has never been as clear as it is right now. And yet, the temptation to run—toward the comfort of distance, toward the lie that I can handle this alone—whispers in my ear like an old, well-worn tune.

But I don't run.

Instead, I find myself stepping closer, leaning into his touch as though the act of doing so might make me feel a little less fractured. A little more like the woman I used to be before everything unraveled. His gaze never falters, and in the depths of those dark eyes, I see the unspoken promise. He's not going anywhere. Not yet. And maybe, just maybe, I don't have to carry this burden alone anymore.

I let out a breath I didn't realize I was holding, my fingers curling around his wrist, the pulse beneath his skin strong and steady. I'm not sure if it's his calm that soothes me or the fact that I'm finally allowing myself to be vulnerable, to admit that maybe I can't fix everything by myself. Maybe I don't have to.

"I don't know where to start," I whisper, the words barely more than a confession. It's a raw admission, one I'd never thought I'd say aloud, not to him, not to anyone. But here we are, standing amidst the wreckage, in a place where the truth is all that remains. My voice cracks, just for a moment, and I feel the sting of tears hovering just beneath the surface, threatening to rise. But I refuse to let them fall—not now, not when I'm so close to something that could heal.

He doesn't answer right away. Instead, he steps closer, his body aligning with mine so perfectly, like we're two pieces of the same puzzle that, despite the disarray, just might fit if we give it enough time. He's quiet for a moment, and the space between us seems to stretch, but it's not uncomfortable. It's the kind of silence that asks questions, not answers. The kind of silence that makes everything feel possible, even when it's hard to believe.

"You don't have to start anywhere," Jaxon says at last, his voice low and steady, but there's something in it—something that feels like more than just words. There's an understanding there, one that reaches into the broken places I'm trying so desperately to keep hidden. "You don't have to have it all figured out. Not yet."

I swallow hard, trying to hold it together long enough to let his words sink in, to let them make sense. The weight of everything is still there, heavy on my chest, but somehow, in this moment, I don't feel so alone in it. I nod, though I don't fully understand what he's offering me. What I'm offering him, I'm not sure. But there's something about the way he's looking at me, like he's waiting for me to find my way, even if that means stumbling a little along the way. And maybe that's all I need right now. Someone to catch me if I fall. Someone who believes in me, even when I don't know how to believe in myself.

The silence stretches between us again, but this time, it doesn't feel quite as suffocating. There's a tension in the air, but it's not the kind of tension that makes me want to run. It's the kind that makes me want to lean in further, to let myself be seen, even if it's just for a moment.

"I'm afraid of what happens if I can't fix this," I finally admit, the words spilling out before I can stop them. "Afraid that I'm not... enough. That I'll let you down."

Jaxon's eyes soften, and for the first time since we've met, I see a flicker of something in his gaze—something vulnerable, something human. It's the look of a man who's been through his own battles, who's felt the weight of failure and loss, and yet, he's standing here, in front of me, offering me his strength. I'm not sure why, but in that moment, I believe him when he says it.

"You're more than enough," he says, and the words, though simple, settle over me like a blanket, wrapping me in warmth. "More than I ever expected, more than I ever thought I needed. But here you are, showing up. And that's all I could ever ask for."

For the briefest of moments, I think I might laugh—because isn't it funny? Isn't it almost comical how we've both been walking around carrying these mountains of fear, pretending like we're the only ones who are struggling to hold everything together? It's almost too much, this weight we've both been dragging behind us. But instead of laughing, I let out a shaky breath, my hand slipping into his. It's a quiet promise, one that doesn't need to be spoken aloud. A promise that we'll figure it out, no matter how messy it gets.

"You make it sound easy," I tease, the words slipping out with more lightness than I expect. It's a moment of humor, a breath of fresh air in the middle of everything that's been suffocating me. But I mean it, too. Jaxon has this way of making the impossible seem within reach, even when the path ahead is as unclear as the fog rolling in outside.

He grins, that wry, familiar smile that always manages to soften the edges of my anxiety. "It's not easy. But nothing that's worth it ever is, right?"

I laugh, the sound feeling strange on my lips, but comforting at the same time. It's a laugh of surrender, of acceptance. Of stepping into the unknown together, no matter how daunting it seems. And in that moment, I realize that maybe this is what healing feels like. It's not some grand revelation. It's not a single, earth-shattering moment of clarity. It's just this—a quiet understanding between two people who are learning how to trust again. How to show up for each other when everything around them is falling apart.

And maybe, just maybe, that's enough.

The weight of his hand on my cheek feels different now, not the warm, comforting touch it once was, but an anchor, holding me steady as if he knows I'm teetering on the edge of something too vast to comprehend. The debris of our shared battles litters the hall, the charred remnants of everything that once was, and for the first time in ages, I feel the pull of something deeper, more complex than the simple rush of adrenaline that had once defined us.

"You're not broken," Jaxon says softly, and his voice is steady, unshaken by the chaos that swirls around us. "But I'm starting to think I am."

I meet his gaze, but I don't say anything right away. There's a vulnerability in his words that stuns me, something raw and human that I didn't expect. In the past, Jaxon had always been the strong one—the one with the answers, the one with the plan. But now, standing here with the remnants of our lives in ruins around us, he's just a man. A man who's as unsure as I am, as afraid of the unknown as I've always been.

I search his face, trying to reconcile the person I thought he was with the one standing in front of me now. For a moment, I almost don't recognize him. He's different, more open than he's ever been before, and it shakes me to my core. And then I realize, with a sinking feeling in my chest, that maybe I've been running from the same truth for too long. That in all my self-doubt, I never stopped to consider that he might need me just as much as I need him.

"I'm not... I'm not sure how to fix this," I admit, the words tasting foreign in my mouth. The vulnerability stings, but it's also freeing, like something has cracked open in me that I didn't even know was there. I feel exposed, but it's not the terror I expected. Instead, there's a strange sense of relief, as if I've just put down a weight I've been carrying for years. "I don't know if I even can."

His gaze softens, and there's an understanding in his eyes that makes my throat tighten. "You don't have to fix anything. Not tonight, not here." He takes a step back, his hand still lingering in the air like it's unsure where it belongs. "We'll get through this, but only if you stop trying to shoulder it all alone."

There's something about the way he says it—simple, matter-of-fact—that almost feels like a challenge. Not the kind that demands an immediate response, but the kind that leaves a door open, a crack in the walls that I've spent so much of my life building.

But I don't know how to walk through it. Not yet.

I look down at the shards of the mirror at my feet, the edges sharp and dangerous, the glass glinting in the dim light. It's a small thing, but something about it feels significant. It's broken, just like me, just like us. I wonder if I can ever gather all the pieces of who I used to be and rebuild myself. If I'll ever feel whole again, or if that's even possible.

"You make it sound so easy," I say, finally breaking the silence. It's almost a laugh, but it doesn't reach my eyes. Instead, it feels more like the weight of something I haven't admitted to anyone, not even myself. "Like everything can just be swept away, and we'll be fine."

Jaxon doesn't smile, doesn't try to reassure me with empty words. Instead, he takes another step closer, his body filling the space between us until I can feel his warmth, his pulse, everything he is just inches away. He's no longer the impenetrable wall I once thought him to be. The edges of his strength are softening, and for the first time in a long time, I realize that maybe that's the only thing I've needed from him all along.

"You're right," he says, his voice quiet but steady. "It's not easy. But it's worth it. I don't know how to fix everything either, but we don't have to fix it all at once." He tilts his head, searching my face, his eyes never leaving mine. "We just have to start somewhere."

The room feels smaller now, the air thick with the tension between us. I know what he's saying, and I want to believe him. I want to believe that we can take it slow, piece by piece, and build something new from the wreckage. But there's a part of me that's terrified of what it would mean if we try and fail. Terrified of what happens when everything I've built, every wall I've put up, starts to crumble.

"I don't know how to let go of all the things I've been holding onto," I confess, the words tumbling out before I can stop them. There's a heaviness in my chest, a pressure that won't let up. "I don't know how to stop running from everything I've done, everything I've been."

Jaxon doesn't say anything at first. Instead, he just looks at me, like he's waiting for me to finish. His presence is a quiet assurance, but there's something else there too—something that feels like a question, like he's asking if I'm ready to step into the unknown with him.

"Maybe," he says after a long pause, "we don't have to let go of everything. Maybe we can carry it, together."

I feel a shiver run through me at the thought. The weight of everything we've both been through, everything we've survived—it feels too much to carry on our own. But the thought of carrying it with him, sharing the burden, somehow makes it seem a little less daunting.

I open my mouth to speak, but before I can form the words, a noise cuts through the quiet, sharp and sudden. My pulse spikes, my body stiffening in instinctual reaction. I turn toward the sound, but the room is still and empty, the only light coming from the broken remnants of the chandelier overhead.

I know I've heard something. I know we're not alone.

Chapter 21: The Weight of Tomorrow

I woke to the faint scent of earth and saltwater, the two mingling like old friends, a reminder that the world, despite everything, still existed outside of the cocoon I'd created in my mind. The blinds were half-drawn, letting in just enough light to make me squint, but not enough to disturb the heavy sleep I'd barely pulled myself from. I stretched, my limbs stiff from the unyielding mattress that had become more of a relic than a comfort, and then I turned toward the spot where Jaxon had slept.

Empty.

The sheets were rumpled but not enough to suggest he'd left in a hurry. No, it was the quiet that settled around me, the absence of the steady rhythm of his breathing, that put a knot in my stomach. I had grown used to the sound of it—the simple rise and fall that soothed even in the worst of times.

I stood, my bare feet meeting the cold wood floor with a shock, my body groaning with the protest of a life lived mostly in motion. There was a fire in my chest—impossible to ignore—and the thought of seeing Jaxon, of hearing his voice, pushed me toward the kitchen. The quiet of the house was unsettling, far too silent for something that should have been a home, not a mausoleum.

The sun had barely broken the horizon, casting the room in a pale, washed-out light. The whole house felt frozen, like everything was caught in a moment before the storm. Except that the storm was long gone. The Wraith—its control, its reach—had been nothing more than a memory for weeks. Or so I thought.

I found him by the window, his back turned to me as he watched the ocean, his posture as rigid as the rocks below us. Jaxon's dark hair was tousled from sleep, and his fingers, white-knuckled, gripped the edge of the windowsill like it was the only thing holding him to this world.

I said nothing at first. What could I say? He hadn't even turned around when I entered. We were supposed to be rebuilding, supposed to be finding our way out of the wreckage. So why did everything feel so fragile?

"Are you going to brood all day?" I asked, my voice hoarse with the weight of a thousand unspoken things.

He didn't flinch. Instead, his head slowly turned, eyes meeting mine, but they were distant, as if he wasn't really seeing me at all. The ghost of something darker passed across his face, something I couldn't name, and before I could speak again, he lifted his chin, staring past me to the horizon.

"Do you ever wonder if we've truly won?" His voice was quieter than I expected, and it carried a tremor of something far deeper than doubt. It was fear.

"Won?" I couldn't help but laugh, though it felt strained. "Jaxon, The Wraith is gone. We're free. Isn't that what we wanted?"

"We are free," he agreed, but there was something in the way he said it that made my stomach churn. "But what happens when the thing you've spent your whole life fighting for is over? Do you just move on? Pick up the pieces?"

I moved toward him, taking slow steps, unsure if I was walking toward him or away from him. "You pick up the pieces," I said firmly. "You start over."

He didn't respond, and for a moment, I thought he might not. His gaze shifted to the ocean again, his eyes narrowing as if searching for something in the distance that would give him the answers he craved. The tension between us was thick enough to suffocate, but neither of us seemed to know how to break it.

I took a breath, steadying myself. "We'll rebuild," I said again, as if saying it aloud would make it real. "We'll rebuild this—this place, this life, together."

Jaxon's lips twitched, but not in a way that was comforting. It was more like he was holding something back, a truth he couldn't or wouldn't say. His eyes flickered toward mine, and in them, I saw the ghosts of everything we'd survived. It wasn't enough to erase the past, no matter how hard we tried.

"I don't know if we can," he said, and there was a quiet conviction in his tone that made me stop. "What if we haven't even begun to understand what we've lost?"

The question landed like a heavy weight in my chest. We hadn't just lost The Wraith; we'd lost so much more in the process. Pieces of ourselves we could never reclaim. Pieces of the people we used to be, before the fighting, before the chaos.

"Maybe we never will," I said, finally standing beside him, close enough to feel the heat of his body, the familiar scent of him that still made my pulse quicken. "But we have now. And that has to be enough."

He didn't respond, his fingers slowly uncurling from the windowsill. Instead, he turned to me, his eyes searching mine, as if trying to read something I hadn't even known I was hiding.

"Does it feel like enough to you?" he asked softly.

The question hit harder than I expected, but I forced myself to meet his gaze. "Not yet. But I'm trying. And I need you to try too."

There it was. The thing that had been hanging between us, unspoken but ever-present. I wasn't just fighting for survival anymore. I was fighting for a future, a future that didn't seem so impossible when I was standing next to him. But the doubt, the shadows that still clung to us, were like chains, holding us both back.

"We're not done," I said, a quiet promise. "But we will be. Together."

The days had begun to feel like a series of slow breaths—long and drawn-out, each one lingering just a moment too long before the next one came. I could hear the wind in the trees outside, their branches creaking in a way that felt less like nature and more like the weight of something forgotten, some warning we had missed. Jaxon and I hadn't spoken much since that morning at the window, not about anything that mattered. We had settled into a new routine, one where the quiet between us was comfortable, but not quite enough to quell the unease simmering beneath the surface.

The mornings were the hardest. When the sun first rose, it seemed to shine brighter than it ever had before, bathing the house in golden light as if trying to wash away the ghosts of the past. But then, the shadows of the afternoon would creep in, long and stretching, reminding me that nothing about this new life was truly free from the past. I could feel it like a weight on my chest, this constant undercurrent of something looming just out of reach.

It was late afternoon when I found myself in the kitchen again, staring at the small pile of dishes that had accumulated over the past few days. I used to be someone who couldn't stand clutter—who would clean and tidy before I could think clearly. But now, I found myself avoiding it, not wanting to confront the chaos of my own mind in such a tangible way. There was something oddly comforting in the disarray. The mess, in its way, was proof that we were alive, that we were trying.

Jaxon entered silently, his footsteps barely making a sound against the worn wood floor. I turned to greet him, but before I could say anything, he lifted a hand, his fingers brushing the edge of my sleeve as he passed. He was always so close, but still, it felt like a lifetime since I'd felt his warmth press against mine in any real way. The touch was fleeting, a whisper of something I couldn't name, but it left a trail of heat behind, one that I couldn't ignore.

"Dinner's in thirty minutes," I said, the words falling out of me before I could stop them.

He nodded, his jaw set in that way that made him look more distant than he ever truly was. "I'll be in the garage. I need to finish fixing the generator."

The generator. The never-ending project that had become his obsession since the storm had knocked out power weeks ago. We didn't need it—there was still enough light to get by, and the water was still running—but Jaxon had thrown himself into it like it was the last task on a list he couldn't abandon. It was like he was building something to replace the world we'd lost, but in doing so, he was constructing walls around himself. I didn't blame him. I had my own walls, built carefully over years, and they were still there, looming between us.

"Okay," I said, my voice tight even to my own ears. He didn't look back as he disappeared into the garage, the door sliding shut behind him with a soft click.

I turned my attention back to the counter, where the same forgotten dishes waited. The clink of plates and silverware was oddly soothing, a rhythmic sound that filled the empty spaces. But no matter how hard I tried to focus on something as mundane as washing dishes, my mind kept drifting back to the feeling that something was wrong. Something was waiting, hiding just out of sight.

The kitchen door creaked open again, but this time it wasn't Jaxon. It was Delilah, one of the few people I could still rely on, and even then, I often wondered how much I truly knew her. She was standing in the doorway, arms crossed over her chest, her lips curled into a half-smile that didn't quite reach her eyes.

"We need to talk," she said, her voice laced with a seriousness I wasn't used to hearing from her.

I set the dish in my hand down with a clink and turned to face her, the sudden shift in the air making my pulse quicken. Delilah didn't do "serious." She didn't even do "worried" unless the world was about to fall apart. And it had felt like that for months.

"What's going on?" I asked, my voice low, barely above a whisper. My hands were still wet, the water leaving a cold trail down my wrists.

Delilah hesitated, her gaze flicking toward the closed door of the garage where Jaxon was working. "It's about him," she said, her voice dropping an octave. "And you."

I stiffened, unsure of what she meant but instinctively knowing that it wasn't good. "What about us?"

"Something's not right. I've been watching him," she continued, her eyes narrowing as though she were searching for something in the space around her. "He's not himself, not really. And neither are you."

I swallowed, trying to keep the wave of defensiveness that bubbled up from spilling over. "What do you mean, 'not myself'?"

Delilah's gaze softened, but only slightly. She was never one for sugarcoating things. "You know what I mean. I'm not the only one who's noticed. The way you both... hold back. The way you look at each other like you're both waiting for something to go wrong."

I opened my mouth to argue, but nothing came out. It was like she had reached into the deepest parts of me and pulled out the very thoughts I'd been trying to bury.

"We're fine," I said, though it sounded hollow even to my own ears. "We're just... adjusting."

"Are you?" she asked, her eyebrows raised skeptically. "Because it looks to me like you're both afraid. Afraid of the future, afraid of the past, and most of all, afraid of each other."

I felt the weight of her words settle in the pit of my stomach. I wanted to argue, to tell her that she was wrong, that we were rebuilding, slowly but surely. But the truth was, I wasn't sure anymore. Was I afraid? Or had I simply stopped believing that the world could be anything but broken?

Delilah stood there, watching me, her eyes holding something unspoken, something urgent. I didn't know if she was trying to warn me or simply making an observation, but I had a feeling I wasn't going to like whatever came next. The world felt smaller all of a sudden, the walls closing in.

Delilah's eyes bore into me, unflinching, her arms crossed over her chest, as if she were waiting for me to break under the weight of her words. I could feel the air between us crackle with the tension of an unspoken truth, one that had been simmering for far too long. The kitchen had never felt so small, its walls pressing in, its light too bright, too harsh.

"You know I'm right," she said, her voice not unkind, but firm. "You're both holding your breath, waiting for the other person to shatter. And it's not just about Jaxon. It's about you too. You're afraid of losing him, of losing... everything. But you're also afraid of getting too close, because you don't know how to survive that."

I shook my head, the words stinging, but I couldn't bring myself to argue. She was right, and I hated that she was.

"I'm not afraid," I muttered, but even I could hear the lie in my voice. The truth was, I had been terrified for so long that it felt like a second skin. Terrified that what we had was fragile, that the peace we'd fought for would slip through our fingers like sand. And every time I reached out, every time I tried to grasp something real, the fear tightened around my chest, suffocating me.

Delilah's gaze softened, but the flicker of concern never left her eyes. "You're still running from something, you know. From yourself, from him, from everything you've ever believed in. That's what's eating at both of you."

I opened my mouth to respond, but the sound of the garage door opening interrupted me. Delilah stepped back, and without another word, she turned toward the door, slipping through it before I could even form a response. I stood there for a long moment, my heart beating so loudly in my ears that it drowned out everything else.

I wasn't ready for this. I wasn't ready to face whatever had been waiting, lurking beneath the surface. I had spent so long running from it, pretending that everything was fine, that now the very thought of confronting it felt like a betrayal. Betrayal of Jaxon, of everything we had started to rebuild.

The sound of footsteps brought me back to the present, and I turned just as Jaxon entered the room. He stopped, his brow furrowed, eyes catching mine with that same searching look. It was a look that always left me feeling exposed, vulnerable, as if he could see right through me, right to the parts of myself that I'd spent years burying.

"Delilah?" he asked, his voice steady but laced with something I couldn't place.

"Yeah, she just... left," I said, my voice sounding off even to my own ears. "She's fine."

Jaxon didn't reply, but his eyes flickered with the same tension that had been between us for days, for weeks, since everything had changed. Since the world had stopped spinning on someone else's terms, and we were left to rebuild our own.

There was a pause, a stretch of silence thick with things unsaid, before he crossed the room to me. His presence filled the space, large and inevitable, just as it always had. And yet, I found myself wishing for distance, wishing I could take a breath without the weight of him hanging over me.

"You okay?" he asked, his voice softer now, almost hesitant.

I nodded quickly, but the words caught in my throat. I wasn't okay. I wasn't even close. But I couldn't say that to him. I couldn't add to the burden that had been building between us for so long.

"I'm fine," I lied again, smiling just a little, hoping it would convince him, hoping it would convince me.

But Jaxon didn't buy it. He stepped closer, his hand brushing against my shoulder, his fingers warm and gentle. I shivered, but not because of the touch. It was because I knew, deep down, that nothing would ever be the same again. Not for either of us.

"You're lying," he said, his voice low, a wry smile pulling at the corner of his lips. But there was no humor in his eyes, only the same sadness that mirrored my own.

I swallowed, the lump in my throat growing. "I'm not lying."

He didn't say anything for a long time. Instead, he simply reached out and took my hand, his grip firm, grounding me in a way that both terrified and comforted me at once. "I can't help you if you won't let me in," he said, his voice quiet but steady.

The words hit me like a punch to the gut. I knew, deep down, that he was right. But the fear—the ever-present fear—held me in place, stopped me from opening up, from giving him all of me. I had spent so long guarding my heart, guarding myself from pain, that I wasn't sure I knew how to let go anymore.

"I'm not sure how to do this," I whispered, more to myself than to him, though I knew he heard me.

Jaxon's thumb traced circles on the back of my hand, the motion slow and deliberate, as though he were trying to remind me that we could still find our way back to something real. Something unbroken. But the truth was, I wasn't sure there was any unbroken part of me left.

"I'm not asking you to be perfect," he said softly. "I just need you to be here. With me. In whatever way you can."

I wanted to say something, to tell him that I wasn't sure I could give him anything, but the words stuck. Instead, I found myself leaning into him, just a little, as if the contact could somehow bridge the gap between us. But it didn't. It only made it worse. Made it all too real.

A loud bang echoed from outside, sharp and unexpected, followed by the screech of metal on metal. My head snapped toward the window, the sudden sound jolting me out of my own thoughts. Jaxon's hand tightened on mine, his gaze narrowing in response to the noise. It was only when I saw the look on his face—tight, determined, fearful—that I understood.

Something was wrong. Something was happening. And I wasn't ready for it.

"I'll go check it out," Jaxon said, his voice clipped as he pulled away from me, his expression hardening. But I could see the flicker of unease in his eyes.

Before I could say anything, he was gone, disappearing through the back door and into the growing darkness. I stood there, my heart racing, my mind spinning, as the echoes of that bang hung in the air like a threat.

And then, just as the door clicked shut behind him, I heard it—a faint, familiar whisper in the back of my mind. A voice I hadn't heard in so long. One that I thought was gone.

It's not over yet.

Chapter 22: Unmasking the Threat

The neon lights of New Chicago never quite go out, even in the early hours of morning. The streets hum with a tired energy, the sound of tires skimming cracked pavement, the distant rumble of low conversations in alleyways, and the occasional thud of doors slamming shut. In the city's belly, it all felt the same—chaotic, restless, and just a little bit dangerous. But that morning, the air felt different. Heavier. Like something was pressing down on my chest, but I didn't know what yet. I wouldn't have known it then, but that was the moment everything would change.

It started with the message. No name. No signature. Just a string of numbers and symbols that meant nothing at first glance. But to Jaxon, it was a call to arms, a whisper of something hidden, a thread pulled at the very fabric of the world we thought we'd patched together. He didn't need to say much. The dark furrow of his brow and the set of his jaw told me everything I needed to know.

"We're not done," he muttered under his breath, his eyes scanning the encrypted message on the screen. His voice was quiet, but the tension wrapped around it like a second skin, a tension I could feel crawling up the back of my neck. "We missed something. And now it's coming back."

I leaned in beside him, the familiar scent of leather and pine filling my senses as I slid into the chair next to him. "What does it mean?"

"Everything," he said, his voice so low it barely rose above a whisper. "It's The Wraith. Or at least what's left of them."

The words hit me like a cold gust of wind. The Wraith. A shadowy figure from our past. The mastermind of a sprawling criminal network that had been like a ghost—slipping through our fingers every time we thought we'd cornered it. But that was before, when we had the luxury of thinking it was over, of believing that the chaos had finally settled, that we were safe.

Clearly, we were wrong.

I didn't need to ask why it had to be us. Jaxon didn't do things halfway. He didn't ignore danger. He hunted it. And right now, it was hunting us. Without a word, he powered up the old motorcycle parked outside, and the rumble of its engine echoed down the alley. I followed him instinctively, the hum of the bike vibrating through my body as we sped toward the heart of the city.

New Chicago wasn't the glistening future the brochures promised. The city was a labyrinth of steel and concrete, the grime of the underworld curling between the cracks of its sleek exterior. There were no clear lines between good and bad here; everything was blurred, every deal tainted. And now, buried somewhere in that twisted mess, was the piece of The Wraith's empire still lurking in the shadows. My pulse quickened as we weaved through the maze of streets, every corner holding the promise of an ambush. I could almost hear the echo of footsteps behind us, the weight of a thousand eyes on our backs.

We followed the trail—slow, deliberate. Every clue we found felt like a breadcrumb that led deeper into a forest of deceit. An old contact. A whispered name. A location scrawled in code, half-wiped from the face of a wall. It all pointed to the same place. A warehouse on the edge of the city, buried under layers of secrecy and forgotten by time.

The sun had barely set when we arrived. The place was abandoned, or at least that's what it seemed. The rusted gate creaked open under Jaxon's touch, and I stepped in after him, my boots crunching against broken glass and debris. The scent of oil, metal, and mildew clung to the air. It was a forgotten place—until we set foot in it. Then, it felt alive with the weight of ghosts, both old and new.

The inside of the warehouse was dim, shadows playing tricks on my eyes. The beams overhead groaned under their own weight, and every footstep seemed to echo louder than the last. I couldn't help but feel the tension creeping up my spine, curling around my ribs like an iron vice.

"Stay sharp," Jaxon's voice broke the silence, low and deliberate, the sound of it grounding me in the chaos. I nodded, my hand instinctively resting on the grip of my sidearm.

We moved like shadows through the space, our every breath a quiet invitation to danger. I could feel it, the pull of something unseen, waiting. My pulse quickened. A shift in the air. Then—footsteps. Not ours.

"Show yourself," Jaxon called out, his voice commanding, and for once, I didn't need to look at him to know he was smiling. He thrived in moments like this, when the darkness turned into a playground for the brave.

From the far corner of the warehouse, a figure emerged, tall and cloaked in the kind of darkness that even the dim lights of the space couldn't dispel. The man stepped forward, his face half-hidden in shadows, his eyes gleaming like chips of ice. He didn't speak at first, but I could feel his presence pressing against me, filling the room like a silent storm.

"Is this the part where you explain yourself?" I asked, my voice tinged with more annoyance than fear. I wasn't sure if that was brave or stupid, but at that moment, I didn't care.

The figure chuckled, the sound like dry leaves scraping against pavement. "You think you know everything, don't you? The Wraith was never just one person. It was a network. A system. And some of us are still… functional."

Jaxon's hand twitched, but he didn't reach for his weapon. "That's not what you're here for, is it? You're not just a remnant.

THE RUSE

You're the key to something bigger." His words weren't a question. They were a statement.

I watched the man's expression shift, the corners of his mouth pulling tight. The moment stretched between us, thick and dangerous.

"You're late," the man finally said. "But I've been expecting you."

I should have known it wouldn't be that easy. The way the man's lips curled, the way his eyes didn't quite meet mine—they gave away more than he realized. And yet, despite everything, I couldn't shake the nagging sense that we were both playing a game none of us understood.

He took a step forward, his boots scraping the concrete floor in a slow, deliberate rhythm. The smell of stale air and gasoline clung to everything, a constant reminder of the underbelly of New Chicago, where even the light seemed to struggle for dominance.

"I hope you've come prepared," he said, his voice deep and smooth, like he'd practiced his lines a thousand times. His gaze flickered to Jaxon, then back to me, his smirk never wavering. "You're not the first ones to chase ghosts."

Jaxon didn't flinch. I, on the other hand, was starting to feel the weight of our situation pressing down. Something about the way the man spoke—calm, confident—made my skin crawl. It was the kind of certainty you didn't just acquire. It was earned, honed through years of manipulation, strategy, and an almost terrifying understanding of the game we were all caught in.

"We're not here for stories," Jaxon replied, his voice cutting through the thick silence. "We're here for answers."

The man's smirk flickered, almost imperceptibly. "Answers? I'm afraid those are hard to come by. The Wraith was never about answers. It was about control. Power. And as long as there are people willing to play, it never ends."

It was a statement that made my stomach tighten. Control. Power. Two things I'd spent most of my life trying to avoid, and here, in this empty warehouse, they hung in the air like an impending storm.

Jaxon took a step forward, his shadow casting long against the walls, "Who are you? And what do you know about the Wraith?"

The man chuckled, a dark, throaty sound that did nothing to ease the growing tension. "Who am I?" he repeated, almost amused. "That's a story you'll have to unravel yourself. But I'll give you this—there's more to the Wraith than you think. You think you've seen it all, but the truth is, you've only seen a fraction."

A fraction. The word hung in the air like a challenge. I could feel Jaxon's presence beside me, solid, unwavering, but I also felt the weight of the unknown pressing down on us both. This wasn't just about finishing something that had started years ago; this was something new, something we hadn't even begun to understand.

"And why should we trust you?" I asked, my voice sharper than I intended. "You're just another link in the chain, aren't you?"

The man's eyes locked onto mine, piercing, as if measuring my every word. "Trust?" He repeated the word as if it were foreign to him. "Trust is a commodity. One you'll find in short supply the deeper you go. But I'll tell you this—if you want to know the truth, the one thing you can trust is the game. And in this game, there's no way out. Only survival."

There was something about the way he spoke—something that made me shiver. Survival. I had heard it before, from the people who lived on the edge, in the places where you didn't ask questions unless you were ready for the answers. The kind of survival that didn't leave room for second chances.

The silence stretched between us again, and I could feel the weight of it, like the heavy hands of fate, slowly tightening. Jaxon

THE RUSE

shifted beside me, his eyes never leaving the man, the muscles in his jaw flexing with tension.

"Enough of this," he said finally, his voice cold, controlled. "What do you want?"

The man's smile was slow, almost calculated, and for a moment, I almost believed that whatever came next would be the end of us. But it wasn't. Instead, he reached into his coat, his movements smooth and deliberate, like he was trying to draw out the moment. I didn't breathe, didn't move, not even when he pulled out a small, black device, the kind you'd see in spy movies—the sort of thing that made your heart race without you even knowing why.

He clicked a button, and a holographic display flickered to life in front of us, illuminating his face in ghostly light. The image was fuzzy at first, a jumbled mess of shapes and colors, but then it cleared.

A map of the city.

But this wasn't just any map. It was marked. With symbols. Red circles. Lines drawn in a jagged, chaotic pattern.

"It's all connected," the man said, his eyes glinting with a mixture of pride and something darker. "These marks? They're locations. Safe houses. Drop points. The remnants of The Wraith's empire. And they're all still active."

I felt the floor shift beneath me. A sinking feeling in the pit of my stomach. "You're telling me there are more?" I asked, my voice coming out hoarse despite the calm I was trying to project.

"More?" The man repeated, his gaze flickering to the hologram. "The Wraith wasn't just one person. It wasn't just an organization. It was a system, a network of influence. You're looking at the heart of it. But the real question is, why hasn't it died? Why hasn't it all come crashing down?"

He took a step closer, his voice dropping to a dangerous whisper. "Because some of us never left. And we've been waiting for the right moment. A new leader. A new vision. And that, my friends, is where you come in."

I met Jaxon's eyes. His jaw was clenched, his expression unreadable, but I could feel his unease vibrating between us like an electric current. He was already calculating, already thinking three steps ahead. But I wasn't so sure we were ready for what was coming next.

Not by a long shot.

The map flickered before us, glowing faintly in the dim warehouse light like some sort of twisted treasure chart. Red circles. Jagged lines. It was more than a blueprint; it was a game board, and every piece, every symbol, was an open invitation to chaos.

I wanted to step forward, to demand the answers I needed, but something in the back of my mind told me to hold back. This wasn't just another cryptic message. It wasn't some leftover piece of The Wraith's broken empire. This was something else entirely.

Jaxon seemed to feel it too. His eyes never left the man standing in front of us, but the tension in his jaw was undeniable. "A new leader?" he repeated, his voice an edge sharper than a knife. "And you think that's us?"

The man smiled, a cool, calculating smile, one that didn't reach his eyes. "Not 'think,' my friend. I know."

I couldn't help it. I laughed, a short, incredulous sound that bounced off the walls like a ricochet. "And what makes you so sure?"

He paused, the smile lingering just long enough to unsettle me. "Because I've been watching you. Both of you. Long before you even knew who I was."

I saw Jaxon's hand twitch. Not for a weapon, but for control—he was measuring the man with that intense focus of his, and I could almost hear the calculations running through his mind. His instincts were deadly, and they were sharpening by the second.

"I don't have time for this," I snapped, stepping forward, matching the man's cool gaze. "You either give us what we want, or we walk. There are plenty of other places in this city where you can disappear."

The man's lips twitched, as if amused by my words. "Ah, but you won't. You never do. You can't afford to." He waved a hand toward the hologram, where the red circles continued to blink ominously. "These aren't just random spots. They're hubs. They're critical points that keep the network alive. And those who control them? They control the city. You think you can walk away, but the moment you do, you'll become part of the game. You'll always be one move behind."

I could feel my heartbeat thumping in my chest, the adrenaline already spiking. "You're a strategist," I said, the words rolling off my tongue as a quiet realization hit me. "You've been setting this up for a while, haven't you?"

The man didn't answer immediately. Instead, he took a small step back, as if savoring the moment, watching us both with a mixture of amusement and something darker. "It's never been about survival," he said, almost conversationally. "It's about control. Always control."

The weight of those words hit me harder than I expected. Control. It was a concept I had danced around for so long—both the pursuit of it and the fear of losing it. And now, standing in this forgotten warehouse, I realized how deeply rooted it was in every corner of this city, in every twisted deal, in every life it had ruined.

Jaxon exhaled, the sound sharp, like he was releasing more than just air. "I didn't come here for philosophy."

"Then you came for the wrong reasons." The man's tone was laced with finality, the kind that made my stomach churn. He straightened up, his dark silhouette blending into the shadows like he was part of the very darkness that surrounded us. "But maybe you're right about one thing. You can't walk away. Not after what's coming."

I looked at Jaxon, his face unreadable, his body tense as if preparing for something I couldn't see yet. He turned back to the man. "What are you talking about?"

Before the man could answer, the lights overhead flickered. Once. Twice. The cold hum of the old warehouse seemed to grow louder, the air around us vibrating with the kind of tension that made every nerve in my body snap to attention. And then the door at the far end of the warehouse burst open with a crash.

I spun around, my instincts firing before I even processed the movement. Figures poured into the room, all wearing black, faces obscured by masks. The sound of heavy boots hitting the concrete echoed in the space, creating a heartbeat that drowned out everything else. A dozen bodies, maybe more, all moving with precise coordination. There was no hesitation in their steps. No fear.

For a split second, I felt the world tilt beneath me, the gravity of the situation settling like a heavy weight on my chest. The man had known we were coming, had expected it. He hadn't just set us up for a conversation. He'd set us up for a trap.

Jaxon's hand shot out, grabbing my arm, pulling me back to him as he assessed the situation with lightning speed. "Don't move," he whispered, his voice rough with urgency.

I didn't need to be told twice. My hand slid to the grip of my gun, fingers curling around the cold metal, my body primed for the inevitable confrontation.

The masked figures formed a circle, closing in around us. The man stood just behind them, his expression still unreadable, but now there was something else. Something deeper in his eyes that made my blood run cold.

"This isn't just a game," he said, his voice carrying across the room with an unsettling calmness. "This is the beginning. And you two? You're in the center of it."

I didn't look at Jaxon. I didn't need to. We had been through enough together to know what came next. But the sinking feeling in my stomach—the one that had been gnawing at me since the moment we stepped into this trap—told me that whatever we were facing, it was bigger than we'd imagined.

And for the first time, I wasn't so sure we were going to make it out.

Chapter 23: Shadows of the Heart

The city hummed below us, a low, steady pulse that thrummed through the bones of the concrete beneath my feet. The moon was a thin slice of silver above, its light caught in the haze of city lights. I stood on the rooftop, the wind threading through my hair, tugging at the hem of my jacket. My fingers were numb from the chill, but it wasn't the cold that made me tremble. It was him. Jaxon.

He stood a few paces away, the glow from the streetlights casting his face in shifting shadows, giving his features an otherworldly quality. There was something about the way the light caught the sharpness of his jaw, the hard edge of his brow, that made him seem like a man who existed outside of time. A man who belonged to the dark. But tonight, in the vastness of the night sky and the sprawling city that never truly rested, he felt like the only thing solid in a world that felt too fluid. Too dangerous.

"I'm not good at this," I said, my voice sounding too small, too fragile against the roar of the distant city. I knew I had to say it, knew I had to say it to him, but the words caught in my throat like stones. There were so many things that had remained unsaid between us, so many things I had kept hidden, even from myself. Love wasn't something I was familiar with, not in its truest sense. Trust was foreign. It had always been easier to let the walls remain, to let the shadows guard my heart. But tonight, for reasons I couldn't explain, I wanted to let him in.

Jaxon turned to face me, the soft curl of his lips barely visible in the dim light. He didn't speak right away, didn't rush to fill the silence with hollow words. He simply stood there, the quiet between us as thick as the night air, letting me gather my thoughts, my courage.

"I don't know how to let people in," I continued, my words thick with the weight of years of being closed off. "I've always kept everyone at arm's length. Love, trust... it's not a luxury I've ever had. Not really. Not the way I should have."

He took a step forward, then another, until we were inches apart. My breath caught in my chest, the heat of his presence pulling me into him like gravity. His eyes never left mine, and I saw something there—something soft, something real—that made my heart stutter.

"I'm not asking you to let me in all at once," he said, his voice a gravelly whisper that seemed to slide under my skin. "I'm not asking for promises you're not ready to make."

I could feel the pull of his words in my bones, felt the way they both soothed and stirred. Jaxon wasn't asking for everything. He was asking for something more dangerous—he was asking for trust. And the worst part was, I could feel myself wanting to give it to him. I could feel the walls I had spent so many years building starting to crumble, piece by piece, as his gaze held me captive.

"I'm scared," I admitted, the confession slipping out before I could stop it. It was a weakness I wasn't accustomed to showing, but it was there—raw and unshielded. "I'm scared of what'll happen if I let go. Scared of... losing control."

Jaxon's hand reached out, warm and steady, and he took mine in his. It wasn't a move of passion, not at first. It was a quiet offer, a gesture that felt almost reverent. He didn't force anything, didn't push for more than I was willing to give. His thumb brushed lightly over the back of my hand, grounding me in a way that felt so simple, yet so monumental.

"Maybe control isn't what you need," he said, his voice low and intimate. "Maybe it's trust. Maybe it's surrender."

The word felt like a shock of electricity, jolting through me. Surrender. I wasn't sure if I was ready for that. If I ever would be. But the way he said it—like it wasn't a weakness, like it was something strong, something necessary—made me wonder if I had been wrong all this time.

I wanted to pull away, to retreat into the safety of what I knew, but there was something in his touch, something in the weight of his words that held me fast. "And what if I can't give you that?" I asked, my voice almost a whisper.

He leaned in closer, so close that I could feel the heat of his breath on my cheek, the brush of his lips near my ear. "Then we'll figure it out together," he murmured, his voice like silk, his words a promise. "But I'm not going anywhere."

The way he said it—so sure, so unwavering—struck something deep within me. A part of me wanted to fight it, to tell him that nothing was ever as simple as it seemed, to remind him that people always left, no matter how much they promised to stay. But in that moment, with the city below us and the stars above, I couldn't deny the truth that was beginning to bloom in my chest.

I didn't know what would come of this. I didn't know what the future held, or whether I could ever truly let go of the past that had clung to me like a shadow. But I knew one thing with unshakable certainty—I didn't want to walk away from him. Not tonight. Not now.

His hands found my face, cupping it gently, and he kissed me—not with the desperation of someone trying to claim me, but with the quiet reverence of someone who knew the fragility of what we were building. The kiss was slow, like the first rays of dawn creeping over the horizon, tentative but sure. And for the first time in a long while, I allowed myself to be lost in it.

The shadows of my past still lingered in the corners of my mind, whispering doubts, reminding me of the pain that had shaped me. But in that moment, with Jaxon's hands gently holding me, with his lips against mine, I let them fade into the distance. I wasn't sure what love looked like, but for the first time, I was willing to let it find me.

The city buzzed beneath us, an electric pulse of life that seemed to stretch out forever, humming with the weight of a million unspoken stories. I could feel the rhythm of it deep in my chest, thrumming beneath my skin. It had always been like this, this feeling of being too small to fit in such a vast, noisy world, and yet, somehow, impossibly part of it. I'd grown used to it, the solitude and the noise mingling, drowning out the emptiness in my heart with the distant roar of life.

But now, with Jaxon standing there beside me, that solitude felt different. His presence was a weight I hadn't anticipated, one that grounded me in ways I couldn't explain. His hand still held mine, warm and steady, and despite the looming shadows of my past, despite the doubts and fears twisting in my stomach, I felt a strange sense of calm in his touch. Like maybe, just maybe, I wasn't alone after all.

"So," I said, breaking the silence that stretched between us, my voice sounding more uncertain than I meant it to, "what happens now?"

Jaxon didn't answer right away. Instead, he watched me, as though he were weighing my words, deciding whether or not I was ready to hear whatever it was he might say. The city lights flickered behind him, casting faint reflections across his face. His jaw was tight, his expression unreadable for a moment, but then he sighed, a soft exhale that made the tension between us ease just slightly.

"What do you think happens now?" he asked, his voice low, but not in a way that made me shrink. More like it invited me in, asking me to be brave enough to voice whatever fears I was hiding.

I could feel the walls starting to rise again, instinctively, but I pushed them down with a force I didn't know I had. He was right. This was my moment to speak up, to stop running. The truth tasted bitter on my tongue, but I forced it out anyway. "I think I'm scared," I admitted, swallowing hard, feeling exposed. "Scared of what this could mean, scared of how quickly everything is changing. I've never let someone in like this. Not like this."

He nodded slowly, as if the admission didn't surprise him. As if, perhaps, he'd been waiting for me to say it aloud. "Yeah," he said quietly. "I get that. But that's okay."

His words hung in the air between us, weightless and delicate, like a fragile thread stretching taut. "I'm not asking you to figure it all out tonight. I'm just here. Whenever you're ready."

I blinked, taken aback by the simplicity of his response. But it was the sort of simplicity that made everything I'd been struggling with seem a little less complicated, a little less impossible. Maybe I didn't have to know everything. Maybe all I had to do was be here. Be with him.

But just as I opened my mouth to speak, something in the back of my mind shifted, dark and familiar, like a storm cloud rolling in. I pulled my hand away from his, startled by the sudden rush of cold air between us.

"I don't know if I can do this," I blurted, my words tumbling out faster than I could stop them. "I don't know if I can trust anyone. I've... I've spent so long building these walls around myself, you know? It's easier to just keep people at a distance. Easier to push them away before they get too close. That way, they can't hurt me."

The words felt raw as I said them, like peeling back a layer of skin to expose the soft, vulnerable parts beneath. It had always been easier to push people away, to keep things light and casual, because real connection? Real intimacy? That was dangerous. That was where things got messy. And I couldn't afford to get messy. Not again.

Jaxon's face softened, and he stepped closer, but he didn't try to touch me. Instead, he simply leaned against the low wall of the rooftop, watching me with an intensity that made my breath catch. "I get it," he said quietly. "Trust is hard. I know that better than anyone."

I felt the weight of his words, heavy with something I couldn't name. The vulnerability in his voice was so raw, so unguarded, that it made me ache. "You don't know everything," I replied, my voice trembling. "You don't know how deep it goes, how far back this goes."

"I don't need to know everything," he said, his voice steady, but there was something in his eyes, something unspoken, that told me he wasn't just talking about me anymore. "I just need you to know that I'm not going anywhere."

I wanted to laugh, bitter and sharp, but I bit it back. That was the problem, wasn't it? People always said that—always promised they weren't going anywhere—but in the end, they did. They always did. And yet, standing here with him, something in my chest cracked open. A tiny seed of hope, fragile and delicate, began to take root.

"I don't know how to do this," I said, my voice small now, vulnerable. "I don't know how to let myself trust. But I think... I think I want to try. With you."

The words were a breath, a fragile offering, and I felt myself holding my breath as if waiting for some sort of judgment, some sign that I'd said the wrong thing, that I was still too broken, too messed up to deserve whatever this was. But Jaxon didn't look at me like I was broken. He didn't flinch at my admission of fear. Instead, he gave me a soft smile, the kind that made my heart flutter in ways I couldn't explain.

"You don't have to have it all figured out, not tonight," he said again, his tone warm. "You just have to take one step forward. And if that step is with me, I'll be right there with you."

The quiet settled around us, thick and comforting. For the first time in as long as I could remember, I allowed myself to believe that maybe, just maybe, I wasn't walking this road alone.

The silence between us deepened, curling around the words we hadn't spoken, the questions left unasked. I could feel my heart, heavy with a thousand things left unsaid, trying to break free from the walls I'd built around it. It was a strange sensation, a mix of fear and hope, like standing at the edge of a cliff and wondering whether you should jump or turn back. The world felt impossibly close, yet impossibly far, and for the first time in a long while, I wanted to reach out and touch it. To feel something real.

Jaxon's fingers brushed mine again, just the slightest of touches, but enough to make me feel like I might shatter if he let go. I met his gaze, not sure if I was expecting reassurance or an ultimatum, but what I found was something softer. Something more profound.

"You don't have to be perfect," he said, his voice rough, but gentle, as though he knew I was still holding onto something. "Hell, I'm not perfect. We both know that. But I want to try. To figure it out with you. No pressure, no rush. Just... us."

His words hung in the air like a lifeline. No pressure, no rush. I let them settle into me, the warmth of them, the unexpected tenderness that came with the honesty in his eyes. But there was still something gnawing at me, something I couldn't quite shake off. My past, those shadows that never seemed to let go, whispered in the back of my mind, reminding me that things like this—trust, connection, vulnerability—were never as simple as they seemed.

"You say that like it's easy," I muttered, pulling my gaze from his, trying to regain some semblance of control over the chaos inside my chest. "But it's not. It's never been easy."

He sighed, the sound low and understanding, like he could feel the weight of my hesitation pressing against him. He reached up, cupping my cheek gently, his touch warm and steady. I let him. There was something about him, something that made it almost impossible to resist.

"I know it's not," he said softly. "But sometimes... sometimes the hardest things are the ones worth fighting for."

The words struck me in the chest like a sudden gust of wind. It was as if the air around us shifted, a subtle change that was barely perceptible but heavy with significance. I could feel the gravity of the moment, the weight of what was being offered between us. And yet, I couldn't shake the uncertainty that lurked at the edges of my thoughts, the sharp prickle of fear that refused to let me be fully present, fully trusting.

"I want to believe you," I whispered, more to myself than to him. "I really do. But there's this part of me... I don't know if I can make myself believe that this will be different."

Jaxon was quiet for a long moment, his hand still resting against my cheek, his thumb tracing the curve of my jaw in slow, soothing strokes. "I'm not asking you to believe right away," he said, his voice low and steady. "I'm just asking you to give it a chance. To give us a chance."

The words were a balm to the raw places inside me, the places I'd kept hidden for so long, and yet, the shadows still lingered. I wanted to trust him. I wanted to let go of the doubt, to stop clinging to the remnants of past hurts and disappointments. But there was a part of me that couldn't shake the fear. The fear that this—whatever this was—was too fragile to hold. That it would slip through my fingers, just like everything else I'd ever tried to keep.

And yet, despite that fear, there was something else. A pull, something deeper than reason or logic. Something that made my chest ache in a way that felt both terrifying and comforting.

"I'm scared of getting hurt again," I admitted, the words slipping out before I could stop them. "I've spent so long building walls around myself, keeping people out. It's easier that way."

Jaxon's expression softened even more, his thumb still moving gently along my skin, as if trying to soothe the storm inside me. "I get it," he murmured. "But you don't have to do this alone."

I looked up at him then, really looked at him, and something in the quiet strength in his eyes made my heart stutter. Maybe it wasn't about being alone. Maybe it was about learning how to trust again. To let someone in, even if it felt impossible. Maybe, just maybe, I could find a way to make peace with my past and take a step forward into something new. Into something real.

But just as I started to believe it, just as I started to feel that fragile flicker of hope, something shifted. A sound in the distance, faint but unmistakable. A voice calling my name.

I tensed, the sudden intrusion snapping me out of the moment like a cold slap. My gaze darted toward the edge of the rooftop, where the sound had come from. The world around us seemed to hold its breath, waiting.

"Do you hear that?" I asked, my voice barely above a whisper.

Jaxon stiffened, his eyes narrowing as he strained to listen. His hand dropped from my face, his body suddenly alert, every muscle tense. The sound came again, louder this time, unmistakable. A voice. A voice I recognized.

"Ella..."

The air seemed to crackle with tension as I turned toward the source of the sound, the words hanging in the night like a warning, a promise of something that was about to change everything. I had no idea who it was, but I could feel the pull of it, the way it knotted up the space between us, the way it unsettled the fragile peace we'd started to build.

Jaxon's hand found mine again, tight and urgent. "Stay close to me," he murmured, his voice low, a shadow of something else creeping into it. "Something's not right."

And just like that, everything shifted again. The world I thought I understood suddenly tilted, and the sense of security that had just begun to settle in me shattered like glass.

Chapter 24: The Calm Before the Storm

The sun had slipped behind a veil of clouds, casting the small town in a muted light that felt both peaceful and ominous. We didn't speak much as we made our way to the little café tucked between a bookstore and a laundromat, but it wasn't an uncomfortable silence. It was the kind of quiet that wrapped around you like an old sweater—familiar, warm, and comfortable in its own way, especially after the whirlwind of events that had become the new normal for us.

I pushed open the door, the bell above it tinkling like a gentle promise, and a rush of warm, aromatic air filled my lungs. The scent of freshly brewed coffee mixed with the faint sweetness of cinnamon rolls and chocolate croissants, and for a moment, it was easy to pretend that life wasn't a constant series of explosions, both literal and metaphorical. The barista behind the counter, a young woman with purple-tipped hair and an exuberant smile, greeted us with an enthusiasm that almost seemed out of place given the tense undertones we carried. But her lightness was a welcome contrast, something to hold onto as I tried to reset my spinning mind.

Jaxon ordered first, his voice low but firm as always. He glanced over at me as he waited for his coffee, his dark eyes flickering with a hint of something I couldn't quite place—perhaps it was relief, or maybe just an inkling of distraction. Whatever it was, it made him seem more... human. More like the person he'd been before we found ourselves tangled in this mess.

"What's it like for you?" I asked suddenly, without thinking. The question slipped out like a secret I hadn't even known I was holding. I wanted to know what it felt like to live with the weight of so much responsibility on his shoulders, to carry the kind of knowledge he did without shattering beneath it.

He raised an eyebrow, his lips quirking into a half-smile. "Like a vacation, obviously."

"Right," I said, chuckling at his sarcasm. But then, after a beat, I couldn't help myself. "Seriously, Jaxon. You've got this whole 'cool and collected' thing down, but I'm guessing it's not always like that. Tell me—what's it like when you're not... being the hero?"

His smile faltered, but only for a second. Then it was gone, replaced by that careful mask of his. "I'm always the hero, Lila. It's just—well, it's just the way it has to be."

I frowned, watching him for any sign of something more—anything that might explain the guarded nature that had become second nature to him. But there was nothing. He was an enigma wrapped in a layer of steel, and I wasn't sure how much more of it I could take.

"I'm not sure if I believe you," I said softly, my voice barely above a whisper. "But if you're right, then maybe you deserve this moment. Just a moment, you know? To breathe."

For a long moment, there was nothing but the hum of the café around us, the clink of spoons against ceramic mugs, and the soft murmurs of conversations that sounded so far removed from everything we'd been through in recent days. I closed my eyes for a moment, letting the peace of it all wash over me, and for a heartbeat, I almost believed that things could return to normal. That I could sit across from him, sipping my coffee, laughing at some absurd remark he made, and never have to face the storm that always seemed to be lurking just around the corner.

The barista placed our cups on the counter, snapping me from my reverie. I reached for mine, cradling the warm ceramic in my hands as I inhaled deeply. The bitterness of the coffee wasn't a distraction—it was a reminder that some things hadn't changed, even if everything else had. Jaxon reached across the table, giving me a small, knowing look as he took his own cup in hand.

"You know," he said, a hint of a smile playing at the corners of his mouth, "for someone who insists on being a realist, you sure do dream big."

I laughed, not because it was funny but because it felt good. To laugh at anything, to have a moment that was just ours, unmarred by the mess we were in. "Big dreams," I echoed, stirring my coffee idly. "Maybe that's the only thing left worth holding onto."

"Then don't let go of them," he said, his voice steady, the words weighted in a way that felt too much like a warning.

I opened my mouth to reply, to try and lighten the mood again, but before I could speak, the sharp, jarring sound of a distant explosion rattled through the windows. It wasn't a dull thud—it was a violent, shaking force that seemed to ripple through the air itself. The room stilled, the air thickening with a collective intake of breath.

Jaxon's eyes darkened, his hand already moving to his side, fingers brushing against the handle of the concealed weapon beneath his jacket. I barely had time to process what had happened before he was standing, his chair scraping loudly against the floor.

"We need to go," he said, his voice cold and commanding. There was no hesitation in his tone—only an urgency that snapped me to attention.

I didn't ask any questions, didn't even try to process it. I simply stood, leaving the cup behind as I followed him out the door, my heart pounding in my chest. The world outside had already started to crack under the strain of whatever had just happened. The once-calm street was now filled with shouting, panicked voices, the air thick with the smell of smoke and the distant sound of sirens. The calm had shattered, and in its place, there was only chaos.

And somewhere in the midst of it, I could feel the storm coming.

The blast had barely rippled through the air before Jaxon was already on the move, his body coiling like a spring, his eyes scanning the street with a predator's intensity. There was no time for hesitation. No time for questions. It was the kind of reaction that had been honed over years of survival, years of living in the shadow of chaos.

I barely kept up as he navigated through the crowd, pushing past startled pedestrians and the occasional delivery truck that had come to an abrupt halt at the sound of the explosion. The air felt thick, charged with something more than just the acrid smoke that began to snake its way toward us. It was as if the very pulse of the city had shifted, a shift I could feel deep in my bones.

"Where are we going?" I asked, breathless, as I tried to match his quick pace. My heart thudded wildly in my chest, the adrenaline already rushing through my veins, but there was still an edge of disbelief tugging at my thoughts. Was this really happening?

He didn't answer right away, his focus unbroken, but I could see the lines of tension on his face, could feel the weight of the decision that was already taking place in his mind. "The source," was all he said, and in those two words, there was nothing but certainty. There was no room for doubt. He wasn't asking. He was telling. And somehow, that made everything feel even more urgent, more immediate. The calm we'd briefly shared now felt like a distant memory, a dream from a life that no longer existed.

As we rounded the corner, the sight of the street ahead stopped me dead in my tracks. The explosion had sent a shockwave that had splintered a nearby glass storefront, leaving shards of it glittering on the sidewalk like dangerous confetti. People were running in every direction, some screaming, some frozen in place, too terrified to move. The cacophony of sirens had already begun to fill the air, but it was the underlying tension—the knowing—that gripped me the hardest. There was something deliberate about this chaos. Something calculated.

Jaxon didn't slow down, didn't even glance back as I stood there for a moment, trying to process what I was seeing. It was only when he reached the corner of the block that I snapped back to reality, my legs pumping to catch up with him.

"What's going on?" I asked, the words coming out too quickly. My mouth was dry, but I couldn't stop myself. I needed to understand, needed some semblance of clarity before everything spiraled completely out of control.

"This wasn't just a random blast, Lila," he said, voice low, like he was talking to himself more than to me. His eyes flicked to the shadows that clung to the edges of the alleyway as we passed, scanning for any signs of movement. He was preparing for something. Whatever was coming next, he wasn't about to let it take him by surprise.

I felt a chill, not from the wind that had begun to pick up, but from the cold certainty that was creeping into his tone. It was as if he knew something I didn't—and if that were the case, I hated that I was being kept in the dark.

"Then what is it? What do we do?" My voice was sharper now, frayed at the edges. I wanted answers, not half-spoken riddles that only made the storm brewing inside me worse.

Jaxon finally glanced back, his gaze softening for the briefest moment as our eyes met. "We go to the source," he repeated, his tone still calm but edged with something darker now. "And we deal with it before it escalates."

It was then that I realized how much I depended on him in moments like this, how much his steadiness, his unwavering composure, held everything together. Even when everything felt like it was breaking apart, he was the anchor, the still center in a storm that had no clear end.

But that thought barely had time to settle before the ground beneath us seemed to shift again. The rumble of another explosion echoed in the distance, closer this time. My skin prickled with unease, and I had to force myself to keep moving.

"You're not telling me something," I said, more quietly this time, forcing the words through the tightening knot in my throat. "You don't just... 'deal with it.' Not like this. What aren't you saying, Jaxon?"

He didn't respond immediately, but I caught the flash of hesitation in his eyes before he turned away, taking long, purposeful strides toward the source of the blast. He was trying to shield me from something, I realized—something he didn't want to drag me into, no matter how deep I was already in it. But I wasn't naïve. I knew better than to believe I could remain on the periphery of whatever this was.

"I'm trying to keep you safe," he said, his voice tight now, the words rougher than they had been before.

And suddenly, I wasn't sure if he was talking about the explosion, or something else entirely.

We made our way through the maze of streets, the air becoming more charged with every step. The city, always so alive with noise, was eerily quiet now, like it was holding its breath. I could feel the tension in my chest building, the weight of the unknown pressing down on me, suffocating and yet invigorating at the same time. There was no turning back from this.

Finally, Jaxon stopped in front of a dilapidated building—a warehouse, I realized, with its rusted, corrugated iron sides peeling in the corners. The place was dark, save for a few flickering lights that barely cast any illumination on the street around it. The silence hung thick in the air, like it was holding some dark secret, and I couldn't shake the feeling that something terrible was about to unfold right before us.

"Stay close," Jaxon murmured, already reaching for the handle of his jacket. I could see the subtle movement of his hand—preparing for whatever came next, whatever lay within that darkness.

THE RUSE

My breath caught in my throat as I followed him into the shadows. The calm had passed, and with it, everything I thought I understood about the world around me. This was something else entirely.

The cold bite of the night air hit me as soon as we stepped into the alleyway. I followed Jaxon closely, the weight of what we were about to face settling heavily on my chest. The shadows swallowed us whole, and the city's usual hum felt distant, as though we had crossed into some other world where the rules didn't apply. The flickering streetlights cast erratic glows on the cracked pavement beneath our feet, and the soft thud of our shoes was the only sound that dared to break the tense silence between us.

"I don't like this," I murmured, my voice betraying the anxiety I was trying so hard to mask.

Jaxon didn't reply immediately. He didn't need to. His silence spoke volumes—his jaw tight, his hand brushing over the cool metal of his gun under his jacket. He was preparing for something. Something big. But what?

"What aren't you telling me?" I asked, more sharply than I intended. "Don't keep me in the dark, Jaxon. I'm not some bystander in this mess."

He shot me a quick glance, his eyes narrowing as though measuring whether or not he should share anything more with me. His lips pressed into a thin line. "It's not about keeping you in the dark. It's about keeping you alive."

There it was again—the subtle protectiveness in his words. The same instinct that had kept me at arm's length from the beginning. As much as I hated it, I couldn't deny that he was right. I didn't belong in his world, not really. His world was dangerous, filled with shadows I was still too naive to fully understand. But somehow, despite knowing better, I couldn't bring myself to walk away. Not now. Not when it felt like everything was about to fall apart.

We reached the front of the warehouse, its large, rusted doors creaking in the wind like an old man complaining about the cold. The place was a ghost of something long forgotten—except it wasn't forgotten. Whatever was happening here, whatever secret it was hiding, it was alive and waiting.

Jaxon moved closer to the building, his steps measured and deliberate. I followed, staying as close to him as I dared without feeling like I was stepping on his heels. I could feel the tension in the air, the kind that prickled my skin and made my heartbeat thunder in my ears. Something was about to happen. Something that would change everything.

Jaxon motioned for me to stay back as he reached for the door. It didn't budge. He cursed under his breath, trying the handle again. No luck.

I stepped forward, the urge to help, to do something, pushing me past my fear. "We need to get inside," I said, trying to sound like I wasn't about to lose my nerve. "Can't we just—?"

"We wait," he cut me off, his voice hard. "It's safer that way."

I opened my mouth to argue, but something in the way he looked at me—his gaze filled with both frustration and something else, something that felt like sorrow—made me close it again. I hated that he thought he could protect me from this. Protect me from him, maybe. But I wasn't going to sit back any longer.

We stood in silence for a long moment. The world around us felt like it had been paused, suspended in time. I could hear my breathing, shallow and uneven, as though my lungs didn't quite know how to process the air. I glanced at Jaxon, who was still focused on the door, his stance unyielding.

Then, in an instant, the moment cracked.

A muffled sound—like the snap of a twig underfoot—came from inside the building. My pulse quickened. The hairs on the back of my neck stood at attention. I could feel the shift, that shift in the air that preceded something terrible. Something was wrong. The building had been too quiet for too long.

Jaxon straightened, his hand now visibly gripping the gun under his jacket. "Get back," he whispered urgently, voice low enough that only I could hear it. He didn't have to say more. His warning was clear.

But I didn't listen. I couldn't.

The door swung open with a screech that sent a jolt through me. A shadow moved inside, swift and silent. Without thinking, I rushed forward, but Jaxon's arm shot out in front of me, his hand firm on my chest. I looked up at him, confused and angry.

"Not yet," he said, his voice tight, as though even the smallest crack in his cool demeanor would betray everything he'd been trying to hold together. "Stay behind me."

I wanted to argue, to insist that I could handle this. But the look on his face, a mixture of urgency and something deeper—something I couldn't place—made me swallow my words. He wasn't just protecting me. He was protecting something else.

And that's when it hit me. He wasn't scared for me. He was scared for us.

Before I could fully process the weight of that realization, a figure stepped into the doorway. Tall, broad-shouldered, and clad in dark clothing, the person was an immediate threat. My heart leapt into my throat as the figure stepped forward, just enough for me to see the glint of something cold in his hand.

"Well, well," the voice was familiar, too familiar. It was a low, dangerous drawl. "Looks like you're already making yourself at home, Jaxon. That's a little bold, don't you think?"

My breath caught, my stomach dropping to my knees. I knew that voice.

But I didn't know how to survive it.

Before I could react, before I could ask anything, the man raised his arm, and the world around us plunged into darkness.

Chapter 25: The Rising Tide

The air in the room was thick with the hum of tension. Every time Jaxon slammed the file down onto the table, a shiver ran through me, like the soft scrape of nails across a chalkboard. He was losing his cool, and that was dangerous. I watched him, the sharp angles of his face carved in frustration, a muscle in his jaw twitching like it always did when he was about to speak—no, snap. I didn't need to hear him to know he was pissed. It was written all over him, in the tightness of his shoulders, the way his fingers rapped against the wood like a countdown.

"What do you think?!" he snapped, his eyes blazing at me. "I've checked every angle—every damn one—and nothing makes sense. The deeper we dig, the more people we have to look over our shoulder for. Do you have anything?"

It wasn't the kind of question that expected an answer. It was the kind of question that came when you were running on fumes, where the frustration built until you couldn't hold it in any longer. And yet, there was something in the way his voice cracked on that last word, something raw and desperate, that kept me from simply nodding and staying quiet.

I leaned in, lowering my voice. "We keep going. That's all we can do." My words were careful, measured, but inside, my heart was beating too fast. I hated seeing him like this. Hated seeing him so close to breaking. The walls were closing in on both of us, and there wasn't a way out. Not yet.

"Great," Jaxon muttered, raking a hand through his hair, the dark strands sticking out like he'd been pulling at them all night. "Keep going. Right. Because that's working."

I stood, moving toward the window to give him some space, trying to ignore the way the late afternoon sunlight bounced off the dusty glass, casting long, restless shadows across the room. The silence between us hung like a heavy curtain, but even in it, I could feel the pulse of something unspoken, something heavy and warm. Maybe it was just me, but I couldn't shake the growing sense that every second we spent together now was drawing us closer to something bigger than we realized. And it was terrifying.

The world outside felt different now. The usual bustle of the city had taken on a muffled quality, like we were on the verge of a storm. You could almost hear the impending crash if you listened closely enough. I could see the gray clouds creeping in from the west, a stark contrast to the orange and pink that had painted the sky just hours earlier. It wasn't the kind of sunset that made you want to linger and enjoy the view. No, this one felt like a warning.

"Are we sure we can trust her?" Jaxon's voice broke the silence. The question was soft, almost hesitant, like he was trying it on for size. I didn't turn to face him, but I felt the weight of his eyes on me, trying to gauge my response.

The woman he was referring to, Iris, was someone we'd met only days before. Smart. Calculated. And just a little bit dangerous. She had been helpful—at least, we thought she had been—but when you started peeling back the layers of who she really was, things got murky. Everyone had their secrets. But Iris? She seemed to have a whole damn vault of them, locked away and buried so deep it was hard to know where to even begin.

"I don't know," I admitted, my voice quiet. I could feel Jaxon's gaze on the back of my neck, sharp as a knife. "I don't think we can trust anyone right now. Not completely."

Jaxon grunted in agreement, though his tone was a little too raw, a little too pained. I turned back to face him, taking in the lines around his eyes, the dark circles from sleepless nights. He was unraveling. Slowly, but surely. And no matter how much he wanted to push it down, to ignore it, I knew it was eating him from the inside out.

"You're doing too much," I said, my voice firm. "You need to sleep."

He scoffed, but there was no real heat behind it. "Sleep is for the weak."

"Right. So when was the last time you ate something other than coffee and frustration?"

That made him laugh, though it was bitter, like he didn't really believe me. His shoulders dropped ever so slightly, just enough that I could see the exhaustion that had settled into his bones. The hard shell he'd built around himself was starting to crack, but I didn't know how to fix it. Not yet. All I could do was wait, keep my distance, but be close enough to catch him when he finally broke.

I took a step toward him, careful not to push too hard. I didn't want to make it worse. "Jaxon," I began, trying for softness, "this isn't just about you anymore. It's about us. And I'm not going anywhere. But you've got to let me in. We need to do this together."

He exhaled sharply, his breath coming in fast bursts. I couldn't tell if he was angry or just overwhelmed, but whatever it was, it seemed to settle into something more like resignation. Slowly, Jaxon lowered his head into his hands, rubbing his temples like it was the only thing keeping him grounded.

"I just want to fix this," he muttered, his voice rough.

I walked over and placed a hand on his shoulder, offering a small squeeze. "We will. I promise. But you're not in this alone."

His eyes met mine, and for the briefest moment, the wall between us crumbled. For all the things we hadn't said, for all the truths we hadn't yet uncovered, there was a quiet understanding that lingered in the space between us. It wasn't enough to solve the puzzle or stop the chaos that was unfolding, but it was something.

And it was the one thing that might keep us both from falling apart.

I tried not to dwell on the soft pressure of Jaxon's hand on my shoulder, how it lingered just a beat too long, how my pulse quickened every time our fingers brushed. The air between us was becoming charged, but I wasn't sure if it was the threat of what we were uncovering or something else entirely. Whatever it was, I couldn't afford to get distracted. Not now.

The next few days bled into one another, time warping into something strange and almost surreal. We had managed to corner a few more leads—distant, half-formed things that felt like wisps of smoke that would vanish at the slightest touch. But that wasn't what kept me awake at night. It was the growing realization that we were in deeper than I had first thought. And every time I felt like I had a grip on the situation, the ground would shift beneath me.

By midday, the sense of urgency was almost palpable in the small, cluttered office we were using as a base. Paper strewn across the desk, coffee cups stacked like little monuments to sleeplessness, and the faint hum of a nearby fan struggling against the suffocating heat. It had been weeks since the explosion, but the destruction still loomed over everything, like a shadow you couldn't shake.

Jaxon paced, his boots heavy on the floor as he shuffled through another stack of papers. I could hear his breathing, steady but shallow, like he was holding something back. I resisted the urge to ask if he was okay. It was a question he'd never answer honestly, and I didn't need him to. Not now.

"What if we're missing something?" he muttered, running a hand through his hair.

I raised an eyebrow, looking up from the mess of files I was trying to organize into something that made sense. "Like what? Another dead end?"

"No," he snapped, his eyes catching mine for just a moment. "I mean something we haven't even considered."

I paused, setting the papers down carefully. The tension in his voice wasn't lost on me. "Such as?"

He gave a sharp shake of his head, the frustration in his movements almost violent. "I don't know. Maybe it's not about what we're looking at, but who."

The words hung in the air, sharp and cold, like the sudden shift of a storm. It wasn't a new thought, but it felt different coming from him. Jaxon had always been the one to hold things close to the chest, preferring to work alone even when there was no reason to. But this—this was something else. Something personal.

"Who?" I asked, not daring to move too much. "Are you thinking it's someone we trust?"

His eyes met mine, steady, calculating. "I'm thinking it could be someone we've overlooked."

That was the moment I knew I had to trust him, even if it was against every instinct I had. He was onto something, even if it didn't make sense yet. We'd been looking at the wrong people for too long, too focused on the immediate danger. There was someone, or something, lurking beneath the surface, waiting for us to make the mistake of looking in the wrong direction.

"Iris," I said quietly, more to myself than to him.

Jaxon's head snapped toward me, his expression hardening in that way it always did when he was trying to keep his emotions in check. "What about her?"

I swallowed, the weight of what I was about to say pressing against my chest. "She's too clean. Too polished. Someone who fits in just a little too well."

The suspicion that had been niggling at me for days finally clicked into place. Iris's carefully curated answers, her smooth demeanor, her ability to slide into any conversation without missing a beat—it wasn't normal. She wasn't normal. It had never sat right with me, but I had ignored it, thinking it was just my overactive imagination. Now, I wasn't so sure.

"You think she's playing us?" Jaxon's voice was low, dangerous.

I nodded. "I do. I think she's hiding something."

There was a long silence, and for a moment, I thought Jaxon would argue. But then he just nodded, a sharp, decisive motion that told me he agreed.

"What's the plan?" he asked, the crackle of determination back in his voice.

I didn't have an answer yet. But I knew one thing for sure: Iris was more than just a helpful ally. She was a piece of the puzzle we hadn't even realized we were missing, and whatever game she was playing, we needed to figure it out fast.

By nightfall, the weight of the mystery felt like it was suffocating me. The faint glow of city lights outside our window did little to ease the sense of unease that had settled in my stomach. I had spent too much time in the darkness, too many hours trying to make sense of all the lies and half-truths that had been thrown at us. And yet, there was still no clear picture, just a blur of moving parts, all of them dangerous.

Jaxon was leaning over the desk, his focus unwavering as he combed through another set of documents. I could hear the soft rustling of paper, the faint tap of his fingers against the desk, his breath steady but thin. It was as if he was hanging by a thread, the slightest movement, the smallest gust of wind, could make him snap.

"I think she's got something we don't know about," I said, unable to hold back the words any longer.

Jaxon didn't look up. "We'll find out soon enough."

The certainty in his voice made something stir in me. I hadn't expected him to sound so confident, so sure of himself. But then again, I had learned by now that Jaxon wasn't someone who half-heartedly went after a problem. If he was focused, if he'd latched onto something, he wasn't going to let go until it had been solved.

"I don't know if I can trust her," I admitted, more to myself than to him. "Something doesn't feel right."

Jaxon's head snapped up, his eyes locking with mine. The intensity in them made my pulse quicken, the way he always seemed to see straight through me, to the parts I kept hidden. For a moment, I almost forgot to breathe.

"You don't have to trust her," he said softly, his voice lower than usual. "You just have to watch your back."

I nodded, though I wasn't sure which part of the conversation he meant more. Trusting Iris, or trusting myself. Either way, I knew one thing for certain: things were about to get a lot more complicated. And no matter how much I wanted to step away from it all, I wasn't going to let Jaxon face it alone.

We had been working for hours, the evening pressing in on us like a thick, humid fog. The flickering fluorescent lights overhead buzzed steadily, and the scent of stale coffee filled the room, blending with the sharp tang of ink and paper. There was no noise except for the occasional shuffle of papers or the low murmur of Jaxon muttering to himself as he paced the length of the small room, his frustration growing palpable.

The weight of everything—of the lives lost, the friends we didn't know we had, and the ones who might not be what they seemed—was beginning to sink in. And it wasn't just the case that was weighing on me anymore. It was the pull I felt toward Jaxon. Every time I looked up from the mess of files in front of me, my eyes would settle on him, his jaw clenched, his brow furrowed. I hated it. I hated that I couldn't focus, couldn't keep my head in the game. That I was watching him fall apart and not knowing how to stop it.

"Do you ever feel like we're just going in circles?" I asked, breaking the silence, my voice sharper than I intended.

Jaxon stopped pacing and shot me a glance, a half-smirk playing at the corner of his lips. "I think we've been in circles since the explosion. You're asking the wrong guy."

I sat back in my chair, rubbing my temples. The weight of my own exhaustion made it hard to think. I wasn't sure if it was the case, or the constant strain between us, or the way he looked at me when our hands brushed, but everything felt out of sync. Like we were teetering on the edge of something neither of us could define.

"I'm serious," I said, trying to keep my tone light despite the tightness in my chest. "I mean, we keep uncovering all this stuff, and we're still no closer to figuring out who's behind this. Or why. Or how we're supposed to stop it."

"I know." He ran a hand through his hair, clearly trying to keep his composure. "It feels like we're fighting shadows, doesn't it?"

It wasn't the first time he'd said something like that. The case had turned into a maze of half-truths, suspects who seemed too perfect to be guilty, and allies who were starting to feel like liabilities. There was something about Jaxon in those moments, the vulnerability he tried to bury under his tough exterior. And it was that, more than anything else, that had kept me rooted to this chaos. The sudden, inevitable truth that we were both in over our heads.

I stood up and stretched, a tightness in my back I hadn't noticed until now. "So, what's the next step?"

Jaxon turned to face me fully, his expression unreadable. "The next step is we get answers. And I think it's time we stop asking the wrong questions." He paused, letting that hang in the air between us. "We find out what Iris knows. And we do it tonight."

My stomach did a quick somersault. There had been moments—small, fleeting ones—when I thought maybe I could trust her. When her smiles were warm, her presence felt like something familiar, something safe. But now? Now it felt like I had been blinded by her charm.

"Are you sure?" I asked, more to myself than to him.

"No," he said flatly. "But we don't have a choice."

There was a hard edge to his voice that told me this wasn't a decision he'd come to easily. He was just as uncertain as I was, but neither of us had time to be. The weight of our choices felt heavier with every passing hour, and I knew this wasn't just a simple case anymore. This was personal. The conspiracies, the lies, the hidden alliances—it was all circling in on us.

I met his gaze and nodded. "Then we do it your way. But we need to be careful. This could backfire."

"Careful's not going to keep us safe. It's going to keep us in the dark. I don't have time for that."

His words sliced through the air, raw and sharp, and I found myself holding my breath. There was a dangerous resolve in him now, a fire that had been smoldering since this whole mess started, and it had ignited into something unpredictable. I didn't know whether I was scared of him or the truth. But either way, I was in this, locked in with him, no way out.

Hours later, we were standing in front of Iris's apartment building, the world outside dark and quiet. The weight of the night was settling in, the streets empty except for the occasional car driving past. I could feel the cool night air pressing against my skin, and I tucked my hands into my jacket pockets to keep them warm. It was too still, too silent. And that feeling—the one that whispered of impending danger—was crawling up my spine.

"I don't like this," I muttered under my breath, keeping my voice low.

Jaxon didn't respond, his eyes scanning the building with an intensity that made me uneasy. We hadn't discussed what we were going to do once we were inside. It didn't matter. We both knew the game was changing, and we had no idea how to play it.

"You sure she's here?" I asked, glancing at the building's entrance.

Jaxon nodded, though his jaw was tight. "I checked. She should be."

We stood there for a moment, the tension thickening in the air between us. I was about to speak when I heard the unmistakable sound of footsteps—quick, light, purposeful—coming from behind us.

I spun around, my heart leaping into my throat, but it was too late.

A figure stepped out of the shadows, and for a heartbeat, I thought it might be someone we knew. A friend, an ally, maybe even someone we could trust.

But the smile on their lips wasn't the one I had hoped to see.

"Did you really think you could find out what I was hiding?" The voice was smooth, low—like honey, laced with venom.

I knew the voice. I knew it. And my stomach dropped.

Before I could even move, a gun pressed to my side.

Chapter 26: Collateral Damage

I felt it before I saw it—the rush of tension in the air, thick and suffocating. Like the world had gone quiet, even though the constant hum of the city never really stops. We were in the midst of it now, my fingers still gripping the hilt of the blade I had snatched just minutes before. My chest burned, lungs fighting for air, but there was no stopping. No time.

The alley was narrow and slick with rain, the puddles reflecting a distorted version of reality, the neon signs from nearby shops painting everything in fractured red and blue. Jaxon was ahead of me, just out of reach, but close enough that I could hear his breaths—sharp, shallow gasps cutting through the night like a knife. I couldn't help but focus on the way his back tensed, his movements precise, calculated, every step a warning.

"You don't have to do this," I called to him, but my voice was swallowed by the roar of my own heart.

He glanced back, those dark eyes piercing through the shadows. He knew. He always knew. But he didn't answer. Because in his world, silence was a weapon. The Wraith's world had made him that way.

I took a breath, steadying myself against the cool stone wall, and then pushed off, trying to make my steps light, but the sound of my boots on wet pavement seemed deafening. I caught up to him just as he rounded the corner, his silhouette lost in the mist rising from the street. There were only a few steps left to go.

I hated the Wraith's organization. I hated what they did to people, how they twisted the lives of anyone who got too close. But somehow, I hated the way Jaxon had been pulled into it even more. I had tried to protect him from it, tried to pull him back from the edge, but when it came down to it, he always felt like the only thing that mattered was the mission. The job.

"You think we're getting out of this?" I asked, my voice a little too sharp. His shoulders tightened, a visible flinch.

"Don't start, Lila," he said through gritted teeth. His voice was colder than I had heard it in weeks, and the distance between us seemed to stretch, despite the fact that we were so close. Too close, really.

But it was too late to back down. There was nowhere to run now, no way to escape the reckoning that had been building ever since we'd first set foot on this path. The Wraith's people had been following us for days, getting closer, relentless. We had no choice but to face them.

Then, the crackle of a radio. I froze. Jaxon stopped too, a glance shot toward the sound, alert, the muscles in his jaw twitching. The air around us shifted—charged, like we were standing on the edge of something volatile. I swallowed hard, my grip tightening on the blade, heart pounding as the distant thrum of engines came into earshot.

"Get down!" Jaxon snapped, and before I could process it, he was pulling me toward the ground, a hard shove that knocked the wind from me. I hit the pavement with a sickening thud, pain shooting up my side.

The gunfire came next—fast, sharp, and deadly.

I didn't hesitate. Reflex took over. I pulled the knife from my side and threw myself toward Jaxon, moving in sync as we took cover behind a pile of crates. It was just the two of us against an entire organization of ruthless killers. No big deal.

"You good?" he asked, his voice low, the tension in his body still palpable. He had his back to mine, fingers poised, ready. Always ready. Always calculating.

I nodded, forcing myself to focus through the pain. I couldn't afford to slow down now, not when everything we had worked for—everything we had survived for—hung in the balance.

THE RUSE

"I'm fine," I muttered, though it was a lie. The blood dripping from my side said otherwise. But I couldn't let him see that. Not now.

We moved together, fluid and practiced, the world spinning around us as we fought for the only thing that mattered: survival.

I caught sight of the lead enforcer, his heavy footsteps echoing like thunder. I didn't hesitate. There was no time to hesitate. I sprang forward, the blade flashing through the air, aimed at the heart.

But before I could reach him, I heard it—the sound of a gunshot, too close. A sharp pain exploded in my shoulder, and everything went black for a second.

"Lila!" Jaxon's voice was frantic now, but there was nothing I could do. The blood flowed, warm and thick, soaking into my shirt. My knees buckled, and I barely managed to stay upright, leaning against the crates for support.

"I'm fine," I whispered through gritted teeth, but it was a lie again. I could feel myself slipping, the world starting to tilt, as my vision blurred. The stinging in my side wasn't helping. Nothing was.

Jaxon's face was a mask of fury as he reached for me, pulling me close. His breath was shaky against my skin, his words a tangle of frustration and fear.

"I won't let them take you," he said, his grip tightening on my arm, but there was no escape. No getting out of this.

I wanted to say something. To tell him I was sorry, that I should've never dragged him into this mess. But the words caught in my throat. I couldn't make a sound, couldn't even feel my legs anymore.

In the silence that followed, the weight of my choices hit me harder than any bullet ever could. I had done this. I had dragged him in. And now, I might lose him forever.

I closed my eyes, waiting for the inevitable.

But then, I heard the sound of footsteps. This time, they were different. The kind you can't fake. Soft, hesitant, but sure. I opened my eyes, blinking against the fog in my head.

And there, standing in the doorway of the alley, was the last person I ever expected to see.

Jaxon's expression flickered—surprise, disbelief, and something else I couldn't name. His grip on me loosened, just for a moment. Long enough.

And in that moment, everything changed.

The figure in the doorway wasn't who I thought it would be. It was a woman—sharp-featured, with hair dark enough to almost blend into the night, and eyes that burned through the haze like twin stars. She didn't look like someone who would be standing in an alleyway at midnight, surrounded by blood, bullets, and chaos. No, she looked like she belonged on a stage, a carefully rehearsed part in a play that was far beyond the likes of me. But her presence in that moment was undeniable, like a ghost pulling the strings.

Jaxon didn't move at first. He simply stared, his chest rising and falling, his breath sharp, strained. And for a beat, I wondered if he recognized her. If he'd ever been haunted by someone like her before. Maybe it was someone from his past. Maybe he wasn't the only one with a complicated history, after all.

"Lila," he said softly, as though he couldn't quite believe what he was seeing. His hand was still on my arm, but his focus was now entirely on her, and I felt that small, dangerous shift in the air, that ripple of something unspoken between them.

I didn't know what to do with that—didn't know if I was angry or hurt or just... too tired to care. The woman, meanwhile, wasn't waiting for an invitation. She stepped into the alley with a measured grace, her heels clicking against the wet concrete with every step.

"You should've known this was coming, Jaxon," she said, her voice smooth, almost too perfect for the situation. "You thought you could outrun your past, but it's always right behind you, isn't it?"

Her words stung, but I wasn't sure why. Maybe because they were true. Jaxon had spent too long running from whatever darkness followed him, and I had been foolish enough to think we could outrun it together. The cost of that illusion was spilling out around us now, and it tasted bitter in the back of my throat.

Jaxon didn't respond right away. He stood there, tense and still, like a man holding back a storm. His eyes darted between me and the woman, but whatever had been said between them in the past, whatever weight lay there, he wasn't sharing it with me. Not now, not when it mattered.

I could feel the blood pooling in my side, warm and sticky, but somehow, the pain wasn't the worst part of it. The worst part was knowing I had dragged Jaxon into this mess. Knowing that this fragile thread between us—this thing I couldn't even name, but I felt it in every beat of my heart—was about to snap.

I swallowed the bitterness rising in my throat. "Who are you?" I asked, trying to keep my voice steady, but even to my own ears, I sounded too raw, too exposed.

The woman smiled, but it wasn't a friendly smile. It was the smile of someone who knew exactly how much power they held over you, someone who'd played this game far longer than you ever had.

"You don't remember me, do you?" she asked, almost mockingly, as if I should've known. But I didn't. I had no idea who she was or what she wanted, but I could see the way Jaxon's body shifted, the way his eyes narrowed at the sound of her voice.

It was all coming together now—the silent, weighty conversations we never had. The things he hadn't said. The ways I'd ignored the shadows that followed him like a second skin. This woman, this stranger, wasn't just a random threat. She was a part of that shadow, a part of the life I had tried so hard to pull him away from.

"Jaxon," she said, stepping closer, "you and I both know this isn't over. Not by a long shot."

The tension in his body grew, coiling tighter, and for a moment, I thought he might actually snap. But then, to my surprise, he turned back to me, and there was a look in his eyes—a raw, vulnerable look that made my heart stutter in my chest.

"I need you to get up," he said quietly. "Now."

"Excuse me?" I blinked, unsure if I had heard him right. He had his back to the woman, but I could feel the energy in the air crackling between them.

"I'm not going anywhere without you," he added, his voice steady but there was a subtle urgency underneath, a crack in his calm exterior. "We need to move. Now."

I didn't understand. Why was he still thinking about escape when there was no way out anymore? We'd crossed the point of no return days ago, and now it was too late to run. All we had left was the wreckage of our choices.

But there was no time to argue. I felt him pull me gently but firmly, his hands strong around me despite the wildness in his eyes. And then, before I could even take another breath, the woman spoke again, her tone light, like she was merely offering a suggestion rather than a warning.

"You won't get far, you know," she said. "Even if you do manage to escape this night. The Wraith has eyes everywhere. The damage you've caused—it's bigger than you think. It's not just me who's been waiting for you, Jaxon. We all have. You can't outrun us."

The words hit like a slap. The Wraith? That name had been whispered through the streets, a shadow of terror. But hearing it—feeling it—suddenly felt more real than any ghost story ever had. It wasn't just a name. It was an entire network of people willing to burn everything to the ground to get what they wanted. And now, we were in their sights.

I looked at Jaxon, his face hardening, and it struck me—he wasn't afraid. But I was. Because I knew the truth now, as clear as the ache in my side. There was no way out. Not without sacrifice. Not without paying a price far heavier than either of us had anticipated.

Jaxon was already moving, his hand gripping mine as he led me toward the narrow exit at the end of the alley, but I couldn't shake the feeling that we were walking straight into a trap. That no matter how fast we ran, how hard we fought, it wouldn't be enough.

Because love—love had made us vulnerable. And in the end, it was going to cost us everything.

The streetlights flickered overhead as Jaxon pulled me through the darkened alley, his fingers gripping mine with a desperation that made my chest tighten. I tried to ignore the coldness creeping along my spine, the ache in my side that deepened with every step, and instead focused on the feeling of his hand against mine. It was an anchor, a lifeline in the chaos that was quickly closing in around us. But even that, as much as I hated to admit it, couldn't keep me from the truth.

The woman's words echoed in my mind, her voice too calm, too certain: The Wraith has eyes everywhere. I wasn't sure what was worse—the reality of it or the knowledge that Jaxon knew all too well what it meant. I had thought we were past the worst of it, that maybe we had a chance to breathe, to figure things out without the constant threat of death hanging over us. But that was a lie, a false hope built on the flimsy assumption that we could outrun our pasts.

"Where are we going?" I asked, my voice barely more than a whisper. My legs felt like lead beneath me, each step more difficult than the last, and I wondered how much longer I could keep up before my body gave out completely.

"Shh," Jaxon replied, glancing over his shoulder. His jaw was tight, his eyes scanning the darkness, as though he expected enemies to materialize from the shadows at any moment. "Just keep moving. We're close."

I didn't know if he meant close as in "we're almost there" or close as in "we're about to be surrounded by a dozen armed men." Either way, I wasn't sure how much more of this I could take. The world around us felt like a pressure cooker, everything closing in, and I was standing at the boiling point, waiting for it to explode.

My head spun, and I stumbled slightly, the pain in my side flaring up as I tried to steady myself. I didn't even know where we were going anymore. I just trusted Jaxon's instincts, and even that was becoming harder to do. Was it the right choice? Had I made the right choice?

He turned sharply down a side street, and I followed without question, though every instinct in my body screamed at me to stop, to look behind us. To look for the danger that was sure to be creeping ever closer. We had no idea what kind of firestorm we were running from, but I knew we weren't out of the woods yet. Not by a long shot.

"Are we... are we really doing this?" I asked again, this time louder, as though speaking the words might make them less real. Maybe if I said it enough, it would go away. But the moment the words left my lips, I regretted them.

Jaxon's grip tightened, and for a brief second, he looked at me—really looked at me—as though he could see right through the mask I had carefully placed over my face.

"We don't have a choice," he said, his voice low and steady. But there was something in it that made my pulse spike. Something that didn't quite add up. "This is the only way. We have to go to ground."

I didn't respond. What could I say? That I was terrified? That I wasn't sure if I could trust him anymore? That maybe, just maybe, we were in over our heads? No, there was no time for those questions. Not now.

THE RUSE

We kept moving through the streets, the wind picking up, rattling the leaves in the trees above us. The city felt empty at this hour—quiet, almost like it was holding its breath, waiting for the storm to hit.

And then, I heard it. A sound in the distance. A car engine.

I froze.

Jaxon's hand jerked me to a stop, his eyes narrowing, his posture instantly alert. He was already calculating, already three steps ahead, but this time, even he couldn't ignore the fact that we were both running out of options.

"I think we've been followed," he muttered, his voice barely audible. "Shit."

I felt a cold rush of fear shoot through me, and I instinctively pressed myself against the side of the building, my body shuddering from the effort of remaining quiet. Jaxon had already moved into the shadows, his form melding with the darkness, but I couldn't help but feel the weight of every second that passed. It was only a matter of time before the hunt would catch up with us, and when it did, there would be no more running.

The sound of the car grew louder. The unmistakable hum of an engine, followed by the screech of tires as it came to an abrupt stop not far from where we stood.

My heart beat in my throat, and I could feel the panic clawing at my chest, threatening to overwhelm me. It was too late to hide. Too late to run.

Jaxon cursed under his breath, his hand still gripping mine. "Stay close," he whispered urgently.

I barely nodded, too frozen to speak, too terrified to move. My entire body trembled as I waited for the worst to come.

The headlights flashed in the alley, casting long shadows that seemed to stretch for miles. The vehicle stopped just a few feet away, and I could see two men stepping out of the car—tall, muscular, their movements fluid as they scanned the area. It was as if they knew exactly where we were, knew exactly where to look.

And then, one of them looked directly at me.

My breath caught in my throat, and I squeezed my eyes shut, hoping against hope that they couldn't see me. But it was no use. They were too good. They'd been trained for this. For us.

The first man smiled—slowly, deliberately—and then said the one thing I never expected to hear.

"You didn't think you could run forever, did you, Lila?"

And just like that, I knew. We weren't running anymore. This was it.

Chapter 27: Love Among the Ruins

The first thing I noticed when I woke up was the air. It wasn't the sharp, sterile scent of the hospital room I'd been trapped in for weeks. No, this air smelled like salt and earth, like the promise of a storm that never quite came. My room was small, tucked in the corner of Jaxon's cabin, its wooden walls worn smooth by time and the salt of the sea. A slight breeze fluttered the white curtains by the open window, carrying the distant hum of waves crashing against rocks below. I tried to sit up but my body rebelled, each movement a reminder of my fractured ribs, bruised limbs, and the weight of what had happened to bring me here.

I was supposed to be dead. The thought lingered, chilling and relentless, even now. The memories of the explosion, the screams, the chaos—Jaxon's hands desperately pulling me from the wreckage, his voice steady as he told me to stay with him. But it was the silence after I blacked out that haunted me the most. I'd been so close to giving up, to letting go of the fight. But I hadn't. I was here now, and it was more of a miracle than I cared to admit.

I tried to push myself further up the bed, wincing as my ribs screamed in protest. That's when I felt him. The weight on the bed shifted and I turned to find Jaxon, his face shadowed by the dim morning light but his presence unmistakable. He was sitting on the edge of the mattress, his hand brushing against mine as if he couldn't help himself, as if touching me was the only way he knew I was still real.

"Hey," he said softly, his voice rough from days of worrying, or perhaps from something more. His lips twitched, trying to offer a smile, but it faltered as his eyes studied me with an intensity that nearly stole my breath away. I'd seen him fight battles—real ones, life-and-death ones—but this look was different. It was the kind of look I never thought I'd see from him. A look of vulnerability, of fear, so raw that it made me ache in places I hadn't realized were sore.

"I'm okay," I whispered, the words tasting foreign in my mouth. I wasn't sure if I was telling him or trying to convince myself.

"No," he muttered under his breath, shaking his head slowly. "You're not okay, but you will be. You're here, and that's all that matters."

His fingers curled tighter around mine, and I let him pull me gently into his arms, careful not to touch the spots where the bruises still marked my skin. His embrace was solid and warm, a refuge from the storm I'd been trying to outrun. It was the kind of warmth that seeped deep into your bones and made you wonder how you ever survived without it. For a while, neither of us spoke. The silence between us was comfortable, heavy with unspoken truths and a love that seemed to stretch out, infinite and uncertain all at once.

"Jaxon," I murmured after a while, pulling back slightly to look up at him. He met my eyes, his gaze unwavering despite the faint tremor in his jaw. I could see it now—the weight of everything that had happened, the toll it had taken on him. "Do you ever wonder if we're just... broken?"

His brow furrowed, and I could see the confusion flicker in his eyes. "What do you mean?"

"I mean, all of this," I gestured vaguely to the room, to our lives, to the wreckage that we'd somehow managed to claw our way through. "The chaos, the fights, the things we can't fix. I don't know if we're strong enough to survive this."

Jaxon let out a long breath, his hand smoothing my hair back as he looked away, out toward the window, where the ocean seemed to stretch forever into the horizon. His voice was steady when he spoke again, though there was an edge to it, something fierce. "Maybe we're not. Maybe we're two people who were never meant to be put back together after everything that's happened. But here's the thing..." He turned back to me, his gaze piercing, and for the first time in what felt like ages, I saw the old fire in his eyes—the one that made him seem invincible. "You and I, we've already survived worse than this. The rest of the world can't break us. Not when we're together."

The words settled between us like a pact, a promise neither of us could break. The past few days had been filled with the quiet hum of recovery, the healing of bones and skin, but what had been broken in my heart and mind wasn't so easy to fix. And yet, as I looked at him, the certainty in his voice settled some of the storm inside me. We might not have all the answers, but we had this—whatever this was.

I opened my mouth to respond, but the words stuck in my throat, tangled in the mess of emotion that swelled inside me. It wasn't enough to say that I loved him—that I always would. Because I knew that love wasn't something you simply declared; it was something you showed, day after day, in the small, quiet ways you held each other together when the world tried to tear you apart. And in that moment, as I rested against him, our hands still tightly clasped together, I realized I wasn't afraid anymore. No matter what came next, I was ready to fight—not just for him, but for us.

And maybe, just maybe, that was enough.

The first time I ventured out of the cabin after days of being holed up in bed, I was greeted by a sun that felt too bright for my battered eyes and a wind that seemed to laugh at my fragile attempts to stand upright. The beach, only a short walk away, stretched out before me like an old friend who hadn't been around in far too long. The sand, white as sugar and soft beneath my feet, felt different now—familiar, but tinged with the weight of everything that had happened.

I paused, breathing in the air as though it could fill in the cracks in my soul. The sea was wild today, its waves churning and crashing in a frenzy, much like the turmoil inside me. My body still ached—there were days when it was a dull, constant throb, and others when it flared up like a burn—but I had to keep moving, had to keep pretending I wasn't broken. That's how I'd always coped. Pretend long enough, and maybe, just maybe, you'd start to believe the lie.

Jaxon was at my side, as always, but today there was something in his step that caught my attention. He was walking with a kind of deliberate calmness, his eyes fixed ahead. I knew that look—the one that meant something was brewing in his mind, something he wasn't ready to voice just yet. He was always trying to protect me, to shield me from the parts of the world he couldn't control. But this time, I wasn't so sure he was protecting me from the world. He was protecting me from himself.

"You're quiet," I said, my voice catching the way it always did when I tried to breach something too close to the surface.

He glanced at me, his lips curling into a half-smile, the sort he used when he didn't want me to know he was holding something back. "I'm just letting you catch up to me. You've been in bed for a while."

I narrowed my eyes at him. "I'm fine. You know, I can stand on my own two feet." I took a step away from him, testing my balance. He didn't say anything, but I saw the way his jaw clenched, the way his eyes tracked my every move. The need to protect me was like a physical thing with him—something tangible, a heavy cloak that hung between us whenever the world was too much.

And yet, in this moment, I couldn't help but feel the distance. It wasn't in the physical space, but in the space between the words we hadn't said, the things we hadn't confronted. The last few days had been full of quiet, careful healing—of tender touches, of whispered words, of promises both spoken and unspoken. But we hadn't talked about the bigger things. The things that would decide whether we were really strong enough to endure everything that had happened.

THE RUSE

I wasn't sure what I was waiting for—some grand gesture or declaration of love that would somehow make everything okay again. But as I stood there, the waves crashing at my feet, the realization hit me: It wasn't about the grand gestures. It was about the quiet moments, the unspoken words, the way he held me when I was falling apart. That was love, wasn't it? The quiet understanding that you didn't always have to say everything, but you had to be there. Every day. No matter how hard it got.

"Jaxon," I said again, this time more firmly. I reached out, grabbing his arm gently, pulling him to a stop. "What's going on in that head of yours?"

He sighed, a long, slow exhale that carried with it all the weight of everything he'd been carrying. "I'm not sure you're ready to hear it."

"Try me," I said, forcing myself to meet his eyes, even though they seemed to burn through me. "I can't fix what I don't know."

He looked at me for a long moment, his gaze flicking to the horizon before he spoke again. "You don't know what it's like, waking up every morning thinking you might lose everything. I've spent days wondering if the woman I love would ever be the same again. If we'd ever be the same."

I felt the blood drain from my face, my pulse quickening as the reality of his words slammed into me. "I—" My voice faltered, and I had to take a steadying breath before I could continue. "I'm still here, Jaxon. I'm still the same person. Maybe I'm broken, but I'm still me."

He didn't say anything for a moment. His eyes softened, but there was something else there too—something darker, something I couldn't name. "You don't get it. I'm scared. Scared of losing you. Scared of not being enough for you."

My heart stuttered in my chest. I hadn't expected this. It was always me who had the doubts, the insecurities, the fear that we wouldn't survive this. To hear him say it out loud, to admit that he wasn't immune to those same feelings—it was like watching a dam break, the flood of emotion rushing out of him before he could stop it.

"You've always been enough," I whispered, stepping closer to him. "More than enough. You're the one who saved me. Don't you see that?"

He shook his head, a bitter laugh escaping his lips. "I don't know if I can be what you need. Not after all this."

The words hung between us like a heavy mist, thick with unspoken fears, the kind of fears that could destroy everything if given the chance. But something shifted in me, something fierce and unyielding. Maybe we were both scared. Maybe we both had doubts. But if there was one thing I knew for sure, it was that I wasn't walking away from this.

I reached out, cupping his face with my hands, forcing him to meet my gaze. "We'll fight for this, Jaxon. Together. I won't give up. And I don't want you to either."

His eyes softened, the tension slowly leaving his body. For a moment, we stood there, in the silence of the world around us, letting the truth of what we were saying settle between us. The path ahead wouldn't be easy, and the scars we carried—both the ones visible and the ones hidden deep—would never fully fade. But we would carry them together. And that was enough.

The next few days felt like a strange kind of limbo. I was no longer entirely broken, but neither was I whole. Each morning, I woke to the same world, the same sun filtering through the same curtains, the same endless stretch of ocean below. The rhythms of life—the slow creak of the cabin's wood, the distant call of gulls—played on, unaffected by the chaos that had nearly unraveled us.

It was the quiet that unnerved me. The way Jaxon would look at me, as if searching for something he couldn't find. Or maybe he was waiting for me to ask the questions that hovered between us, unspoken. Sometimes, I'd catch him staring at me across the room, his gaze intense, as though he could unravel every single thought I was trying to hide. I wasn't the only one trying to heal; he was carrying something too. But what? I had no idea.

I spent hours each day pretending to read, but my thoughts were scattered, like shattered glass, slipping through my fingers no matter how hard I tried to piece them together. Jaxon never pushed me, never asked if I was okay beyond the usual, careful inquiries. And I didn't ask him the questions that were creeping up inside me—about the explosion, about what we were, about whether the person he was now was the same one I had fallen in love with.

It was strange how quickly everything could feel so fragile. One minute, we were both charged with this wild, undeniable intensity—fighting against the world, fighting for each other. The next, I couldn't shake the feeling that we were teetering on the edge of something. Something that could either pull us apart or make us stronger. And I wasn't sure which was worse: the idea of being broken, or the thought of pushing Jaxon away when he was the only thing keeping me from falling completely apart.

I was sitting on the porch one afternoon, staring out at the water, trying to keep my mind from running too far down that road when he came up behind me, his steps slow and deliberate, like he was testing the ground between us. Without a word, he sat down next to me, the familiar scent of him—a blend of woodsmoke and salt—immediately filling the space between us. His hand brushed against mine, not in a gesture of comfort, but in the quietest way, almost like a question. I turned toward him, meeting his eyes. For a moment, neither of us said anything. It was one of those moments that felt pregnant with the weight of everything we hadn't said yet.

"I don't know what's wrong with me," he said quietly, breaking the silence at last. His voice was strained, like he was trying to find the right words to say, but not sure how. "I should be with you, right now. I should be trying to fix things."

I shifted, pressing my palm flat against the weathered wood beneath me, feeling the rough texture against my skin. There were a million things I wanted to say. I wanted to tell him that he didn't have to fix anything, that all I needed was him. But it wasn't that simple, was it? Nothing ever was. Especially when it felt like we were both living with our hands tied.

"Jaxon," I said, my voice soft but firm. "You don't have to fix anything. You've already done enough."

He turned to me, his face inscrutable, and I felt the weight of the unspoken question settle between us once more. He was waiting for something I wasn't sure I was ready to give him. He needed assurance, and I needed it too, but neither of us seemed willing to speak the words that would set us free.

"Do you ever think we're just... too damaged?" he asked suddenly, his voice low, like he was afraid the wind would carry the question away before I could answer. "That maybe we've both been through too much? That maybe we're just too broken to be fixed?"

His words hit me like a punch. The thing I hadn't wanted to acknowledge, the doubt I had buried deep inside me, now spilled out into the open. I wanted to deny it, to tell him that we were stronger than our scars, that we could still find a way to make it work. But I couldn't lie to him—not when he was looking at me like that, his eyes filled with that impossible mix of fear and hope.

"You know, sometimes I think we might be," I admitted, my voice trembling slightly. "But I don't know if that's a reason to give up. Or if it's just a reason to try harder."

There it was—the truth. The part of me that wasn't sure if love could survive everything we had put it through. If it was really enough to simply love each other when the world had already beaten us down.

He ran a hand through his hair, the movement frustrated, almost desperate. "But what if we're just fooling ourselves? What if this is all just some... some last-ditch effort to hold on to something that's already gone?"

His words stung more than I'd expected. Because deep down, I was afraid he might be right. I was afraid that the us we had fought for, the love that had once burned so fiercely, had been extinguished in the wreckage we'd left behind. That we were clinging to memories of something that couldn't survive.

I wanted to say something that would fix it. I wanted to be strong for both of us, to tell him that love was enough. But as I sat there, feeling the sun on my face, I realized something. Maybe it wasn't about the love we had before. Maybe it was about the love we could build now, out of the ruins of our past, if we were brave enough to face the uncertainty.

"I don't know, Jaxon," I said quietly, my voice a whisper against the wind. "But I know one thing: I'm not ready to give up yet."

The words hung between us like a fragile thread, neither of us sure whether it would hold or snap. And in that moment, with the ocean roaring beneath us and the weight of our unspoken fears pressing in on both sides, I couldn't help but wonder—was it enough? Would it ever be enough? The answer felt just out of reach, as elusive as the tide, pulling me in deeper with every passing second.

And then, just as I thought I might finally find the courage to speak the truth that had been building inside me, there was a sound—faint, almost imperceptible—but unmistakable.

A knock at the door.

Chapter 28: The Final Confrontation

The air was thick with tension, as though the very atmosphere around us was holding its breath. We were standing on the precipice of something irrevocable—something that would change everything. I could feel the rough texture of the concrete beneath my boots, the remnants of a forgotten world where I used to find comfort in the smallest of things. But comfort had long since slipped away, replaced by something far fiercer, far more demanding. This wasn't just a battle for survival. No, this was something more personal—more visceral—than I had ever dared imagine.

Our enemy, a shadowed figure wrapped in layers of deceit, stood before us like the storm we knew was coming but had never quite prepared for. The Wraith's legacy was now a twisted thing, a carcass of an empire left to rot at the hands of someone who had no idea how to wield power with finesse. The leader, his back turned to us, surveyed his domain, that arrogant, indifferent posture that had always irked me. The world he had inherited, my world, was nothing but a chessboard to him—a thing to be broken apart, reshaped in his image.

And there was no one else who could fix it but us. Well, mainly us—although I was certain that Liam would have preferred the full burden of it all to fall squarely on his broad shoulders. He didn't say anything as we approached, his gaze steady, locked onto the figure in the distance, but I could sense his impatience. He was more than ready to bring an end to the charade. The faintest hint of a grim smile tugged at the corner of his mouth. For all the gruffness and self-assurance, I knew him well enough to understand that beneath it all, Liam carried an urgency that I could feel in my bones.

I glanced at him, taking in the sharp angles of his jaw, the unwavering steadiness of his hands. There were still faint traces of exhaustion around his eyes, the kind that no amount of sleep could undo. It didn't matter. He had carried this fight for longer than I had, and now, I was by his side, ready to carry it with him—whatever it took.

"We do this together," I whispered, the words more of a promise than a question. A vow.

Liam's gaze flickered to mine, and something unspoken passed between us—an understanding forged in the fires of everything we had endured. His lips parted in something that could have been a laugh, if not for the weight of the moment.

"Always," he murmured back. "Always."

The figure before us turned slowly, his eyes like two cold pits of nothingness, calculating, watching us with the detachment of someone who had never once doubted his own superiority. He was older than I remembered, though the years seemed to have done little to erode the sharpness of his features. His black suit, tailored to perfection, seemed to absorb the light, giving him the aura of something both immovable and untouchable. And I hated him for it.

"So, we finally meet," he said, his voice a smooth, eerie lull that made the hairs on the back of my neck rise. He didn't move, didn't flinch, as though he had all the time in the world. "I expected more from you," he added, a sneer creeping onto his face.

Liam took a step forward, his presence commanding. The fire in his chest was palpable, even from where I stood. "You're running out of time," he growled. "This is where it ends."

The figure's smile never wavered, and he raised a hand, dismissing us with a flick of his fingers. "Endings are overrated. I'm just getting started."

I felt my pulse quicken, the weight of everything crashing into me. The finality of it, the utter hopelessness that this had been building toward for so long. I wasn't just fighting for my life anymore. I was fighting for everything I had built, everything I loved, everything I had allowed myself to believe in. And that made this moment, this fight, the most terrifying of all.

I shifted, stepping to the side to give Liam space, but not too much. He glanced at me, the briefest of glances, and in that look, I knew that he was going to do whatever it took. He would burn through the walls of hell if that's what it took to protect us.

There was no more room for words. With a speed that caught me off guard, Liam lunged forward, his movements precise and calculated. He wasn't just fighting the man in front of us; he was fighting every ounce of betrayal, every scar, every injustice that had led us here. I saw the fury in his eyes as he blocked a blow, then delivered one of his own, and my heart thudded in my chest, an unrelenting rhythm that matched the violence of the struggle.

I joined in, moving fluidly as we became one—our actions synchronizing without a single misstep. I didn't think. I just reacted. I fought because it was what I was born to do, because this fight was for everything that mattered. With every swing of my fist, I could feel the world shifting beneath my feet. The fight wasn't just external—it was internal, too. And somehow, in the chaos of it all, I found myself tethered to him. To Liam. His strength, his anger, his absolute refusal to let go. We moved as though we were one soul in two bodies, a force of nature no one could stop.

But just as quickly as the moment exploded, it faltered. The figure in front of us had been waiting for this. He smiled as if he had anticipated our every move, his eyes gleaming with something that felt far too familiar—like he had already won. "You think this is it?" he taunted. "You think you can stop me now?"

I didn't have an answer for him. Not yet.

But I would.

The silence that followed was a strange thing, like the world had decided to hold its breath and wait for the outcome. The room seemed to stretch and pull in on itself, each beat of my heart like an

THE RUSE

echo of the madness unfolding around us. For a moment, everything slowed—the air, the tension, the very floor beneath my feet.

Liam's face was a mask of determination, every inch of him taut with the promise of battle. His hand still gripped the hilt of the weapon he'd wielded with such expert precision moments before, though now, even as his chest rose and fell with steady, measured breaths, I could see the glint of something darker in his eyes. The kind of exhaustion that came from fighting for so long. The kind that told you there was no turning back, no reprieve. His jaw clenched, and I knew without asking that he wasn't thinking about the fight anymore. He was thinking about us—what this meant, what we were willing to lose in order to end this nightmare once and for all.

The man before us took a step forward, his calm a contrast to the storm we had just weathered. His confidence was unsettling, like a shadow that draped itself over the room. "Is this really the best you can do?" His voice was honeyed, smooth, yet it held a sharp edge that cut through the air. "I must admit, I'm disappointed. I thought you would offer me more of a challenge."

Liam's response was low, a rumble of fury in his chest. "You're running out of time, old man."

I stood beside him, but I didn't feel the need to speak. The words seemed pointless. All the pleading, all the reasoning, had been exhausted. We had tried diplomacy. We had tried to understand. But this man was beyond reason. There was no "negotiating" with someone who had spent their entire life sharpening their blades in the dark, waiting for this moment—the moment when they could step into the light and claim their twisted version of victory.

His gaze flickered briefly to me, and for the first time, I felt a prickle of something akin to fear. It wasn't fear for myself, but fear of what he might say next. Fear of what he might reveal.

"You know," he said, his lips curling into a smile that wasn't remotely warm, "I've often wondered what it would be like, to be you." He looked at me, his eyes narrowing. "To feel what you feel. To have what you have. A love so strong it burns everything in its path."

My heart stuttered, an involuntary reaction to the way his words wrapped themselves around my chest, squeezing tight. I knew exactly what he was doing—he was trying to get under my skin, trying to make me doubt. But I wasn't going to fall for it. I had lived through enough to know the difference between fear and reality.

I let out a breath, steadying myself. "You'll never understand," I said, meeting his gaze without flinching. "Because you don't know what love is. You only know how to break things. But you won't break us."

The smile faltered for just a second, and I saw something flicker behind his eyes. It wasn't anger—it was something darker. Something colder. He took another step forward, closer to the edge of the chaos we had created together. I could feel the pulse of the impending clash in the very air between us. And though every muscle in my body screamed to move, to react, to strike first—I held back. Waiting. Watching.

This was the part of the fight that mattered most. Not the violence, not the power of the blows, but the moment right before the final strike. The moment when everything would pivot on a knife's edge.

Liam stepped forward, his boots hitting the ground with a deliberate, almost menacing thud. His eyes met mine again, and I could see the promise in them. A promise that no matter what happened, we would find our way through this. Together.

"Stay close," he said, his voice rougher now, the weight of the battle pressing down on him.

I nodded, more instinctively than consciously, and followed him. His presence was like a shield around me, though I knew he would never let me be the one in danger. It had always been like that—Liam would throw himself into the fire without a second thought to keep me safe. But I wasn't some helpless bystander. This was my fight too.

The figure in front of us narrowed his eyes, his smile slipping into something far more calculating. "You think you can stop me?" he asked again, his voice a whisper, but this time the words carried a different weight. "The world doesn't work the way you think it does. There are always more pieces to move. More angles to exploit."

Liam didn't flinch. "I've heard enough of your lies."

And just like that, everything changed.

It was impossible to say exactly how it happened—the shift, the moment when the scales tipped—but suddenly, the room seemed to explode into motion. Liam lunged forward with all the force of a predator in its prime, but this time, there was something new behind his movements. A desperation. A need to end this. To make sure that, no matter what, we wouldn't be here again.

I didn't hesitate. I was beside him in an instant, moving with a fluidity I hadn't known I was capable of. Every move, every twist, every strike was guided by something I couldn't name. A force beyond the fight itself.

I saw it then—the flicker of uncertainty in our enemy's eyes. The brief hesitation that gave me the opening I needed.

In that split second, the world slowed again. I felt the weight of our connection, the bond between us that was unspoken, yet so strong it could break anything in its path. And in that moment, I knew one thing for sure: this fight would end the only way it could. With us, together. No matter what.

The world had condensed into a space so small, so confined, it felt like we were holding our breaths, each of us waiting for the inevitable strike. Time had become elastic—stretched thin and taut, holding us in a moment that seemed to last forever. I had fought beside Liam more times than I cared to count, but there was something different about this fight. Something that made every punch, every step, every sound of our feet hitting the ground reverberate deep into my bones.

Our enemy, his face still unreadable, adjusted his stance as though the chaos unfolding around him was little more than a mild inconvenience. He had grown accustomed to this—manipulating people, pulling strings from the shadows. But he had underestimated the strength of what he was up against. The sheer force of us. Together.

I could hear Liam's steady breathing, steady like the rhythm of a heart that had been through more battles than any one man should endure. His hand brushed mine for a brief moment—just a flicker of a touch—but it was enough. It anchored me. It reminded me why we were here. Why we couldn't afford to fail.

"You think you've won," the man said again, his words languid, the edge of disbelief cutting through the cool indifference in his tone. "But you haven't. You never will."

I shot him a look that would have made most men flinch, but he didn't even blink. Instead, he stepped closer, and my hand instinctively went to the weapon I had kept concealed beneath my jacket. His eyes locked on mine, and for a split second, I felt that familiar prickle of unease. There was something about the way he looked at me—like he could see straight through every wall I'd spent years building. And I hated him for it.

"I've learned more from this little game than you'll ever know," he continued, his voice now a low drawl, like he was explaining something simple to a child. "Your love? It's your weakness. Your strength? Your downfall."

His words sliced through the air, hanging heavy with the weight of a man who had convinced himself that every piece of this twisted puzzle had already been solved. He didn't know us. He didn't know what we were capable of.

I felt Liam tense beside me, his muscles coiling as though he were ready to spring into action at the first sign of danger. His gaze never wavered from the man before us, but there was something else in his eyes—something unspoken, as though he were trying to figure out how this would end. If it would end.

"Is that what you tell yourself every night?" I asked, my voice sharp and cutting through the silence. "That our love is our weakness? It's not. You'll find that out soon enough."

The man chuckled, but there was no humor in it. Only coldness. "You don't get it, do you? I'm the one who controls the strings. I'm the one who decides what happens next." His eyes flickered to Liam, then back to me. "You're both so certain. So confident. But you're nothing but pawns."

I felt the muscle in Liam's jaw flex, the only outward sign of his growing frustration. I knew what was coming. I knew the second Liam let his temper slip, the battle would escalate into something raw, untamed. And we couldn't afford that right now. Not when we were so close.

"We're not your pawns," Liam said, his voice low and dangerous. "We're the ones who checkmate."

Without another word, Liam lunged at him, the movement so fast I barely had time to react. I followed, adrenaline surging through me like a pulse of fire. The sound of our feet hitting the ground was drowned out by the crash of steel meeting steel. I had no idea how much time passed as we collided with him, as we fought with everything we had left. But I could feel it—the shift in the air, the moment when the balance tipped. The moment when he realized he had miscalculated.

The man staggered back, his expression finally breaking into something that resembled concern—just a flicker, but it was there. And that's when I knew. We had him.

I moved faster now, the fight taking on a rhythm of its own. My body reacted before my mind had time to process. And as Liam delivered blow after blow, I stayed beside him, my strikes purposeful, controlled. I could feel the burn in my muscles, the weight of exhaustion pressing on my shoulders, but there was no stopping now. There was no room for hesitation.

The man's gaze flashed with panic—real panic—for the first time. And I wanted to savor it. I wanted to watch him unravel, piece by piece, as the foundation he had built began to crumble around him.

Then, with a movement so swift it was almost imperceptible, he reached into his jacket, pulling something out—a device, small but deadly. I recognized it immediately, the gleam of danger in his eyes telling me everything I needed to know.

"Don't," I shouted, but it was too late.

He pressed the button.

The world erupted in an explosion of sound, of heat, of shattering glass. My heart stopped, caught somewhere between shock and a desperate, helpless scream. The blast rocked the building, sending a shockwave that knocked us off our feet. I collided with the ground, the air knocked out of my lungs, but my mind didn't stop racing.

Liam's voice cut through the ringing in my ears. "Get up!" he shouted, pulling me to my feet with a force that sent a jolt of adrenaline straight to my core.

But when I looked up, everything had changed. The room was gone, reduced to rubble and smoke. The enemy was gone, too—vanished into the chaos, leaving nothing but a cold, foreboding silence in his wake.

I turned to Liam, my breath ragged. "Where is he?"

But Liam didn't answer. His gaze was fixed on something beyond me—something that made his face drain of color.

And then I heard it.

The unmistakable sound of footsteps, approaching from the darkness.

Chapter 29: A New Dawn

The city is a symphony of motion, every street and alley pulsing with the energy of its rebirth. Morning light spills across the cracked asphalt, casting shadows long and sharp, as if the night itself has only just released its grip. Jaxon's hand is warm in mine, steady in a way I haven't quite gotten used to. He doesn't speak, but there's a quiet understanding in his touch. Like we've both finally stopped running, finally stopped pretending that we can outrun the ghosts we've collected along the way.

Above us, the sky is a canvas in motion, hues of orange and pink bleeding into each other. It's a reminder that everything changes, whether we're ready for it or not. The city, once bruised by violence and loss, is beginning to stretch toward the sun. Buildings that once stood silent and defiant in their decay are slowly being reclaimed, their skeletal frames kissed by the warmth of hope. People move about, eyes focused and determined. Their strides have purpose now, the kind that only comes after surviving something that almost destroyed them.

I take a deep breath, savoring the air that smells faintly of rain, old wood, and the promise of something new. The lingering scent of gunpowder is still there, tucked into the folds of the streets and in the corners of the buildings. It's an odd mix, that smell of destruction paired with the lightness of renewal. It's like the earth itself is trying to erase the traces of what's come before. But the city knows better. It remembers. We all do. And I think that's why it's still standing—because it refuses to forget. It wears its scars like a badge of honor. Maybe, in a way, we all do.

Jaxon shifts beside me, his thumb brushing lightly over my knuckles. I turn my head toward him, finding his gaze already fixed on me. His eyes, dark and steady, seem to hold more than just the reflection of the city around us. They hold a thousand untold stories—some of them mine, others his, and a few that are ours, written together. There's something about the way he looks at me now, something unspoken, but understood in the very marrow of my bones. His jaw tightens, a subtle movement, but it's enough to make my pulse quicken.

I'm not sure when it happened, when we shifted from surviving to living, but somewhere in the chaos of it all, it's happened. I don't need to ask him about the past. I don't need to know what he's done, who he's hurt, or what has been broken. The truth is, none of that matters anymore. What matters is the steady pressure of his fingers wrapped around mine, the way our breaths sync when we're close. In this moment, it feels like we're invincible, like nothing can tear us apart. And maybe that's enough.

The wind picks up, sending a chill across my skin. I shiver slightly, but I don't pull away from Jaxon. There's something about standing here with him, in this quiet space between what was and what's yet to come, that makes everything feel more tangible. The world feels like it's at the edge of something great, something unstoppable. And I think, for the first time in my life, I believe that we're meant to be part of that.

I laugh, low and soft, surprising myself more than anyone else. It's not a laugh I've heard in a long time—one that's free, without the weight of fear or regret. Jaxon glances at me, the corner of his mouth lifting in that quiet, familiar smile. The one that says, "I get you." It's the kind of smile that could make me do anything.

"What's so funny?" he asks, his voice hoarse from the remnants of the night.

I shake my head, still smiling, even though I don't have a real answer. "I was just thinking," I say, my voice light, almost teasing, "how much I've hated the sound of silence. And now... now I can't get enough of it."

He raises an eyebrow, but there's no judgment in the movement—just curiosity. "And here I thought you liked noise. You know, explosions, sirens, chaos."

I laugh again, louder this time, the sound cutting through the stillness of the morning. "Yeah, well, you can only handle that kind of thing for so long."

Jaxon pulls me closer, his arm slipping around my waist as if to anchor me in this moment, in this world that feels more real than anything we've known. His chest is solid against my back, his warmth a contrast to the crisp air. He presses his lips to the top of my head, a gentle, fleeting kiss, as though he knows I need it to settle into the calm that's finally creeping into my veins.

"We've made it this far," he says, his voice quiet but firm. "We'll make it further. Together."

I don't respond immediately. It's not that I don't agree; it's that I need a moment to fully absorb the weight of what he's saying. He's right. Everything we've done, everything we've fought for, has led us here. We're standing at the threshold of something new, something we've earned. And even though I know the world won't be perfect, and the shadows of our past will always be there, I also know that we're stronger than anything it can throw at us.

The silence settles between us again, but this time it's comfortable, peaceful. There's no need for more words. We've both said everything we need to say. And the truth is, the world feels a little less overwhelming with his hand in mine, with the knowledge that we're not alone in this fight anymore.

The sun climbs higher, casting a golden light over the city, and I take one last look at the skyline, the jagged edges softened by the dawn. Whatever comes next, whatever challenges the future holds, I know this much: it won't break us. Not anymore.

The morning stretches out before us, full of promise and quiet anticipation. Jaxon's fingers tighten ever so slightly around mine, a silent vow that whatever happens, we're in this together. The stillness of the moment is almost too much to bear, yet I find myself clinging to it, unwilling to rush forward. There's something in the way the city stirs, like it's waking up with us, shedding the remnants of what once held it in darkness. Even the air feels different, charged with the kind of hope that rises like steam from freshly broken earth.

As we begin walking down the quiet street, the sounds of the world come alive around us. Birds chirp in the distance, their songs soft and tentative, as if unsure whether it's safe to be loud yet. The soft scrape of tires against pavement and the faint hum of distant voices drift in from nearby alleyways. There's a sense of movement everywhere—small shops beginning to open their doors, the creak of metal gates being raised, the faint shuffling of those just beginning their day. It's not the usual chaos of city life; there's no frantic rush, no screaming in the streets. Instead, there's a kind of reverence, as though everyone knows they're witnessing the birth of something bigger than themselves.

Jaxon glances at me from the corner of his eye, a half-smile playing on his lips. He's never been one for large speeches or declarations, preferring the quiet strength of his presence. But today, there's something about him—a spark that hadn't been there before, a confidence that feels like it could light the entire city on fire. I don't ask him about it. I don't need to. Whatever he's feeling, I can feel it too.

"Hard to believe, isn't it?" he murmurs, his voice a low rumble against the quiet of the morning. "After everything, it feels like we're standing on the edge of something new."

I nod, the weight of his words sinking in. This isn't just the city changing; it's us too. There's no going back from here. I think we both knew that the moment we chose to stay, the moment we decided that survival wasn't enough. The choices we've made—good or bad—have led us here, standing together at the cusp of a future we never thought possible."

"I know," I reply, my voice thick with the emotions I'm not quite sure how to untangle. "It's like the world's finally letting us breathe again."

Jaxon chuckles softly, his hand brushing against the small of my back as we continue our slow walk. His presence is a constant now, a steady anchor in the chaotic sea of everything that's happened. He doesn't flinch when I lean into him, doesn't pull away when the weight of everything presses down on me. He just lets me be, and that, in itself, is a gift I never expected to receive.

We pass an old café, its windows still covered in grime from the months of neglect. But the door is open, and I can hear the faint clatter of dishes being prepared inside. A woman steps out to sweep the sidewalk, her weathered face crinkling into a smile when she spots us. There's something about her, some quiet dignity in the way she holds herself, that makes me pause for a moment.

"Morning, you two," she calls, her voice rough but warm. "You look like you've been through hell and back."

I'm not sure whether she's referring to the bags under my eyes or the strange energy that surrounds us. But something in her words makes me smile.

"Something like that," I answer, returning her greeting with a wink.

She gives a knowing nod, as if she's seen it all before, as if survival itself has a language that only those who've been through the fire understand. "You'll be all right," she says simply, her broom pausing mid-sweep. "Don't let the past drag you down."

I want to say something, to ask her how she knows, but there's no need. Her words are enough. And just like that, I feel lighter, like the burden of the past doesn't have to carry the same weight it once did.

THE RUSE

Jaxon shifts next to me, his lips brushing my ear. "You ready for the next part?" he asks, his breath warm against my skin.

The question is simple, but there's an undercurrent to it that makes my heart beat a little faster. It's the same question I've been asking myself for days, maybe even weeks. What happens when we're no longer fighting for our lives? What happens when we're free to just... live?

"I think so," I answer, glancing up at him with a look that's part challenge, part curiosity. "But if you're about to suggest I go back to the farm, you've got another thing coming."

Jaxon laughs, a low, rumbling sound that fills the space between us. "No chance. I think we've both earned a little more than that."

The path ahead is uncharted, the way forward unknown, but for the first time in a long while, I feel something that's been missing for a long time: possibility. We've fought, bled, and lost so much already. But we're here, standing side by side, the future stretching out before us like an open road.

There's no rush to move forward, not yet. We both know there's a lot to figure out, a lot of healing that needs to happen. But whatever it is, we'll face it together. And that certainty, that shared resolve, is all I need to keep going.

The city continues to stir around us, the murmur of its life growing louder as we make our way through the streets. There's something in the air today—a feeling I can't quite place, but one I know I'll carry with me as long as I can. The smell of fresh coffee, the crackle of electricity in the air, the soft hum of conversation and laughter from the people around us. It's all new, all unfamiliar, but it feels like a promise. A promise that maybe, just maybe, we'll get to build something better from the ashes.

The city is alive in ways I didn't think possible. The streets buzz with a quiet energy, people moving like ants on their daily march but somehow with a sense of purpose that's new. Maybe it's the promise of a future that feels less like a distant idea and more like a reality that we're all about to claim. Maybe it's the simple fact that for the first time in years, we're all standing on the same side—together.

Jaxon's hand is still in mine, and the steady warmth of his fingers threading through mine is a tether, holding me firm in a world that's still shifting beneath my feet. We walk side by side, not saying much but letting the air between us hum with something unsaid. He doesn't need to tell me that we're both still catching our breath, still coming to terms with what's behind us. And I don't need to remind him that I'll follow him anywhere, even if that means walking into the unknown.

As we round the corner, the sounds of the city intensify—voices rising, laughter breaking out in small pockets, the clatter of construction as the city begins to rebuild itself, piece by piece. There's a familiar sense of chaos, but it's not the same chaos that had gripped New Chicago before. This feels... different. More like a kind of rebirth than a last gasp. Even the buildings seem to stand taller, as though they've learned something from all the years they've spent being torn down only to rise again.

"Think we'll ever get used to this?" I ask, my voice barely rising above the din around us.

Jaxon glances down at me, his eyes thoughtful. "Used to what? The noise, the crowds, or the fact that you're no longer at war?"

"I meant all of it," I reply, lifting my hand to gesture at the mess of people and activity swirling around us. "It's just... strange, you know? The whole world keeps spinning, and I feel like I should be running, still looking over my shoulder. But I'm not. I'm just... here. With you."

His lips quirk upward in that signature, half-smile of his, the one that makes my heart stutter just a little. "Funny, I always thought you were a fan of a good chase."

I laugh, though there's an edge to it, something uncertain. "I don't know. Maybe I am. But sometimes... I think I'd rather stand still for once. See what happens."

The quiet that follows between us feels like a puzzle that neither of us wants to solve just yet. We don't need to say much more. It's in the way we move together, the way the world doesn't feel like it's pulling us apart anymore.

"Speaking of standing still," Jaxon says after a beat, his voice cutting through the haze of thoughts spinning in my mind. "I've been meaning to ask you something."

I glance up at him, my heart giving an unexpected leap. "Yeah?"

He looks at me then, really looks at me, his dark eyes searching, like he's trying to read something between the lines, something that's just out of reach. I feel the moment stretch between us, taut like a wire. "Where do we go from here?"

The question hangs in the air, a simple one but with a weight that presses against my chest. It's the kind of question that can make you pause, make you reconsider everything you thought you knew. It's not just about the city, or our fight, or the people who surround us. It's about us. What happens to us now that the war is over? What happens when we're no longer fighting to survive?

I open my mouth to answer, but the words get stuck somewhere in my throat. I don't know what comes next, not really. I've spent so long fighting, so long clinging to survival, that I haven't stopped to think about what comes after. What happens when the smoke clears and the battlefield is nothing but a distant memory? What do you do with the rest of your life when you've already stared death in the face so many times that it no longer frightens you?

"I don't know," I finally admit, my voice quieter than I intend. "But I think... I think I want to figure it out. With you."

The words hang there between us, and for a moment, I see something flicker in his eyes. Relief, maybe. Or something deeper, something that holds the weight of everything we've been through. It's a connection, pure and undeniable. And in this city, amidst the chaos and the change, it's the only thing I'm certain of.

Jaxon nods, his fingers tightening around mine, and for the briefest moment, the world feels like it's aligned, like it's offering us the chance to choose the next step. He doesn't say anything more, but his gaze says enough. He's in this with me. Whatever it is.

We keep walking, and the city pulses around us like a living thing. I'm not sure where we're headed, but for the first time in a long while, I don't mind not knowing. We pass through familiar streets and new ones, each corner revealing a different slice of life. A couple sitting on the steps of a building, laughing as they share a cup of coffee. A group of children chasing each other down an alley, their voices ringing in the crisp air. The feeling of something new, something better, is everywhere. It's in the way the people are rebuilding, in the way the old cracks are being patched up, brick by brick.

But as we move further down the road, something shifts, an unspoken tension that I can't place. My gaze darts around, scanning the streets, looking for a sign, a signal. And then, out of the corner of my eye, I catch sight of something—a shadow moving in a doorway, someone watching us from behind the grime-covered window of an abandoned storefront.

I stop, Jaxon's hand still clasped firmly in mine. My heart skips a beat as I try to make sense of the movement. The figure remains still, almost too still, as if waiting for something. For us.

"Jaxon…" My voice is low, barely a whisper, but it's enough to draw his attention. His body stiffens beside me.

He doesn't ask what's wrong, doesn't question the sharp edge in my tone. Instead, he shifts slightly, his hand pulling me just a little closer.

"I see it," he says softly, his voice low and careful. "Stay close."

THE RUSE

And just as we take a step forward, the door to the building creaks open, and a figure steps out into the light. A face I never thought I'd see again.

Milton Keynes UK
Ingram Content Group UK Ltd.
UKHW030903011224
451693UK00001B/140

9 798230 333050